"A Walk Through Rain gave voice tions and thoughts as I experienced the The journey the book describes will give encouragement, comfort, and a renewed ———— *chat all is not lost. If your faith is changing, or you're fighting your doubts, you need to read this book."*

- Karen, USA (inspiredtofaith.com)

"Having gone through a faith deconstruction of my own, this story has tremendous resonance. I found myself nodding and recalling so many of the questions and struggles that the two main characters discussed. A fantastic job of portraying the very real struggle of faith crisis and offering a glimmer of hope."

- Dave, USA (ponderingelephant.com)

"This book takes you on a mesmerizing journey where faith, honesty and self-discovery meet. A story that will resonate deeply with thousands of other sojourning people."

- Gayle, Spain

"A Walk Through Rain...invites the reader to approach their own questions about faith with less anxiety. Perhaps even better, it serves to remind us that no one travels the road of spirituality alone, no matter how lonely the journey might feel."

- Sean, USA

About The Author

 Craig grew up in England at a time when Star Wars was the latest thing and home computers had to be plugged into a television set. Because he couldn't go to another galaxy far, far away he stuck with the computers and made a succesful career out of them.

Faith and spirituality have always played a key role in Craig's life, guiding him through various good and bad times, and ultimately leading him to leave England with his wife and three children to start a new life in Spain.

Things don't always go to plan, and maybe that's a good thing. Living in a foreign land, although challenging at times, became a wonderful journey of personal growth, expansion and reconnecting with what's important.

Taking up writing allowed Craig to explore a whole new branch of possibility, and this book is the result. These pages hold a glimpse into the unfolding process of dismantling the false self, uncovering forgotten dreams, and living from a more authentic place inside.

A Walk Through Rain

"A Mesmerizing Journey Where Faith, Honesty And Self-discovery Meet"

C.R. PENNELL

Dedicated to my wife, Kate, and our amazing children – Aidan, Anna-Marie and Matthew.

In memory of Diane.

FOREWORD

Craig's book has come at an important time, a time when so many are searching for a more authentic expression of faith. As the reader enters Dan's world, a world where he moves from paralyzing doubts to acknowledging that he has questions about his questions, there will be so much that resonates with our own spiritual journeys.

As the story recounts the twists and turns in Dan's journey, the interaction between the main characters leaves the reader with a rich source to reflect on. There are nuggets to mine, signposts to guide, perspectives to consider and even disagree with, which makes this absorbing tale of hope much more than just a story.

Your own journey will no doubt take some different turns to that of Dan, and I think that the characters you're about to meet would be delighted to know that was the case...and that their conversations enabled you to walk forward more authentically.

- Martin Scott, author of 'Humanising the Divine'

"You can soar, you really can. You're not supposed to fit in that nest. Look at your wings, you've outgrown your surroundings. It's only up in the air that you'll discover who you really are."

INTRODUCTION

I t's not easy to tell one day from another simply by look-ing outside, just as a cursory glance at the outward appear-ance won't reveal the deeper truth about a person's life. A Tuesday can look very much like a Wednesday, and a hurting soul can seem very much like a man with his life in order.

Daniel Kendrick gripped the handle of the half-open door, resisting an impulse to close it firmly on the outside world and retreat once more into the safety of his home.

Out there, on the other side, suburban life was going on in that relaxed, weekend fashion he'd always been a little jealous of. The gray-haired woman with the cats trimmed her hedge with almost mathematical precision; the couple from the corner house, jogging to their silent play-lists, made another circuit of the block; Big Reg, the next-door neighbor, was still polishing his new car with meticulous care.

Dan didn't need anyone to tell him it was Sunday—every-one knew their place, knew the routine that morning. Everyone, it seemed, except Dan.

On Sundays, at least in Dan's little corner of England, the tell-tale signs spoke of different priorities, different motivations. On Sundays, people had their own ideas about the best way to spend a hard-won day off and were intent on doing the things that were important to them.

Except, of course, when it rained.

When it rained, the carefully crafted worlds fell apart and everyone would retreat inside. But for Dan it had been raining inside for a long time now. He couldn't tell what the important things were anymore, and for him this was all unfamiliar territory.

He'd gone through the motions, of course. He'd waved Kimberly off in the car with Reg's wife, Debbie. Then he'd taken a deep breath, found a smile, and walked over to chat politely about polish, paintwork and the benefits of early retirement. He'd tried, and then he'd made some excuses.

It wasn't that Dan had a problem with his older neighbor, in fact there was a growing friendship between the four of them. It was simply that these days Reg was looking for a deeper conversation. Predictions about the weather had been replaced with reflections on life, love and loss, which would inevitably lead to a show of concern. And Dan, because he was a nice guy who appreciated the sentiment, would assure Reg that he was okay. One day at a time. That was the usual line that seemed to satisfy his neighbor's curiosity. Their friendship wasn't quite at the place where he could be truly honest. Dan wasn't even doing that with himself.

And today was not the best of days.

Leaving Reg to his work, he'd returned inside only to find the house strangely quiet. That was probably why he'd left the door wide open—the empty feeling only seemed to amplify his loss, and it had taken a conscious effort to grasp those runaway thoughts and reminded himself that there was nothing to worry about. His wife would be at church now. Tom, their eldest son, would be deep into his guitar lesson—something to do with a certain girl; and their younger son, Alastair, was working on a school project at a friend's house. Everyone was where they were supposed to be, doing what they were supposed to be doing.

Except Dan.

He didn't know where he was supposed to be anymore.

And he wasn't sure what to do about it.

Sundays used to mean something. Dan's childhood memories were full of early morning expeditions with his mother to the old village church, special times that he remembered with fondness. Even in his teenage years, through all the harsh realities of his parents' disintegrating marriage, church had been a welcome comfort in the background.

When he left home to pursue a career, finding a place to grow spiritually had been a high priority. He wasn't alone in his search. At one of the more active churches in town he'd been introduced to another newcomer, a young woman called Kimberly. Her long, dark hair, green eyes and soft Scottish accent captured his heart, and it wasn't long before they were making commitments to each other and to the church where they'd met.

Commitment comes with a price, naturally, which usually meant sacrificing their spare time. Sundays quickly began to overflow into the rest of the week, with house groups, prayer meetings and anything else that needed willing hands. But that didn't matter; it was all for a higher purpose, and they were happy to serve.

Through all those years Dan had known his place. He'd had a role to play. He had belonged, and it had felt good to be dedicating his life to something he believed in.

Not anymore.

Now he found himself standing in the ruins of a once rock-solid faith.

How was that possible?

The easy answer was the funeral. That was the last time he'd stepped into a church, and there was genuine concern when he continued to stay away. Calls from well-meaning friends, visits from the ministry team, and when that failed, the Pastor himself. They all said the same thing—'You're going through a grieving process'.

And he was, but that wasn't the complete picture. It had been nine weeks since that heartbreaking day on a bitterly cold February morning, with the smell of snow in the air and an ache in the pit of his stomach. Kimberly had given him room to adjust, never pushing him to come back into the *fold*. But she knew it was much more than that and so did he; in his heart, Dan had walked away from church long before he'd laid the white rose on his mother's coffin.

And today would have been her 67th birthday.

The whistling kettle brought his attention back to the present and he realized he was still holding the door handle in a vice-like grip. Screwing his eyes shut he gulped in the fresh spring air, exhaled, then slowly but firmly closed the door. The faint aroma of roasting chicken met him as he stepped into the kitchen. With one fluid motion he threw a fresh teabag in his favorite mug, poured in hot water and added a splash of milk.

As he sat himself down at the table he looked around at the reassuringly familiar signs that spoke of family life—the remains of a hastily-eaten breakfast next to Kimberly's journal; the colorful fridge-magnets holding important memos and encouraging Bible verses; the many and varied shoes on the rack by the back door.

Everything appeared to be the same as always, and Dan seemed to be the same level-headed guy he'd always been, with only the gray flecks in his dark hair speaking of middle-age. But those blue eyes were seeing a different story which was beginning to reveal itself in the ordinary, everyday things. Like the fact that he could no longer be bothered to use a teapot to brew his beloved tea. Or that he'd tidied and sorted the garage twice already this year, clearing a space for no particular reason.

He just wanted space.

Dan checked the time. His wife would return in an hour or so; the boys would get back a little later. They would have lunch together as a family—one of the few things he insisted on, now more than ever—and he'd politely ask Kimberly about the morning service. She'd probably say it challenged her, and then remind him that Pastor Alan wanted to meet with him this afternoon.

He would nod his head in resignation, then they'd probably move on to discussing his plans for tomorrow.

Move on.

For Dan, that was what it was all about now.

If he could just find a way to move on, to make sense of

what he was going through. Then things would change.

They had to.

He sipped hot tea, placed the mug to one side and reached for his laptop. The screen sprang to life and for the third time that day he read the email once again. His fingers tapped out a dull rhythm on the edge of the table. Doubts bubbled away below the surface. His eyes came to rest on the last line.

I'm looking forward to meeting you in person.

It seemed to be exactly what he needed. Those words on the screen held an invitation. An invitation to get away for a few days, seek some answers and see things from a different perspective. But more than that, those words spoke of something he hadn't felt for a long time.

Hope.

Hope that someone he'd never met before could help him with a little thing called *the rest of his life.*

But sometimes, as Dan knew so well, hope can let you down.

***

Joe Mitchel sat staring at the computer screen. The flashing cursor played out its rhythmic reminder of a half-finished sentence, goading him to either write something better or give up and hit the delete key. Any sane individual would have walked away after thirty minutes of failed attempts. But for Joe, this was more than simply putting words on a screen. Writing was his way of shaking the tree of life in the hope that some apples of truth would fall to the ground.

Except today.

Today his grasp on the truth seemed slippery at best, and the tree wasn't giving up her apples.

Joe drew in a deep breath and rubbed his beard. He'd always loved words, and recently he'd found his writing taking on a new sense of purpose that surprised him. When things went well, when he could get the words to stay on the page, they were crafted into articles and published on his blog. Every other week, without fail, for almost two years now.

At least, that was the plan.

He pulled his half-moon glasses from his face and stared through the open window. The late afternoon sun lit up the valley in a glorious display. Pine-clad slopes topped by a rugged ridge-line with a backdrop of snow-capped mountains, on any other day it would be the perfect scene of tranquility. His friends back in the States might have disagreed, but today it all seemed like just another distraction.

Joe sat back, sighed once more, and clasped his hands together on the desk. Escape to a secret valley in the mountains of Spain to write about what moved him. Sometimes it worked, and worked well, but today the spark of inspiration had come and gone, and the space left behind was filling up with the effects of a long day.

His phone buzzed quietly. Almost without looking he reached over and swiped the screen.

"Hey," he said. His voice was mellow and level.

"I hoped you'd be awake. Feeling okay?" The female voice on the other end sounded concerned.

"I'm fine." Joe tried to sound like he *was* fine, but he knew there was no pretending with Sandy—she knew him better than anyone. He set down his glasses on the desk. "Just...trying to stay awake."

"You gotta give it a few days, honey." Sandy's words were kind but firm. "All that travel, we aren't spring chickens anymore."

He missed his wife. He listened to her voice at the other end, rubbing his forehead with his free hand as he smiled to himself. *Spring chickens?*

"Okay, you're right," Joe's voice betrayed his fatigue. "Not doing much, playing with some ideas, you know."

"Writing, by any chance?"

"Well, nothing is really sticking."

"Honey, what time is it there? You only ever write in the

mornings."

"Yeah. Well, I had trouble concentrating this morning," Joe could hear the frustration in his quick reply and immediately put the brakes on. "Finding it a little hard to readjust."

Sandy tried a gentle reminder. "Hey, your readers aren't going anywhere."

"Yeah. I know. I just had this idea. Well, half an idea. I think it flew out the window."

For a moment, Sandy didn't reply. Years ago, an elderly couple had told them that the sign of a good marriage was when you could rest in each other's silence. As the years passed by, Joe had come to understand the truth of that wisdom more and more. Those few seconds of silence brought comfort as though Sandy was right next to him.

"What am I gonna do with you, Joe Mitchel?" Sandy's voice was calm and soothing.

"I don't know. Just missing you."

"I'll be back before you know it."

"Not before our visitor arrives," Joe was quick to point out.

"The English guy? Dan? Well, no. But you'll be fine."

"Yeah, just...it was your idea to invite him."

"But it's you he needs to talk to. And you can survive another week without me."

"I guess. Yeah," Joe reluctantly agreed.

"It'll be good for you. Take him out on a hike, kayaking or something. Think of it as an opportunity."

Joe could hear his own words coming back at him. Sandy wasn't going to let him get away with anything, it seemed. With a shake of the head he brought his attention back to the call. "So how's your mom?"

It was Sandy's turn to sigh. "I think she's okay. The fall shook her up a bit. I guess having me here for a while longer has helped her relax."

"Has she forgiven me? For leaving, I mean."

He was certain that Sandy's mother hadn't gotten over the first time he had taken her daughter halfway across the globe.

Their yearly visits back to California were always a reminder of how much a mother missed her daughter. Having a fall two days before they were due to leave brought back all those feelings, along with some difficult memories. It was right that Sandy stayed a while longer.

"She'll be fine. And you need to take a break! Get outside. Go for a walk. No computer, okay?"

Joe knew she was right. "I will, I'm just..." He could feel *the look* coming across the 6,000 miles that separated them.

"I mean now, honey. As in *right now.*"

"Thought I would try to relax by writing."

"Your blog will still be there tomorrow. And..."

"I know. We had a deal." Joe found himself staring at the floor.

Silence. Joe imagined resting his head on Sandy's shoulder, her arms wrapped around his tired body as he sunk deeper into her embrace.

"I'll check out flights this week," Sandy explained, "but I don't want to commit until I know Mom's back on her feet."

Joe sat back in his chair. "Yeah, makes sense."

"Honey?"

"I'm here," he said softly.

"I believe in you. You know that?"

Joe glanced at the computer screen. He couldn't hide his frustration from Sandy. He'd been through desert times with his writing before, and he knew it was all about pushing through. Only today he just didn't seem to have the energy.

"Joe? Sometimes, words aren't everything."

His were. He was sure his were.

He could sense the waves of love and steady patience in Sandy's voice. "You're tired. Leave it for today. Count jet lag as God's blessing and a reminder from me. Okay?"

"Call me tomorrow?" he asked, but it was more than a question.

"Ditch the screen."

"Love you."

"Love you, honey."

The phone fell silent. Joe kept it to his ear. He could feel another wave of tiredness returning. An invisible weight pulled at his whole body. Keeping his eyes open until evening seemed like a near-impossible task.

He didn't want to be alone.

Slowly he placed the phone down and reached to close the laptop lid. Instead, stubborn determination took over. A quick flick of his fingers and a new document stared in front of him. The cursor flashed its challenge once more, and he gritted his teeth. The only thing he had right now was words, and he was going to write those words. He began to type—long sentences, broken paragraphs, raw thought. It didn't matter what appeared on the screen. This is what he did. He was a writer. Words meant something. Words gave him identity. Words helped him push through, put things right.

Eventually his fingers slowed down.

Sandy was right. Sometimes, words aren't everything. And maybe one day the words might stop. Maybe one day he'd have nothing to say. And when that day came he'd be ready for something new.

"Yep," he said with quiet finality.

Then he silently closed the laptop, pulled on his running shoes, and went in search of some fresh air.

Monday

CHAPTER 1

*"God also spends time wandering
in the wilderness..."*

Somewhere over France, Dan clutched a paper cup tightly and let his thoughts drift across the endless sea of clouds. He tried to relax. It was only a two-hour flight and he was conscious of how far removed he felt, up there in the stratosphere, from the recent events that had led him to jump on a plane to Spain.

It had all started with the blog.

Kimberly had been skeptical at first. *"Who even is Joe Mitchel?"* she'd asked him seriously. *"Some old hermit living in the mountains?"*

She was right to challenge him, he knew it. In his hour of need he had turned not to trusted friends or church leaders, but to someone he'd found through a Google search. There among endless pages of opinions he'd stumbled across one of Joe's articles, and something about the honesty and openness rang true.

As the falling leaves marked the beginning of winter, at a time when hope for his mother's recovery was fading fast, Joe's words had given him a measure of comfort in his soul-searching. On those long drives to and from her home, many times Dan had found himself thinking over something that he'd read. Something he could cling to in order to survive another day.

But sometimes the disorientation and confusion was almost overwhelming. At those times all Kimberly could do was allow him space. He knew how helpless she must have felt, and although he tried to keep it all in, he'd never been able to hide anything from her. And that was a good thing.

It was her idea that he should write to Joe. A few weeks after the funeral she'd found him standing in the lounge, gripping the photograph of his mother, lost in his own swirling kaleidoscope of thoughts. She had gently and patiently brought him back to the present, he had placed the photo back on the shelf, and they'd talked about happy memories.

"It's sometimes easier, telling someone you don't know. There's nothing to prove, no need to pretend everything's okay."

She was right. Joe had been quick to reply and his message full of understanding, even taking the time to share some of his own experiences of loss and grief.

The hole they leave is filled with a thousand little memories, each one bringing healing.

Joe's words, once again, were a great comfort. Receiving a follow-up invitation had been a pleasant surprise, but to then discover that Joe lived in the heart of the Spanish Pyrenees meant Dan was suddenly short on excuses.

Come and stay for a few days. That was Joe's offer. *Relax, slow down, and we're available if you want to talk.*

"You said you wanted to get away when this was all over," his wife had reminded him, her eyes full of concern.

"And I asked you to make sure I did."

"So take the week off. Make the most of it. It'll be okay. She would want you to go."

"I've got to figure some things out."

"I know."

"I'm so...unsure about things."

"Not me, I hope." Kimberly's voice was stern, but there was a faint smile on her lips.

"No." A pause as he closed his eyes. *"Just about everything else, though."*

Kimberly had made some tea. They'd sat on the sofa as Dan flicked through the information Joe had sent him. *"He lives near this little town called Pont de la Cruz. Right up in the mountains."*

"*Ooh, big mountains.*" Kimberly glanced at the pictures on Dan's phone. "*You'll be happy.*"

"*Hmm. I think so.*"

"*I don't need to think about it. I know you.*"

Big mountains. From his window seat he scanned the horizon, hoping to catch a glimpse of white peaks. He could almost sense them drawing nearer as the clouds below began to clear, revealing the patchwork green fields and gentle hills of southern France.

Dan smiled to himself. Somewhere down there, living the expat life in a quaint little French village surrounded by vineyards, was his life-long friend Ryan. Energetic, entrepreneurial Ryan who'd turned up at the funeral with a sad smile and a case of champagne.

Again, it had been Kimberly's idea that he should get in touch with Ryan and see if they could meet up. His friend had been enthusiastic, but then he always was. Ryan suggested that he drive down to Spain. It shouldn't take more than a few hours and they could get together at the weekend, after Dan's visit with Joe.

"*That settles it,*" Kimberly had said. "*Pack your thermals and polish your boots. Always best to play it safe in the mountains.*"

"*You would know from experience.*"

"*Yes, I would.*"

***

Joe placed a large glass of water on the desk next to an old photo of him and Sandy, powered up his laptop, then went to open the inner shutters on the windows. Raindrops on the glass spoke of last night's storm, but morning light streamed suddenly into the room, illuminating the stone walls of his study. The old desk dominated the space, otherwise taken up by a soft armchair on a deep rug, and his favorite guitar resting on its stand.

Taking his place in the high-backed office chair, Joe pulled himself into the desk, took a sip of water, and prepared to work.

His eyes skimmed over the screen. Twelve emails called for his attention but they could wait. This time was always writing time, and this morning, after a week of stops and starts, Joe couldn't wait to get some ideas onto the page. He glanced up at the wooden wall-clock, cleared his throat, and set to work.

Soon the tapping of the keyboard was the only sound, and even that seemed to gradually transform into a gentle background rhythm as the thoughts turned into words, the words turned into paragraphs, and once again Joe experienced the special magic of plucking an idea from the ether and bringing it into reality.

However much we want our faith to provide all the answers, the deeper questions of life belong to the wilderness. We hoped that we could depend on the promised safety and certainty of our religious structures, with all those learned theologians and centuries of combined wisdom and understanding. But when we find ourselves in uncharted territory, as so many of us have in recent times, the old constructs don't seem to fit any longer.

At these times it's important to remind ourselves that we aren't being unfaithful in searching for answers. We are challenged to think outside our boxes as we discover that God is not confined to our often close-minded ideas about him/her and how he/she works. We are challenged to walk uncharted paths, and in doing so we find that God also spends time wandering in the wilderness, patiently waiting for us to lay down our borrowed preconceptions and show up, naked and hungry, ready to find a new way forward.

The clock silently marked off the minutes, but time didn't seem to have a lot of meaning for Joe. Right then he was in his zone. Every now and then he would stop to flick through pages of a notebook or look through the window to ease the strain on his eyes. Then he would continue the tapping of keys as the inspiration continued to flow.

It was mid-morning when Joe finally stopped, exclaimed

"Enough!" to the universe in general, and pushed back the chair. He remained seated, resting his elbows on the arms of the chair, hands clasped together under his bristly chin. He closed his eyes as if offering a prayer heavenward.

Joe knew better than to keep on pushing, he was just glad to have been able to get some work done. It didn't matter if he never published it, he simply wanted to get writing again, and this morning at least he now had something to show for his efforts. Something he felt good about.

He took a long breath, held it, then exhaled loudly through his mouth.

"Done for today, Mitch."

Closing the lid of the laptop, he sat absentmindedly staring at the guitar huddled in the corner, his fingers twitching as if eager to run across the strings. Then he seemed to change his mind. He stood up, glanced out the window, and leaving the quiet sanctuary of his office, headed for the kitchen.

Sandy's Kitchen, as they fondly referred to it, was a bright and cheerful room bathing in morning sunlight. Pine cabinets lined the walls, check curtains lined the windows, and a large cast-iron Aga stove kept the cold spring morning at bay.

Joe filled a mug with coffee, slid open the glass doors, and stepped out onto the patio.

The back yard consisted of a manicured lawn surrounded on three sides by bright flower beds and lines of colorful rose-bushes. A small garden area for vegetables was green with new leaves. The patio, scattered with various rustic chairs and tables, ran along the back and side of the L-shaped house, partly enclosing the yard. A low stone wall, inset with two gated archways, closed off the rest of the yard to the outside world. One of the gates opened up onto the parking area near the garage; the other onto a wide, green meadow.

Joe followed the patio around to the left, along the rear section of the house and then onto a gravel path that ran up to the meadow gate. He leaned on the heavy wooden bars, mug clasped in his hands, and looked out across the bright, cropped grass studded with yellow primroses, to the dark green of the pine trees quickly climbing up until they surrendered to the bare, craggy rock edging the high ridge. Above the ridge, scudding white clouds brushed the blue sky.

Joe never grew tired of this view. In the years that they had lived in this valley, every day seemed to be always a little different. The sun would highlight various colors in the forest, the rain would wash the flowers even brighter, sometimes the meadow would be full of goats busily mowing the grass to a perfect half-inch as the bells hanging around their necks rang a melancholy note.

Joe rarely prayed with words. Even in his previous life, he'd often thought that spoken prayers simply got in the way. In what he considered the true spirit of creativity, his prayers were intermingled with his ideas, scattered into the fabric of his work, or trodden out on a high trail.

But today a spoken prayer seemed like good idea, and even then it was succinct and straight to the point. Joe never had been a convoluted kind of guy.

"God, I think I'm gonna need a little help with this stuff."

A week ago he'd been on the other side of the world, drinking coffee with the Pastor of his old church. That meeting, however well-intentioned, had probably been a mistake. It had played over and over in his mind on the flight back home, and each day since the old doubts and frustrations had been lurking in the background. Couple that with the jet lag and, all in all, the rest of the week had felt completely unproductive.

And Joe hated being unproductive, especially when it came to his work—there was simply too much to be done.

From his place by the gate, Joe surveyed the scene, allowing his thoughts to wander and coalesce as he reflected on the twists and turns his life's road had taken. He remembered standing in this very spot six years ago when he and Sandy were first checking out the area and considering the consequences. It had been a beautiful week in early summer, and he'd spent many hours out on the trails getting to know the valleys. In all the uncertainty of building a new life in a foreign land, one thing had been clear—he could happily spend the rest of his days here.

His early-morning writing had been a wonderful distraction, now he could feel the clouds forming once more over his head. Sandy was far away, which never helped. But the deeper pain, which Joe often felt as a dull ache, centered around their son, Grant, and his continued absence from their lives. Pain, blame, and a frustration that no amount of writing could ever overcome.

Joe tried to ignore the thoughts playing at the back of his mind, just as he'd done countless times over the last few years. If he really wanted to be honest with himself he would have to admit that his high expectations as a father had been a constant barrier. The truth was that he'd always pushed Grant too hard.

But he wasn't going to admit that. He wasn't ready. Not yet.

Now there were more urgent matters at hand. Whatever Joe felt towards his son, there wasn't anything he could do about it right now. The new week had begun, a full day demanded his attention, and tomorrow he had a visitor.

From the back and forth emails, Joe had caught a glimpse of Dan's desperation and confusion. Here was someone walking a very lonely and dark road, but there was sure to be a lot more going on. Things that he and Sandy had seen many times before, and still didn't have concrete answers to.

Joe nodded to himself. Sandy was right, as always—having Dan come to stay for a couple of days *was* an opportunity, a chance to explore some of the deeper questions again and share a little of his own experiences. There was even the possibility that he'd enjoy the company.

He drained his mug and turned to head back inside. With a glance at the roses growing against the wall his mood lightened and he allowed himself a half-smile. He would never turn into a grumpy old man, that much was certain. Sandy would never let him.

CHAPTER 2

"Where is the grace?"

I t was early afternoon before Dan caught his first glimpse of the Pyrenees mountains from the car. He'd seen the peaks from the window of the aircraft as it crossed the border and started the descent into Barcelona. Even at this time of year, there still seemed to be plenty of snow on the whole range stretching away to the east, making them look truly awesome.

The airport had been sweltering in a spring heatwave, a dramatic but welcome contrast to the slowly receding winter that had gripped England for months. Dan was glad of the sunshine, it seemed to warm him right through to his core, and the cobalt blue Mediterranean skies seemed to stretch wide and clear, creating a sense of freedom he hadn't felt for a long time. Pulling his suitcase behind him along the row of gleaming rental cars, he'd felt a growing sense of being in a very wide and spacious land.

For the first time in months, he felt like he could breathe.

Now he could see the mountains looming in the distance through the wide window of a roadside restaurant. Dan stirred his coffee and relaxed, surveying the scene as the occasional truck or car passed by. His attention was drawn to a bright patch of yellow flowers growing on the other side of the road and suddenly he found his thoughts drawn to his mother. She had always loved yellow flowers—buttercups, daffodils, irises.

He clearly remembered the early daffodils in the vase next to her bed a few days before he got the phone call that she had passed away.

Have a good life. That's what she'd said. *Have the best life you can.*

If he'd known then that they would be her last words to him he would have done things differently. Instead, he had smiled bravely, hugged her frail body carefully and told her he'd be back next weekend.

He shook his head. No point going down that road. The pain, for her, was over. For him, maybe it was just beginning.

Wiping his hand across his face, Dan continued to stare out the window, but his attention was still fixed firmly in the past.

How long had it been since those first doubts had begun to penetrate his safe world? How was it possible to be so unprepared for death, the most inevitable thing in life? With all the years of faithful commitment to the church, all the books he'd consumed on Christian growth and prayer, all the meetings he'd been to, the groups he and Kimberly had led.

And yet, in such a short space of time it had all started to unravel.

It was a year ago. He'd walked out of the service in the final song, frustrated with yet another sermon on the goodness of God, and bumped into Pastor Alan in the lobby. As they walked out to the parking lot, Alan had asked how his mother was doing. The ministry team had been praying for her, he'd said. And yes, he'd made sure to include her in the bi-monthly email. Yes, Dan appreciated the prayers. And no, the chemotherapy didn't seem to be working.

But it was Alan's parting words that had really got to Dan.

Alan had jumped in his car, and before closing the door had tried his best to sound like a church leader should. *"She just needs to have more faith, Dan. God uses faith, it's like fuel."*

He remembered walking back to the car under a cloud, sitting with his head resting against the steering wheel as his fingernails bit into the palms of his hands. *More faith?* How can she have more faith? Wasn't faith a gift? What about the *grace?* What about a *loving God?*

"Where is the grace?" he'd asked out loud. *"Where is the grace?"*

Kimberly found him soon afterwards. Her soft, calming voice had floated gently down to him through the open window. *"Going somewhere without me?"*

Dan blinked. Suddenly he was back in the restaurant holding a torn sachet of sugar. He grimaced at the sight of a thousand white granules scattered over the table.

"No, I hope not," he said to himself, exhaling as if he'd been holding his breath. He closed his eyes for a moment and reached out as best he could to whoever it was that was running the show up there. He wasn't exactly sure these days. Finding words to formulate into a prayer seemed pointless, and he didn't really want to. He just knew he needed some guidance.

He emptied his cup, cleaned up the sugar as best he could, and went to the counter to pay.

As he returned to the car he was feeling better. The somber moment had passed and he was looking forward to getting back on the road. With a couple of hours experience behind him, he was much more confident with driving on the wrong side. The little car was quite fun and sporty, and the last hour or so of the journey up into the mountains promised to be quite an experience.

"Okay," he said to himself. For the first time in years, he actually felt a childlike excitement stirring inside. "Let's discover the Pyrenees."

***

Pont de la Cruz was a small town nestling in a green valley of meadows and woodland, built out of the natural stone and dark slate of the local area. It might have looked drab and austere if it weren't for the window boxes and balconies bursting with flowers everywhere, and the brightly colored triangles of bunting stretched between tall buildings on the main street that crossed over the river. It seemed like the locals were welcoming the sunshine after a long, cold winter. Cafes and bars added more color with their bright parasols, and people of all shapes and sizes sat at tables or looked in shop windows or leaned on the railings of the bridge taking in the views.

The last leg of the drive had been everything Dan had hoped it would be and more. Wide, smooth highways faded into constantly winding roads that climbed ever higher into the heart of the Pyrenees. Forested slopes of dark pine trees rose up on all sides, broken at regular intervals by alpine rivers bursting with ice-cold snow-melt. It was all breathtakingly beautiful, and he'd found himself looking for places to pull over at the side of the road to take in a view down a valley or a snow-covered peak rising above the foothills.

This was true hiking country, Dan decided, and the town seemed perfectly situated to act as a gateway to adventures unlimited. If only he had more than a week to explore.

Having checked into the little bed & breakfast, unpacked and freshened up from the journey, he now found himself nursing a golden beer at one of the many cafes edging the river. The sun was quickly heading towards the mountains, painting the clouds a deep pink, and the mild evening air was filled with the chatter and rush of the river passing under the bridge.

Couples and small groups were out and about looking for restaurants, walking along the stretch of riverside lined with trees—the perfect setting for an Italian Bistro or Pizza parlor. Dan, having eaten a late lunch, was content to watch the world go by with his *San Miguel* and *tapas* that the waitress had persuaded him to try.

Patatas Bravas, he'd just learned, was a typical Spanish snack of deep-fried potato chunks served with a spicy sauce. He'd also enjoyed the smoked salmon on crispy toast, along with some very tasty fried chicken wings. Dan was in no rush. He sat back, and in a rare moment of inner peace, let the evening ebb and flow around him.

Presently the street lights came on, darkness covered the mountains like a blanket, and the long day of traveling began to catch up with him. A blip from his phone caught his attention—a message from Kimberly.

Hope you are settled in okay and eaten something. Remember to be kind to yourself.

Just sitting outside a cafe by the river watching the world go by. Very European!

Very jealous. Next time we go together.

He nodded. Through all the sorrow, the doubts and the questions, Kimberly was there. She seemed at least to understand something of what he was going through, and was prepared to accommodate his efforts to deal with his internal struggles.

Things had been better between him and his wife, that much was certain. All the pressure and stress of the last couple of years had taken its toll, a tension that had permeated every aspect of their lives. The smiles had faded, the laughter replaced with an underlying seriousness even Dan was able to notice.

Kimberly was strong, though. He'd always seen that, but she could still surprise him.

Yesterday afternoon had been a prime example, when their Pastor had *'popped in to say hello'.* There had been little pretense on Alan's part, though. There never was. His presence seemed to fill their small lounge, dressed as he was in his sharp suit. He was there on *Kingdom Business,* which became apparent as soon as Kimberly had placed slices of cake on the coffee table and poured the tea. He'd gotten straight to the point—his latest project, the *'New Beginnings'* course, was in need of a group leader to host the discussions. And Alan had his eye on Dan.

"Your neighbors have already signed up, Daniel. Would be perfect for you."

Dan was caught off guard. He'd assumed Alan was there to check up on him, instead the Pastor was offering him a place on his team. He remembered Reg saying something about a course, but he hadn't paid much attention at the time.

A few years ago he would have jumped at the chance. An opportunity to serve God while being reaffirmed in his climb up the faith ladder. Being on Alan's team was not something to be taken lightly. Their Pastor was highly respected in the town, even influential. He'd written an incredibly complicated theological study on the New Testament, and was often invited to speak at churches in the area. Alan expected the best from everyone, and serving alongside him was seen as a privilege.

Clearly, there was no doubt in Alan's mind that Dan should be ready and willing. But now, well, now things were different. How different was becoming more obvious by the day, and it was all very disconcerting.

Finally, after Dan had tried various angles on the theme of 'just not sure...', Alan had *'played the loyalty card'*, as Kimberly put it.

"The church needs you to get back into the game, Daniel. You don't want to drift, do you? We all know where that leads."

Get back in the game. Was that it? Dan had to admit that Alan could be a formidable persuader when he wanted to be. He had searched around for excuses, but everything sounded lame. He'd felt himself giving in...

"He's not ready, Alan."

Neither Alan nor Dan had noticed Kimberly standing in the corner of the room with her arms crossed and her eyes almost glowing. Was that a hint of *anger* in her voice?

"He can't rush back into things."

Kimberly had left no room for argument, and Alan, to be fair, had taken it well. He'd smiled, agreed, and moved the conversation on to other church matters. But Alan was a man who was used to getting what he wanted, and as he was leaving he took one last shot.

"Remember, it's a life-long commitment, Daniel. It's called church."

"Right. Of course. I'll let you know. When I get back from Spain." That's all that Dan could manage. It was perhaps the first time he hadn't immediately agreed to one of Alan's requests. For

some reason he felt like he'd been disobedient, and it left an empty feeling in his stomach.

As he and Kimberly cleared up the remains of the cake, Dan had noticed how quiet his wife was. She would normally chat about something, and he was usually happy to listen. Yesterday she had seemed preoccupied.

"I'm not going to commit to anything," he'd assured her.

"Good."

"I'll think about it when I'm away."

"Why? The last thing you need right now is him pushing you to get back into things."

"Well..."

"Don't do it because of me, either."

Yesterday now seemed like a long time ago. A couple of hours on a plane, a few hours drive, and here he was in a different world.

Kimberly's words echoed in his mind as Dan paid the bill. She was probably right—getting back into things was not going to solve anything. If he was going to commit to anything he needed to know why. He needed some answers.

He waved a thank-you to the waitress, now busily serving full tables. As he followed the stone path slowly alongside the river to the next bridge it seemed that for many the night was only just beginning. Stars were out, clearer and brighter than he'd seen them for a long time, the river burbled and rushed below him, laughter drifted up from the restaurants. It was all very wholesome and good for the soul, Dan decided.

Mum, you would like it here.

Standing there on the bridge, the sound of the river seemed to wash over his soul in a gentle but persistent flow, telling him truths that he couldn't quite hear. He could feel the dirt and grime that had built up inside, sense the raw, exposed wounds. Life had been unkind. He couldn't get away from the fact that he'd been carrying some heavy burdens, and the weight had been wearing him down for a long time. He needed rest. He needed to lay things aside. He needed to decide what, if anything, to pick up again from the confusion that was his life.

At least here, with no pressure to be anywhere, he could slow down. At least here, surrounded by mountains, he could find the space to breathe again. And maybe, just maybe, get some things sorted out inside.

Gazing up once more to the star-filled sky, he felt the faint stirrings of hope rise within once again. Maybe tomorrow would hold some answers.

It had to.

Tuesday

CHAPTER 3

"Wasted years...wasted hopes...wasted prayers."

L ike most of the buildings huddling together in the narrow streets of *Pont de la Cruz*, the bed & breakfast was an unpretentious four-story house with thick stone walls, narrow shuttered windows and steeply sloping roof to deal with the winter snows.

From Dan's room the small balcony offered an uninterrupted view across to the old church—an impressive Gothic structure sitting firmly on a rise behind the town. Beyond that, tree-clad hills climbed up to low mountains topped with cloud, and beyond them, the higher peaks glowed in the rays of the morning sun.

Content to stand and gaze, Dan's thoughts gradually turned to the day ahead. He had arranged to meet Joe Mitchel today, which was the whole point of him coming all this way. But from this high window, looking out on a very different part of the world, his personal troubles seemed, at least for a moment, a million miles away.

The idea of taking off for the day flickered briefly through his mind, but it wasn't just Kimberly he'd have to answer to, at the end of the day it was himself. Besides, there was even the possibility that Joe would actually be able to give him something to go forward with.

'*God can handle your doubts*' was a line Joe used often in his articles, and even if it was nothing more than sentiment, for Dan it felt like a lifeline to a drowning man.

"Well," Dan muttered, "maybe today things will change."

Breakfast-time in the small dining room was pleasant and quiet. His host, an energetic Spanish woman in her 60's, brought fresh coffee and a large plate heavily laden with toasted baguette, butter sachets, strawberry jam, a small croissant, and a large slice of heavy sponge-cake sprinkled with sugar that seemed oddly out of place at the breakfast table.

Dan, in between reading the news on his phone, skimming work emails and staring out the window, managed to finish everything.

"You go walking today?" his host asked, topping up his coffee cup.

"Well, driving," Dan explained. He motioned with his hands as if gripping the steering wheel. "Up to the lake."

"Ah, yes, the lake is beautiful," Anna exclaimed dramatically. Then she waved a stubby finger at him as she returned to the kitchen. "But I think is rain later."

Dan checked the weather app, which assured him the chance of rain was low. He also checked the time. It would be a little early back home, but he decided he would send a message to Kimberly now, just in case he didn't have a signal up in the mountains.

Hey I'm going out this morning and meeting up with Joe so will let u know how I'm getting on xx

He sipped good coffee and sat staring absentmindedly at his phone. Doubts remained close to the surface. It had been a long time since he'd talked with anyone about his faith. He even struggled to tell Kimberly what was going on inside. What was he expecting to come from this meeting with Joe Mitchel?

Okay, I'm just going to see how it goes. At least I can go home next week knowing I tried. I have to try.

***

This morning Joe finally felt refreshed. The tiredness of last week was only a memory, and he was looking forward to what the day held.

He flicked through the messages on his phone as he waited for his omelet to crisp up a little more. Sunlight was streaming into the kitchen and the day looked full of promise. But Joe had lived in the mountains long enough to know that you can't trust the weather, especially in the springtime. It would probably rain later, and that would be just fine.

There was a message from Sandy that she'd sent in the middle of the night—*remember you have a visitor today*—and a quick note he'd sent to himself just before heading off to bed.

Enjoying his leisurely breakfast in the quiet warmth of the kitchen, Joe thought over his *note to self*. He hadn't needed the reminder—it had been bubbling away in his subconscious ever since he got up this morning—but it was a practice of his to never miss a nugget of inspiration when it came. He had notebooks full of ideas and snippets of audio recording on his phone that would probably never see the light of day. This one would, he hoped. This one had a pull to it that he had learned to recognize over the years.

Joe made a short to-do list as he finished off his omelet and coffee, cleaned up quickly, and headed for *the zone*.

"*Start the day before the day starts you,*" his father had told him many times. 40 years later he was finally owning that wisdom for himself. This morning he didn't even take the time to open the shutters, he wanted to get his hands on the keyboard. No distractions. No excuses.

We *humans are a strange breed, aren't we? For thousands of years we have wondered at the world, wondered at the stars above, even wondered at our own wondering. And all the time questions, questions, questions. You'd think by now we'd understand how unique and incredible that makes us—little 'gods' walking around on earth...*

"Little *gods*," he said to himself, as if testing the phrase. "Little gods. Some folk aren't gonna like that."

He continued typing. The page filled steadily with words as Joe found himself relaxing into a steady rhythm. After the stagnant mire of the past few weeks, it felt like cool, fresh water for his soul.

...the harder it is to get away from the simple fact that everything is incredibly complex beyond our understanding...

...Worse still for the skeptic, we find that there is reason and order to it all, from the finest detail of subatomic particles, to the grand sweeping galaxies at the farthest reaches of our best telescopes, to the seeds in a sunflower's Fibonacci spirals...

...How can numbers or mathematical patterns be beautiful? How can the vibrations of a string penetrate the soul? And more importantly, why?

Joe's fingers continued to move over the keyboard for a few more minutes, then he sat back, his eyes scanning quickly over the last couple of sentences.

We are faced with a reality that is far too grand for a million lifetimes of exploration. God has truly set eternity in the heart of man. It should be no wonder that we wonder why so often.

"Why," he said to himself, looking around the dark room and noticing the closed shutters. "That is the question, Mitch. Why are you working in the dark?"

Opening the shutters and enjoying the view for a few minutes, Joe nodded. He didn't need to question why today was any different than last week, he simply accepted that this morning he had words, and that was enough.

He checked the clock. Thinking through his to-do list he

figured he had plenty of time to go down to the town to see the mechanic, then get back to meet the English guy. Half an hour more at the laptop and then he'd get going.

Taking his place at the desk like a seasoned pilot might step into the cockpit of an airplane, he soon found himself merging into another world of musings and ponderings, lost in the timeless wonder of the moment.

***

"The lake *eeze* beautiful," Dan said to himself in his best Spanish accent. He stood on the pebbled shore with mountain-tops, bare rocks and cloud-flecked sky all reflected on the surface. Only further out, in the deeper water, was the mirror image faintly rippled by the breeze.

Drinking in the cool, clean air, he looked up and around at his surroundings. Steep, rugged slopes clad with pines formed a wide, fertile valley of small meadows and woodland. Back westward, the way he'd come, the land fell away gradually down to a small hamlet of stone buildings, and nearer by he could see the square bell tower of an old monastery hidden among trees.

Looking eastward, the landscape split around the craggy spur of a mountain, forming two green valleys that rose steadily up to high, rounded summits touched by gray clouds. He observed the northernmost valley with interest. Somewhere up there he would find Joe's place.

Having carefully studied the map on his phone, and once more going over the directions that he'd received from Joe Mitchel, Dan decided that he would leave the car here at the lake and walk up to the house. It should be no more than an hour, he needed the exercise, and besides, he always found some clarity when he was out walking.

And clarity, if he was honest, had been in short supply lately.

Rucksack unceremoniously thrown over his shoulder, Dan set off in good spirits. The scenery didn't disappoint. Grand and uplifting, he felt an expansive sense of freedom as he began his journey. At a steep bend in the single-track road, he was able to look back down through a break in the trees to the lake, glimmering in the sunlight.

Immersed as he was in the dramatic beauty of his surroundings, he couldn't help thinking how unreal it all seemed, how far removed from life just a couple of days ago. Dan soon found himself reflecting on the situation he found himself in. Everything seemed to be confirming his suspicions—he was no longer the person he once was. Something had changed. Something fundamental.

Now all he had were questions.

Pastor Alan's words echoed in his mind once more—*It's a life-long commitment, Daniel. It's called church*

A life-long commitment gone bad. Was this what *backsliding* looked like?

The road continued to roll under Dan's feet and soon passed over a small bridge where he stopped to lean on the barrier. The rushing water, not much bigger than a stream, cascaded down in little waterfalls from one small pool to the next. The constant white noise filled his mind and for a moment he let himself relax. Memories flooded back of happier times in his childhood. Simpler times. He could imagine himself, barefoot, wading into a pool and searching for interesting stones on a hot summer's day.

It's been way too long since I've been out hiking. If only it were that easy, just get away and forget my troubles. Forget who I am.

Turning back to the road, his doubts began to open the door on his frustrations, a jumbled, confusing mess of emotion rising up inside.

Why am I even here? What do I think meeting this guy is going to achieve? Getting some answers? Dumping all my doubts on willing ears? God, I feel so lost right now, so confused about everything. I just want to break out of all this and get on with my life.

He let the words come out, truth mixed with fear mixed with regret. Words that he knew had been lying just below the surface for a long while.

"God, I don't know if you're even listening anymore. I feel let down, abandoned. Where have you been these last two years? Where were you when I needed you? When Mum needed you? Nothing makes sense anymore. I have been putting my heart and soul into church for half my life and I don't even understand what it's for any longer. I've had enough of people pretending that their life is wonderful with Jesus in it, when in fact we're just the same as everyone else. We're just better at hiding behind the facade."

The dull rhythm of rubber-soled boots on concrete soaked into the surrounding trees.

"I don't want to go back to church. I don't want to be part of Alan's little project. I don't want people telling me I need to read the Bible and have a healthy prayer life. I don't want to make excuses for a God of fire and judgment. I don't want to feel like I have to earn your favor, that things aren't going well because I'm not doing it right, not praying right, not putting my heart into it."

As the road climbed alongside green pastures and dark forest, crossing and re-crossing the meandering stream, the late morning skies began to change to gray. Lost in the turmoil of an inner world, spilling out his heart to who knew what, Dan hardly noticed. He continued to let his muddled thoughts flow as raindrops started to spatter on the road at his feet.

Wasted years...wasted hopes...wasted prayers...where does that leave me? Where are you now, God?

It wasn't long before more clouds were building over the mountains and beginning to block out the sun, and presently the rain began to fall with greater force.

Dan lifted his eyes to the cloudy skies as if noticing for the first time that the weather had changed. He stopped and spread out his hands. Rain ran down his face. It was beginning to feel noticeably colder. "Oh, great! Thanks for listening!" he said out loud, half-joking. He would probably see the funny side later, he thought to himself, so why not now?

CHAPTER 4

"What is grace if it isn't complete grace?"

Dan stood at the side of the road. A small car passed by, headlights on and wiper blades flapping crazily against the rain. Rain that was suddenly being blown by a strong wind coming down from the heights. He could feel the cold drops beginning to find a way inside of the collar of his hiking jacket, which he promptly zipped up to his chin.

Looking about him, he weighed the situation. The road twisted away in front and behind, dark forest closed in about him, and the valley sides rose up into cloud. He figured he must be about halfway there, which meant going back to the lake, or pressing on. Maybe he could get a ride either way with the next car, if there *was* a next car on this lonely road.

At that moment the sound of a motor reached Dan's ears. Looking back through the trees he could see a vehicle coming up the road, and presently an old silver SUV came winding around the bend towards him. It slowed down as it approached, saving Dan the trouble of thumbing a lift. The passenger window wound down as the car came to a stop, revealing a bearded face under a worn baseball cap.

"*Hola!* Need a ride?" The voice that reached Dan's ears was distinctly American, and the tone reassuringly friendly.

"Morning!" Dan shouted, relieved to hear his own language. "Are you...are you Joe, by any chance?"

"Sure am!" the driver said with a smile. "Which means you must be Dan from England, right? Jump in, Dan!"

Dan slid the wet rucksack from his shoulders as Joe leaned over to open the door.

"Just about to turn around." Dan climbed in and dumped the backpack between his legs. "Thanks."

"Nice day for a walk," remarked the American as he forced the gear-stick into first and accelerated away with a jolt that made Dan grab the door handle. "I was heading back from town, running a little late this morning."

"Seems like perfect timing."

Joe smiled. "Well, looks like you could do with some hot coffee."

"That,"—Dan wiped the rain from his face—"would be wonderful." He watched as Joe, keeping to the middle of the road to avoid the running rainwater, continued driving at a leisurely pace. "I was about to get very wet, it seems. Well, wetter, if that's possible."

Joe glanced across at his passenger. "You didn't walk all the way up from the town, did you?"

"No. Left the car at the lake," Dan explained. "It was actually a nice walk, until it started raining."

"Some days it rains," Joe said in a low voice, as if thinking to himself. Then he chuckled. "Gotta be a life lesson there, right? I was doing okay until it started raining."

Dan forced a laugh but it sounded more like a strangled cough.

"Best thing to do is keep on walking, in my opinion. Anyway, glad you could make it."

"Thanks for agreeing to see me," Dan said, trying to sound more certain than he felt. Joe's remark had surprised him, and he found himself glancing sideways, wondering who this guy in faded jeans and camouflage jacket really was. A conversation through email was one thing, meeting in person was something entirely different.

"Well, hey, sorry we're not officially open, but you're very welcome all the same." Joe crunched the gears as he turned the car into another sharp bend. "Hope you find it worth your while. It's a long way to come for a cup of coffee."

Dan smiled. That was exactly the kind of thing Kimberly would say when she was trying to cheer him up. He briefly explained that he'd booked in at a B & B for the week. "And meeting up with a friend for the weekend, so hopefully do a bit of exploring."

Joe nodded. As the car slowed again he pointed out a large gray house, just visible through the rain, perched solidly on a rise above the trees. "That's our place, up there."

A simple wooden sign at the side of the road displayed the words *Casa de Gracia.* A rough, puddled track branched off through a pair of high, wrought iron gates set in a stone wall. Joe drove through, immediately stopped at the edge of a wide stream, and opened the door.

"Just gotta shut the gates, as we're closed," he explained, pulling up the collar of his jacket against the rain.

Dan sat watching the stream through swishing wiper blades as Joe, getting wetter and wetter by the second, waded through various puddles, closing the big gates one by one.

"Fixing the automatic mechanism on these gates, way down on my to-do list," he commented as he jumped back in, wiping his hands on his jeans. Joe dropped the clutch and shifted into first gear, but as the SUV started forward into the shallow water the engine stalled with a sudden jolt.

Joe leaned forward to rest his head on the steering wheel. "Manual transmission," he mumbled, then sat up and glanced at Dan. "Sorry about that, wet boots."

Dan smiled as Joe put the gears in neutral and fumbled with the key. The engine coughed, complained, and refused to start. Joe tried again, but there was nothing but tired clicks from the starter.

There was an awkward silence as raindrops spattered on the roof of the car.

"Dead," Joe muttered under his breath.

"Battery?"

"Yeah, it wasn't so great yesterday, which is why I was in town trying to get a new one. Anyways, no big deal, only a short walk up to the house."

Leaving the SUV stuck at the edge of the stream, Joe indicated the way forward. "The water's nice and shallow here so you can ford it in a car, but there's no bridge as such. Just these concrete stepping-stones and a hand-rail."

"That's fine, I like adventures," said Dan lightheartedly, grabbing the rail and carefully stepping up onto the first of four hexagonal islands spanning the stream. It was a simple matter to reach the other side, but the final gap between stepping-stone and dry ground was much wider than he would have expected. He looked back at Joe.

"Ah, stream's a little higher than usual," Joe observed, peering past Dan's shoulder. "Looks like we're stuck here. So, tell me about your life back in England."

Dan smiled at Joe's wry sense of humor. "If it's all the same to you," he said, throwing his rucksack onto the shore, "I'd prefer wet boots and hot coffee. *Then* I'll tell you about England." He took a leap, landing with a splash just short of his target, and stumbled forward on the uneven pebbles.

"Hope you're not going to rate us on Google," Joe shouted.

"Hope this isn't a test," Dan said to himself, turning round just in time to see Joe jump forward gracefully and splash into the water only inches from shore. Reaching out quickly, he was able to grab Joe's arm to stop him slipping backwards.

"Thanks," said Joe. "Don't forget your backpack."

Dan's narrowed eyes followed Joe as he walked up to the track. He nodded to himself then followed along, water squelching from his boots. Joe took the lead, passing an old building that he called 'our ruin', explaining that it had probably been used by shepherds a hundred years ago. At a large rock, the track turned sharply into woodland and began to climb gently up to a sturdy wooden bridge.

Presently the gravel track transformed into a concrete

driveway that turned a sharp hairpin and ran up against a high stone wall. Dan could see rainwater running off roof tiles as they neared the top of the slope, then deep-set, shuttered windows in a rough stone wall. Well-kept shrubs and rose bushes grew neatly along the front of the building. The place had a hint of the luxurious about it, and it may have been something to do with the persistent rain, but he thought it all looked very inviting.

"Home, sweet home. Welcome to *Casa de Gracia*, the House of Grace," Joe announced as he opened the heavy wooden door. "Come on in and warm up."

Dan, shaking raindrops from his shoulders, stepped into a rustic, open hallway dominated by a tiled staircase with ornate wooden balustrades. Rich terracotta tiles covered the floor, and the bare stone walls displayed old farming tools from a bygone era. Archways led off to the left and right.

"I'll take your coat. You can leave your boots in here."

Joe waved Dan through the left archway. He found a cloakroom with numerous winter coats and jackets hanging on hooks, walking boots and hiking shoes of various kinds, and a sturdy wooden table scattered with guidebooks. On the wall opposite the window hung a three-dimensional relief map of the Pyrenees, alongside various framed photographs of people on high mountains. There was a faint smell of worn leather and polish.

"Go make yourself comfortable in the lounge, straight through there." Joe indicated a door on the other side of an archway that led to a corridor, and Dan found himself in a large, comfortable room with a wood-beamed ceiling. Three soft couches huddled together near a large fireplace where a cast-iron stove glowed invitingly. In one corner of the room, bookshelves lined the stone walls, and the rest of the space was occupied by a long, highly polished table with six chairs.

There was a comfortable sense of peace, an almost palpable quiet, and Dan felt immediately at home. His initial doubts about Joe began to fade away as he padded in damp socks over to the fireplace to warm his hands, then sunk down into the couch and stretched out his legs on the thick rug, pointing cold feet towards the warm stove.

"Perfect," Dan thought to himself as he took a deep breath, soaking up the warmth from the fire and feeling his body relax. "Very, very nice."

The door opened and Joe came through. "Hey, warming up? Got you some clean socks, probably want to get those ones off." A pair of thick hiking socks came sailing through the air and landed next to Dan. "More importantly, I got the coffee on. Or I think we have some English tea somewhere."

"Coffee will be great, thanks. I usually have milk and sugar in mine."

"All things are possible, Dan," Joe said in a reassuring tone. "Be right back."

Dan was glad to shed his damp socks, which he placed on the tiled hearth. The clean ones were a little too big but warm, and more importantly, dry. He concluded that putting his trust in the weather app had been a bad move—the last thing he needed right now was a case of pneumonia.

Presently Joe reappeared through the door, balancing a tray which he set down on the low coffee table in the middle of the rug. Two steaming mugs of black coffee, a small jug of milk, sachets of sugar, and a plate of chocolate-chip cookies.

"Help yourself. I warmed up the milk a little, and the cookies are a peace offering. For the episode down at the stream." Joe grabbed his mug, selected the nearest cookie and sat back on the middle of the three couches.

Dan smiled. It hadn't been a great start, but at least it was something to talk about. He leaned forward and poured milk into the dark coffee. "I was just thinking, not the best day to go walking up here."

"That's mountains for ya," Joe said, offering his opinion of the unpredictable Pyrenees weather.

As Dan listened to Joe he couldn't help thinking how out of place this man looked here. Without the baseball cap, Dan could see thick gray hair blending into the flecked beard, and dark gray eyes with deep crows-feet. Give him a Stetson and he'd make a great old cowboy. No, a Sheriff. Definitely a Sheriff.

Looking around the room as he sipped his coffee, it occurred to him how different this felt from the confusing meeting he'd had with Pastor Alan. The sudden change of circumstances was not lost on Dan and he decided to enjoy the relaxed atmosphere. He wanted to know more about how this American writer came to be hiding away in the mountains of Spain.

Joe briefly explained that he and his wife, Sandy, had been there nearly five years, they both loved it here, and over time had slowly adapted to living a new life. "And this little corner of Spain is a world away from what we're used to," he added.

"You run retreats, I read somewhere."

"Well, personally I avoid the term 'retreat'. We try to make it a refuge of sorts. A place for people to find some space. We don't teach or preach, we take a hands-off approach, but we make ourselves available."

"A refuge from the storm."

"Indeed," Joe said softly. "Well, Dan, you are very welcome here. I was talking to Sandy the other night, she said I needed to be sure to tell you, our door is open to you."

"When does she get back?"

"She's still in the States until next week. I only just got back here myself last week. We try to visit family every winter. Sandy's mom especially, she's...old."

There was a pause in the conversation.

Joe leaned forward, his tone was kindly and reassuring. "My mom's been gone ten years now. Sometimes you think you're going to forget them, but you don't. They never really leave."

Dan reached for a cookie and remained hunched forward. Without looking up he said, "It's been a crazy couple of years for me. Trying to be there for my mother. I used to be so sure about who I was, what my life was about..." his voice trailed off, then he looked over to Joe. "I guess I'm looking for some answers."

Joe sat back. "You've been knocked out of your routine, forced to look at life in a different way. It's not surprising. Suddenly everything that seemed so sure is no longer a given."

"That kind of sums it up, yes."

"But you aren't alone."

"Feels that way."

"Of course. And it's completely natural to start doubting God, your faith, and every decision you've ever made. What are you, mid-forties?"

"46," Dan interjected.

"46, and grieving. Got kids, right?"

"Two teenage boys," Dan said with a smile.

"Well, no kidding, Dan. This has to be the hardest time of your life." Joe's eyes seemed to reflect a deep understanding, and his words were reassuring. Dan listened as Joe explained how important it was to not underestimate the very real pain and feelings of loss he was wrestling with. "Pain, and regret for what might have been, if you think about it," the older man concluded.

Dan eased back into the couch once more. "I keep wondering if I've wasted half my life trying to be a good Christian, doing all the right things. And the whole thing seems to have let me down. Which then leads to more doubt..."

"Exactly."

"*Have I missed the point? Do I not have enough faith?* All that kind of thing."

Joe agreed. "Round and round in endless confusion."

"I remember reading that article you wrote, about God's *conditional* unconditional love? Now *that* made a lot of sense to me."

Joe sighed. He was staring into the fireplace as if lost in his thoughts. "Ah, yeah, I got a lot of hate mail over that one." A smile formed on his face but it didn't seem to touch his eyes.

"Well, it got me thinking," Dan paused to gather his thoughts. "I don't want to believe in a God who expects something in return. I don't want to hear that I have to have more faith, love God more, pray more. I mean, if it still depends on me then I'm never going to get there."

"What is grace if it isn't complete grace, right?" Joe banged a fist on his knee. "If there has to be some kind of trade-off then, well…"

"It's not grace."

"Hmm. I should probably do a follow-up to that article," Joe pondered. "It raised a lot of questions. And that's what I try to do —get people asking the hard questions."

"Everything seems to be a hard question right now."

Joe placed his empty coffee mug on the tray, then continued. "You know, Dan, what we're all about here, the bottom line, the reason why Sandy and I do what we do, it's all about creating a safe space. Space for the big, life-changing questions about God and faith and what it all means in the here and now."

Dan nodded his approval.

"We don't necessarily have the answers and we don't pretend to. In a way, the answers aren't really the point." Joe explained. "But I want you to know that from the start. And if you're okay with that, the fact that you may not get all your answers, then I'll encourage you to ask away."

"I have a pretty big list," Dan admitted.

"Alright. Well, listen. This weather is set in for a good while, looks like we're stuck here for the rest of the afternoon, anyways. So here's the deal," Joe rose from the couch and topped up the stove with a couple of logs as he continued. "I'll go fix us a sandwich and more coffee, you relax, and let's just have some good conversation. For me, that's usually where the answers are found."

"Sounds good," Dan said, relieved to be able to talk freely. "Feels like I've been carrying around all these doubts and questions for a long time. Way too long, I imagine. I appreciate it."

"My pleasure," said Joe, gathering the empty cups on the tray and heading for the door.

"Uh, Joe?" Dan called as his host was about to leave the room. "You mentioned that you might have English tea?"

"Coming right up," Joe said with a smile.

CHAPTER 5

"People often want to be told what to believe..."

T he morning rolled steadily into afternoon as the rain continued to fall. Dan was relieved to discover that Joe wasn't one for pretense. It was a refreshing change from the polished lives of the people he had to deal with on a regular basis, and made him wonder if he'd been guilty of the same thing —*don't rub the paint off, Dan, your life might show through.*

Joe had filled in some details of his past—stories from another lifetime, it seemed. Some things Dan had picked up from reading the blog, but others were new to him. He'd gathered that his host was a musician, but he hadn't realized that for many years Joe had been co-leading a successful church.

"Musician, songwriter, and ultimately worship coordinator. It was pretty cool, I have to admit. I had a great team. Couldn't have asked for more."

"So what happened? If you don't mind..."

"No, Sure. It's kind of a long story, but the short version is that I woke up one day."

Dan nodded, waiting patiently for more.

"I began to question what it was all about. This thing we'd built called *church.* All the work putting on a show every Sunday morning. I was pretty sure that if God died nobody there would even notice, the whole thing would just continue to run itself."

"So, what, did you just up and leave?" asked Dan.

"It wasn't that simple, I wish it was. The whole thing was a very painful time. I tried to keep myself working at it but my heart just wasn't in it anymore." Joe leaned forward as if to confide in his newfound companion. "And of course there was Sandy. She was worried that I'd had a mental breakdown or something. In the end, we decided I needed a sabbatical, just to get away and get back on track with God."

"Was it that bad?"

Joe stood up and stretched his back, then walked over to the window to look at the rain. "Probably worse. I was worried that I'd lost my faith and that I was going to lose everything else— my marriage, my career, my house. I would open up my Bible and it was like I was reading Russian or something. I couldn't even pray, and that's pretty scary when you're supposed to be a professional believer."

Dan smirked. *"Professional believer.* Yeah, I know exactly what you mean."

"Well, that was just one more thing to break free from, but when you're in the middle of it all it's very difficult to see a way out. Because of what we've been taught about faith, we're convinced that *we* are the problem." Joe looked over to Dan. *"Is there sin in my life? Am I not reading the Bible enough, not praying enough? What's wrong with me?* That kind of stuff."

Dan was sitting back, looking across at Joe and letting the words sink in. "Yeah, that sounds like me. I think coming here was a last shot at trying to sort myself out."

"Well, for me, I had to get some space between me and my circumstances. I wanted to get someplace I could think and pray. That's how we ended up here."

"A little valley in the Pyrenees," Dan reflected. "Good idea."

Joe explained how they'd come to Spain to get away for a while. How they had done the tourist destinations of Madrid and Seville, then headed for the mountains.

"Sandy's aunt and uncle bought this place about 20 years ago. They were trying to make it work as a bed and breakfast. It was perfect." Joe smiled.

"So you decided to stay?"

"Not so fast," Joe motioned with his hand. He was clearly getting on a roll with his story and enjoying the chance to tell it to someone new. He briefly retold how they had both fallen in love with the place; how he'd found a freedom that he hadn't felt in a long time; how he would get up early to follow the hiking trails up the valley, over the mountains, and down to the town. Sometimes he'd be out all day, sometimes Sandy would come along, but she seemed to know he needed the space to just be.

"So, *then* you decided to stay?" Dan offered.

"Yeah," Joe chuckled. "We decided to stay. Come on, I'll give you the tour."

As Joe showed Dan around the house he gave a continual running commentary of how this place had grown on them in the weeks they were here; how he and Sandy had remembered a dream they'd once had of running a Christian retreat; of how they had returned home with one goal in mind—to figure out the way forward. They had felt sure, Joe explained, that even in all the crazy uncertainty, God was in this somehow. There was a new possibility before them, and all they had to do was find the way.

The house, Dan learned, was built on the site of some old farm buildings. One building had been converted into a workshop and garage, the other formed the back part of the house. The main part was completely new, and every care had been taken to build a modern house that wouldn't look out of place in this beautiful valley. It was all local stone and oak wood beams, and Dan loved how the interior managed to be both rustic and modern at the same time. Upstairs were five large bedrooms, and the loft area had been developed into two self-contained apartments. It was in one of these apartments that they ended up, looking out the window at the weather, which had now turned stormy.

"Got a fantastic view here, back down the valley. We're looking almost west now, and you can catch some amazing sunsets. If you can see 'em," Joe laughed.

"So, how does the story end?"

Joe was happy to explain how they had managed to work something out with Sandy's aunt and uncle. "It was simple. They were finding the place too much work, we felt strongly that this was exactly where we were supposed to be. So it was, in a way, a matter of deciding that there had to be a solution. It was a huge change for us, but I've never done anything in my life I was so sure about, except marrying Sandy."

"And so"—Dan was thinking things through—"you did leave everything behind."

"Yeah, I guess. It took us about a year, all told, but I resigned from the church leadership, we sold our house, said our good-byes, and bought a nice little apartment down in the town. Then, to cut a long story short, we came to live here, and they moved into our apartment."

"And the rest is history," Dan said.

"Well, I hope the rest is the *future*."

"Hmm. Good point. So what *is* the future?"

"Well, there are a growing number of Christians out there that no longer fit into the 'normal way' of doing things. The old, familiar frameworks can't hold them anymore. Their whole world has been shaken, and they need time and space to work out their journey. And that's what we do, we simply facilitate that by creating a safe place to ask questions, and help them on their way."

Dan nodded. "So I'm not the only one to have doubts? That's reassuring, anyway."

"One thing we don't do, though, is tell anyone what we think they should believe. There's an unfolding, a *revealing* that needs to take place, and every one of us is at a different stage along the way. Unfortunately, people often want to be told what to believe, and that," Joe shrugged, "well, that's just exchanging one belief system for another."

"So you kind of see all this as part of a spiritual journey?"

Joe had been gazing through the window, but he turned to Dan and looked him in the eye. "Don't you realize you're on a journey right now?"

"Well, I never thought of it that way, to be honest."

Joe reached out a hand, placing it firmly on Dan's shoulder. "If we're not on a journey we're just standing still. And you aren't standing still because you're seeking answers. You could say it's a *spiritual* journey, but it involves very real struggles."

Dan was only too familiar with the struggles.

"Anyway," Joe continued, lightening up, "this is your apartment. Maybe you'll be able to see a sunset one evening."

"Nice. I'd like that."

"So tomorrow morning I gotta head back to town. Apart from that, I'm at your disposal."

"Maybe I'll tag along," said Dan. "I left most of my stuff at the bed and breakfast. *Casa Anna,* I think it's called?"

"Oh, Anna, yeah, she's a real star. I'll explain that I've kidnapped you for a couple of days, she'll be cool with that. Anyway, get your backpack, settle in and I'll meet you back in the lounge when you're ready."

CHAPTER 6

"To move forward you have to leave some things behind."

Dan had taken up his place on the couch once more, relaxing comfortably into the warm glow that radiated from the fireplace. Rain continued to spatter against the windows, the occasional rumble of thunder echoed in the valley, but the atmosphere in the room was one of peace and safety.

Little by little Dan moved into the space Joe had created for deeper conversation, testing the waters as he attempted to put muddled thoughts and feelings into words. Joe listened patiently, always encouraging with a nod here and a question there, allowing Dan to take his time.

"I know what you mean," said Joe gently as Dan described his slow and steady descent into a quagmire of questions and doubts. "It's incredible how it can all start to crumble so easily."

"Unbelievable. Unthinkable. Was it the same for you?"

"I guess for me it was the hypocrisy. Seeing the widening gap between what we did as a church and who we really were when no one was looking. It's difficult not to judge people who should know better, especially if they are the ones preaching the message."

Dan simply nodded.

"There was a lot going on all at once," Joe continued. "Some-one…a guy in the worship team had an affair. That shook me real hard, it was a helluva mess."

"Nasty."

"Nasty, yeah." Joe was silent for a moment. "A lot of fallout. One thing after another. It forced me to question what this thing called church was really all about. What did my faith mean? What the heck was God doing?"

"But you didn't doubt God in all that? Did you still trust him?"

Joe raised his head as he scanned his memories. "Good question. I doubted God's intentions, sure, but I didn't doubt God as such. Well, maybe for a while."

"I think that's where I struggle," Dan agreed. "What we have doesn't seem to line up with what you read in the Bible."

"No. We still mess up, bad things still happen to good people. We don't seem to be any better than anyone else."

"But we're the ones doing the judging." Dan spoke quietly, staring at the wall.

"Exactly. We've bought into the idea that everything should be better for us believers. Blessings, abundance, answered prayer." Joe gave Dan a sideways glance. "I'm sure you've heard it all a thousand times."

"It's all very…seductive? What am I saying? I sound like Yoda."

A flicker of amusement crossed Joe's face. He reached underneath the coffee table and pulled out a leather-bound Bible. He held it in both hands. "Has this book made you more re-ligious? Or made you more free?" he asked.

Dan considered Joe's question. "I never wanted to be reli-gious. I was always a person of faith."

"Yeah, I used to say the same thing. In reality, what we have is a faith operating inside of a religious box. It doesn't work so well."

"Interesting." Dan's eyes wandered around the room. "I guess religion masquerades as faith, in a way."

Joe nodded in agreement. "In a very real sense. Whenever there's pressure to conform, rules to follow, whenever there's even a hint of fear..."

Everything Joe was saying seemed to be resonating inside. It was uncomfortable, but at the same time he felt a growing sense of relief. He shook his head sadly. "I used to be so sure about it all, like I had this clear path. I knew I was 'saved', I knew I was a child of God, I knew I had a ticket to heaven."

Joe smiled. "Well, we mustn't be too hard on ourselves, Dan. The fact is, for millions of people all over the world, that system works to a point. It *did* work for people like us, for a while. It gave us hope, a place to belong, something to base our life on. It's not that it's bad, it's simply that there are inherent bugs in the software."

"And so long as you don't question things, you can keep going as if nothing is wrong."

"Exactly," Joe agreed. "You and me, and many other people, we've simply woken up to the bigger questions. *Does Christianity have a monopoly on God? What does faith look like in a modern world?*"

"*Why doesn't God answer prayer?*"

"All that stuff," Joe said with understanding. "And you know what? It's okay to ask."

Dan stared at the Bible that now sat solidly in the middle of the table. He hesitated, then reached over and picked it up, studying the gilt lettering with interest. "Nice. You know, it sounds crazy but I don't know what to do with this anymore."

"No," Joe said in a matter-of-fact tone. "That's just normal."

"A friend of mine once told me that God is bigger than the Bible. I think what he really meant was that the Bible keeps God very small."

"Which it can, that's true. It kind of depends on how you approach it," Joe said.

Dan placed the Bible back on the table and remained leaning forward, knitting his fingers tightly together. "I think," he said slowly, "that's what screwed me up in the end. If I couldn't believe the Bible anymore, then I had no foundation."

"Which is not true, by the way," Joe stated, waving a finger in the air. "Ever consider that the reason we have a *personal Bible* is so we can develop a *personal faith?* Otherwise, we'd simply have a set of rules and that would be that."

"Err. No," Dan confessed. "But that's a good point."

"There are other ways of approaching the Bible. One of the first things we try to help people understand is that you don't have to take what you've been taught at face value. What we've been taught about God, what we've been taught about the Bible and its role in our faith, what we've been taught about the place of the church. And just as importantly, what we've been taught about ourselves. It's these four pillars we build our lives on, and any one of them gets a bit shaky you feel it real fast."

Dan took a moment to absorb Joe's words. In his minds-eye he could picture himself standing on a high platform, resting solidly on ornate Greek columns which were cracked and crumbling at the base. He shook his head but the vision remained. "And I suppose it can all come down very quickly. I guess I've been taking a lot for granted for too long."

"We love to think that we have faith all wrapped up. We love the certainty, the black and white of it all. But it seems like it's not as solid as we've wanted to believe," Joe suggested.

"Yeah, I see that," said Dan. He paused, considering the path the conversation was taking. He couldn't think of another person in the world he could talk to about these deep matters. "Suddenly I feel like I know nothing at all."

Joe was nodding his head. "We have to remember, this is *faith* we're talking about."

"Right."

"With faith, you have *some* more certainty over *some* things in your life. A little more clarity maybe, more of a sense of purpose. But to say that we can have all the answers, that we completely know the truth...I just have to remind myself of the facts every now and then."

As Dan nodded in agreement, Joe continued in a softer tone.

"No matter who we are or what we believe, we are all in the same boat trying to find our way, it's just that some of us have begun to think outside the box."

"And I suppose that's nothing new," Dan suggested.

"No, not really."

There was a silence as Dan considered Joe's words. After a few moments, he let his thoughts come out. "I guess I just found it easier to stop. With all that's been going on, I didn't have the strength of will to hold it all together anymore. So I stopped reading my Bible, stopped going along on a Sunday. I don't even know how to pray anymore," Dan finished quietly.

"Would it make you feel any better if I told you this happens to a lot of Christians? From what you've told me it sounds like you've outgrown your spiritual environment, and you've hit *The Wall*."

"The *Wall?*" Dan was curious.

"There's a place we come to in our spiritual walk. It's where we realize that to move forward we have to leave some things behind. And I'm not just talking about church here, I'm talking about our ego, our expectations, our need to belong. Everything hangs in the balance."

Dan rubbed his chin absentmindedly. "Feels more like a desert, to be honest."

"I like the *wall* analogy because there is often a pushing through, and it's easy to bounce back."

"People bounce back?"

"Sure they do," Joe said sadly. "We're talking about having to walk away from family, or that's what it feels like. Our faith will never be the same again. And it's real painful. New birth doesn't come easy."

Dan watched Joe lean forward to top up his coffee. He remained there, studying the mug thoughtfully.

"There's a dying," Joe continued. "A letting go. Sometimes it can feel like you're falling into nothing, falling apart. It's a scary place, like an eagle jumping out of the nest for the first time. Can't blame anyone for wanting to retreat back to what they knew."

"I've felt that pull. Get back to where I felt safe."

"Change is always a challenge. The amount of messages I get from people who are suffering real trauma, you wouldn't believe," Joe was shaking his head. "And I guess you were carrying the weight of your mom's illness at the same time. That's a whole lot to go through on your own."

There was a silence as both men lost themselves in thought.

"So what do I do?" Dan focused on the flames once more. "Is there a way forward?"

Joe sat back and raised his eyes to the ceiling. "I can't give you definitive answers, Dan, it's your journey. But what we *can* do"—he clapped his hands together decisively—"is dismantle the shaky foundations, clear away the rubble, and with the little pieces of gold that are left, we can start building our lives again."

"That's what you did?" Dan asked, looking up. "Sounds like a good place to start."

"Well, that's what I would have done if I'd known back then," Joe explained with a chuckle. "Hindsight is a wonderful thing! But anyhow, that's the approach we always encourage others to take. Dismantle, evaluate and rebuild. And"—he looked over the top of his spectacles—"don't be too quick to throw out the baby with the bathwater."

CHAPTER 7

Every traveler needs a refuge.

"**S**o we aren't going to throw out the Bible just yet?" Dan asked. "Because I've wanted to recently, I really have." He sat opposite Joe at the dining table, steam rising from the plates of spaghetti they were hungrily digging into. It was late, and he could feel the long day starting to wear on him. The warmth of the fire and the glass of red wine probably had something to do with it too, but it was, they both agreed, very good wine.

"It's one of those *big four* questions I wrestled with for a *long* time." Joe's voice was level and steady. He could have talked happily into the early hours, but studying Dan's face it was apparent that the younger man wanted some answers.

"It's certainly been at the core of my life for...I don't know how long," Dan said. "Maybe it's stuck there."

Joe smiled at Dan's honesty. "Well, this is how I see it. The Bible is unique, no doubt about that. It's packed with ancient wisdom. Lots of good common sense, and no question there's powerful teaching to be found in those pages that *can* be a real force for good in the world."

"Okay. I think I'd go along with that."

"Alright. But does it have all the answers? Is it infallible? Is it *true*?"

Dan shrugged his shoulders. "I guess that's what I've always believed."

Joe set down his fork and reached for his wine glass. "The problem is we ask the wrong questions of the Bible. We've been taught to revere it, honor it, and we expect it to behave in a certain way."

Dan agreed. He'd spent many an early morning following study notes and delving into scriptures as if the mysteries of life would somehow unfold before his eyes.

But that was before.

"It's become our essential guidebook to life. But does it contain everything we need to know about God and faith?" Joe asked.

"Well..." Dan hesitated. Questioning the Bible did not sit comfortably with him. "I always understood that it has all the answers to everything we ever need to know. But it's like we have to go digging for it."

"And there's a red line we must not cross, right? You can dig all you want, you can explore different applications of a given text. But you can't question the Bible itself or its central place in your faith." Joe's expression held a question.

Dan's attention moved to his wine. He was mesmerized by the orange flames from the fire dancing in the glass. *You can't question the Bible.* Probably why he'd been avoiding it for months. He nodded thoughtfully.

"So let's just suppose," Joe continued, topping up their glasses, "let's suppose we *do* start questioning it. What do we find? Contradiction, historical inaccuracies, some really weird things. When I started digging for myself I had to decide what to do with all this stuff."

Dan looked across at Joe, pursing his lips. "It feels wrong to even suggest that all is not perfect. I keep looking for the lightning bolt."

Joe smiled and sipped his wine, then continued. "I'm not saying there isn't life-changing stuff in there. That's what I mean by finding the gold. Look at the gospels. They can be very powerful all by themselves. Getting an insight into what Jesus was like, what he said and did. It's radical stuff."

"Okay," Dan agreed. "But isn't that just picking the good parts? What about wiping out nations?"

"I just want to challenge your perception. Can God speak to us through the pages? We've both experienced that, I'm sure. But does God *need* a book to teach us and guide us? If he did, that would be contrary to what's written in the pages. Jeremiah says '*I will put my law in their minds and write it on their hearts,*' so that's pretty clear to me."

Dan lifted a fork-full of spaghetti to his mouth, then paused. How often he'd heard that scripture, and never seen it in that context. "God is bigger than the Bible," he said eventually. "Like my friend said."

"Well, God is certainly bigger than your standard evangelical interpretation of it, that's for sure," Joe was now waving his fork in Dan's direction. "My pastor was forever talking about living a *biblical life.* Kinda his catch-phrase, and we all bought into it, the whole congregation. We were committed to living biblical lives, so naturally, the Bible was our foundation. Of course, in reality, only a very small portion of it was our foundation. I mean, sacrificing sheep is *biblical,* but we didn't do a whole lot of that," Joe laughed.

"You didn't sacrifice sheep? Next you're going to tell me you eat bacon sandwiches! No wonder you lost your way," Dan said with a grin.

"Yeah, no hope for me! But there's a big difference between *biblical teaching* and *Christian lifestyle.* We don't seem to understand how much we pick and choose. A truly biblical lifestyle would be pretty messy."

"Okay, so the question of *is the Bible true...*" Dan was hoping to get at least some kind of clearer answer from Joe, and he felt like it was close.

"Is completely the wrong thing to ask."

Dan nodded. "Because of the way it can be interpreted, or taken out of context?"

"Exactly. Now, ask me if there is truth to be found in the Bible, that's a different question. God is love—I've found that to be true. God is like the perfect parent, sure, in my experience. Absolutely."

Dan nodded. "This is the problem I'm having. There's stuff in there that I just don't get anymore. We say it's infallible, yet at the same time we read the parable of the lost sheep, for instance. It's open to interpretation."

"Yeah, that's a good example. Did Jesus tell that parable? I'm sure of it. Was the parable *true?* No, it was just a simple story. But a story that *conveys* a truth."

"Ah, right. Something doesn't have to be true in order to teach us. That's the power of story, I suppose," Dan pondered, eating the last of the spicy meatballs.

"But if our belief system says the Bible is *true*, if that's where we go to understand what's right and wrong, then there's a whole lot of problematic stuff in there that we have to work around."

"Like most of the Old Testament, I would say. The *before and after* God," Dan said.

"That's the only way we can deal with it. Our experience tells us God is good, God is love, God is forgiving, yet we read that before Jesus stepped in this loving God used to do some pretty nasty things."

Dan was looking inward as he replied. "The nature of God becomes very confusing."

"Very."

"Okay," Dan said. "You said the Bible is one of those foundations. One of the pillars?"

"When you dig a little below the surface, it's actually our *expectations* of it that have become a pillar. We believe it to be ultimate truth, and that's how we approach it."

"You have to believe it all or you can't believe any of it," Dan said. "My Pastor says that all the time."

"Maybe one day he'll think differently," Joe suggested with the hint of a smile.

Dan smirked, and then stopped himself. He'd been where Pastor Alan was, no question. Reaching for his glass, he decided that it was probably time to stop judging others. "Maybe," was all he said.

In all the conversations and arguments Joe had been part of in the last 5 years, one thing was certain—people were very protective about the *Word*. He understood completely that Dan was walking a very fine line, and testing every step. He concentrated on his food for a moment, then put a question to his guest. "You ever found yourself reading scripture because you thought it was the right thing to do? Part of your spiritual discipline?"

"All the time."

"So when you stop reading it, you feel guilty?"

Dan nodded.

"But if we really delve into it we can get confused, lost, right?" Joe suggested. "We end up having to learn *apologetics* so we can convince ourselves that there is some kind of reason for God's strange behavior."

"Oh yes," Dan felt an inward smile forming at the truth of Joe's words. "*Christian apologetics.* How to spin a clever answer that nobody is going to give a damn about. Been there."

"Well, when you think about it, most of us don't have the time or the training to delve deeply into ancient Hebrew and come up with our own interpretation, so we trust in someone else's. We don't really have any choice."

"And I suppose"—Dan was thinking out loud—"in many ways, we assume that the real deep truths have been uncovered over the years by some very wise people."

Joe leaned forward. "We leave life's biggest questions in the hands of theologians. Why? Because it's beyond our understanding? Kind of misses the point of it all, if you ask me."

"Hmm. Should be simple, but it's not."

"But it gets worse."

"How can it be worse?" asked Dan, encouraging Joe to keep going.

"We have ideas about what the Bible says, but many of those

ideas don't even come from the Bible, they come from tradition."

"Such as..?"

"Oh, only some real important stuff. Like going to heaven when we die. A central Christian belief, but try finding that teaching in the Bible."

After all that the two of them had talked about that day, Dan wasn't sure anything was going to surprise him again, but he still raised an eyebrow. "Jesus talks about many rooms in his Father's house. And Revelation...why am I defending this stuff? Go on, enlighten me."

Joe smiled. "The Israelites had a belief that heaven was God's dwelling place. Up there, beyond the sky. But there's no specific teaching in the Old Testament, just vague ideas that get a mention here and there."

Dan could quickly see the amount of questions that little insight might raise. "Interesting. I'd always assumed..." His words trailed off as his thoughts took over.

"But even in the New Testament, there's not much to go on. We read Revelation, all those pictures and visions that we assume speak of the future. But even then, where is heaven located, ultimately?"

Dan didn't have to think about it, the verses seemed ingrained in his subconscious. "Earth. The *new* earth."

"And the old heaven has passed away. Makes you wonder where we get the idea of eternity in heaven."

Dan shook his head in disbelief. "Considering that the Bible covers thousands of years, you'd think there would be more about heaven. If it were important. But if it's *not* that important..."

"Well, I think it's *important,* just not the way it's portrayed. See, when you break it all down, there's a lot of Christian teaching that's based on nothing more than assumptions and ideas borrowed from mythology."

"Ah, okay. Because Jesus talks about the Kingdom of Heaven being within us, which seems to be something very different from a heaven up there."

"Are we confused yet?" Joe quipped. "I think it would be better to focus on what that *Kingdom* means for us right now."

"Rather than believing it's all about having a ticket to get there *later?*" Dan concluded.

"You said it."

There was a natural pause as Dan and Joe both reached for their wine glasses. The older man could see that his companion was busy processing the implications of their conversation. He understood—there was a lot to take in.

"Hmm," Dan said finally. "So, just remind me. *What* did we decide about the Bible?"

Joe laughed, then he put a question back to Dan. "You've read the Book of Job, right?"

"Oh, honestly, I hate Job," Dan pulled a face. "That is the worst."

"Right, you're not alone. I think Job is a great example of how evangelicals fall into a trap of their own making. Job is unlike any other book in the Bible, you know that? It's basically written like a play or something."

"The whole thing seems pretty strange," Dan reflected. "The Devil does a deal with God? What's that about?"

"Confusing, for sure. But it's also very insightful because it paints a picture of ordinary people trying to understand how a good and upright God allows suffering."

"I thought it was about *faithfulness.*"

"So that God can prove a point? Come on! Seriously? We've gotta laugh at this stuff," Joe exclaimed lightheartedly. "If we take it as true then we have some really big problems with the nature of God."

"Yeah, that's interesting. Because it does read more like Shakespeare than scripture."

"I'll take your word for it," Joe said. "If I could, I would prefer to read the Bible freely, without any preconceived ideas. But that's pretty hard to go back to, what with all the history we have."

"So you think Job is more like a parable?" Dan asked, keen to understand more.

"Well, Jesus used parables all the time, of course, and he understood that scripture was open to interpretation. Where is it, the Gospel of Luke? The teacher of the law asks how he can inherit eternal life. And Jesus says, '*how do you read it?*' Basically, *what's your interpretation?*"

Dan sat back in his chair and smiled. "You ever get people throwing stones at you?"

"Not physically," chuckled Joe, looking down at his plate. "Not yet, anyways."

"I must be tired," Dan said, finishing his wine. "I miss the Bible, miss those personal passages. Like God put that line in there just for me at that precise time. I don't really see any other way of reading it."

"The danger," Joe explained, "is that because of a bad experience we lay it aside and never pick it up again."

"That's me."

Joe nodded. "There's nothing wrong with owning a verse if that helps us through at times. But I've done the heaven and hell approach, all the fire and judgment stuff. And now I'm at a place where my understanding, my experience, and I might even say my heart, tells me there is *so much more.*"

"More than how to get saved?"

"Once we move away from our *church-centered* interpretations, and start putting more weight on what Jesus actually taught, what he stood for, then everything changes."

Joe's words raised even more questions, which Dan wasn't ready to look at just then. "Okay, that's worth some thought. Maybe the problem is, like you said, my expectations," he concluded.

Joe fixed his gaze on the last of the wine in his glass. "This is what I believe, and I almost threw the Bible out too. I believe the world needs the wisdom and insights that we find in these ancient writings more than ever. But it doesn't need the *religion*. It doesn't need the rules or the duties, or, come to think of it, the false ideas attached to it that aren't even in there. And that's the problem we face, you and me and thousands of other believers around the world who are losing faith in the old ways—how do we take the practical wisdom and apply it to our lives, and leave all the religious confusion aside?"

Dan placed his knife and fork on the empty plate, covered a yawn and rubbed a hand over his stubbled cheek. "Wow, I've had too many thoughts for one day."

"You have taken a beating, that's for sure. Now,"—Joe began to gather things onto a tray—"I'm gonna clear up. I think you have everything you need in your room. I'll probably be out and about early but I'll leave you some breakfast right here, that sound okay?"

"Sounds great," Dan agreed. "I'll give you a hand."

***

Kimberly sat at the kitchen table, staring into space as she twiddled a pen in her fingers. Every now and then she glanced at her phone, a slippered foot tapping out her frustration on the floor tiles. It was becoming increasingly clear to her that Dan was not going to answer her messages tonight.

Her journal lay open before her, a large notepad filled with scribbles and adorned with sketches, stickers and things she'd cut out of magazines. To the outside observer, it would have looked like a wild riot of words and images. But to Kimberly, this was a treasure-trove of thoughts, ideas and captured inspiration.

This morning's thoughts had centered around a doodle of boot-prints on a muddy track. She'd written some words around it—*New beginning? Unknown destination? Who knows where? Meandering, searching, seeking. Only one way?* She read through them once again, then began to add more.

Questions. So much pain. So much sorrow. Where is the healing? Where…

"Hey, Mum."

Kimberly stopped mid-sentence and looked up to see Alastair heading for the fridge. She smiled, thankful for the interruption. "What are you after now?"

"Just wanted to make a hot-chocolate," her youngest son explained, placing his phone on the countertop and grabbing the bottle of milk.

"Hmm. Easy on the sugar."

"Always."

"Got that project finished?"

"Yeah, nearly there. Heard from Dad?"

Kimberly's eyes flicked briefly to the phone. She shook her head. "I think there's no signal where he is. He'll be doing fine."

Alastair seemed to agree. He placed a mug in the microwave and reached for the cookie tin on the shelf. "He needs a break, I think."

Kimberly put down her pen, closed her journal and sat back. Alastair was always so full on insight, so tuned in to what was going on. At 15 years old, he displayed a maturity that she was proud to see. At the same time, it worried her that he was so sensitive to what was going on. "He does. But he's okay," she reassured him. "These things take time."

"Are you okay, Mum?"

Kimberly narrowed her eyes as she looked at her son. "I am...tired. Long day. And I miss your daddy. I miss him."

Alastair helped himself to the contents of the tin, placing 3 cookies on a small plate and munching on a fourth. "Not really been here lately, has he? I mean, not like before."

Kimberly felt a tightness in her throat. "No. Not in the same way."

Alastair tested his hot-chocolate and found that it was warm enough. He stuffed his phone in a pocket, balanced the mug on the plate, and made to leave. "It'll be good for him, getting away for a bit."

"Yes." Kimberly nodded, her eyes following Alastair through the door. "Yes. I hope so."

***

Even though the long day was dragging at Dan's eyelids, he still wanted to get some thoughts down in his notebook before they were lost to the night.

Four pillars, he wrote. *God, church, Bible and me.*

God seems to have been very distant over the last couple of years. I've had certain expectations that have not been met.

The Bible, Joe seems to think it can be read differently. Again, expectations. Willing to try again?

Church. Alan wants me back 'on the team'. Don't know if I can do that. Kimberly isn't pushing me. Maybe she understands more than I'm giving her credit for.

Me. Who I've been for half my life seems to be crumbling. What does that mean for the next half? What does it mean for tomorrow?

"What *does* it mean for tomorrow?" Dan read his own words quietly, pondering the implications. "That's probably the real question. Because tomorrow will soon become today. And I have to live in it."

He turned out the bedside lamp and stood for some time next to the window, looking out into the darkness. The rain had eased off, the clouds had broken up a little, and now and again bright stars would sparkle in the void.

A thousand miles from home, and only the rain as a familiar companion. But ever since he'd stepped through the door in his wet boots that morning, he hadn't been able to ignore that comforting assurance in his spirit. It was like a warm cloak draped over his shoulders, an invitation to draw closer, and a gentle voice reminding him that he was meant to be here.

He couldn't help but wonder if the assurance went much deeper. That where he found himself right now, with all the doubts, the pain and the sorrow, was exactly where he was meant to be.

Every traveler needs a refuge. It was something his mother used to say whenever his friends stopped by to say hello. In fact, as they were immediately supplied with tea and cookies in abundance, he suspected that was *exactly* why they stopped by.

He smiled faintly as he thought of her, always the mother hen, even to those from another nest.

A traveler in need of refuge.

Yes. That was him right now.

Wednesday

CHAPTER 8

*"It's all about making a decision
and not looking back..."*

The slow, rhythmic sound of water dripping somewhere outside the window seemed to fill Dan's mind. Light was creeping into the room through the half-closed wooden shutters, but it was the dull brightness of a cloudy day. He lay in the soft bed, allowing himself to get his bearings and remember where he was.

Reaching over for his phone, he checked the time—just after 8. He would normally have been up and rushing around for almost an hour by now. Still no signal on the phone, he noticed. He was a little disconcerted that Kimberly had no way of contacting him, and he made a mental note to ask Joe about the internet connection.

Pulling a bathrobe over his pajamas, he opened the inner shutters but the window didn't have much to reveal—a thick fog had filled the valley, obscuring everything except a few ghostly pine trees that marked the edge of the forest. Apart from the persistent drip, there was a stillness and silence about the place.

As he sat back on the edge of the bed for a moment, Dan thought over yesterday's chain of events. Coming here had been a big step outside his comfort zone, not something he would have normally done. He'd found Joe to be very welcoming and easy to talk to, even confide in. He was sharing some deep and difficult matters of the heart with a complete stranger, and there was a rightness to it that Dan could not explain.

Maybe, Dan considered, God was in this, after all. He wondered again whether he was hitting a wall, as Joe had said, or wandering through a desert. Either way, he knew that the last couple of years had been an extremely difficult time, and as far as he was concerned right now, this was exactly what he needed.

Downstairs, the house was quiet. The soft slippers made hardly a sound on the tiled floors, and he wondered if Joe was up yet or still sleeping. A quick look through the door to the lounge answered his question—the fire was roaring, and the table had been set for one. The unmistakable aroma of hot coffee reached his nose.

Sitting down, Dan found warm pastries under a plastic cover, a selection of jams, and enough coffee to kick-start a horse. A folded card next to the plate read *'Make yourself at home. More coffee in the kitchen. You may want this WiFi password...'*

Smiling to himself, Dan quickly set to work loading a croissant with strawberry preserve and pouring himself a *café con leche*. The first taste sent a warmth through his whole body, adding to that reassuring sense of familiarity.

As he savored the wonderful combination of sweet pastry and smooth coffee, gradually his deeper thoughts began to come online and more questions formed in his mind.

Dan wasn't completely sure why he'd reached out to Joe, but he was glad he'd taken notice of Kimberly's promptings. Something about the honesty and openness in Joe's writing had disarmed Dan's safety mechanisms and started him thinking. Thinking, hoping, that maybe there was a better way to believe.

And maybe that was enough for now—finding a better way. Because walking away from a faith he'd built his life around was scary as hell and extremely lonely. Yesterday, on the meandering paths of conversation with Joe, he thought he'd caught a glimpse of this *better way*. A way forward that seemed to have a much bigger God in it than he'd thought possible.

It didn't make sense, but it felt good somehow.

So where was this journey leading? Joe wasn't pretending to have all the answers, clearly, but his approach certainly seemed a million miles away from the same-old stuff he was used to hearing on a Sunday morning. He'd met very few people over the years who'd really made him stop and consider things. It was becoming increasingly apparent that Joe was one of those people.

Dan was just beginning to wonder where his host was when a metallic clanging sound outside offered a clue. Rising from the table, Dan went to look through the window. Beyond the rosebushes, he could see a small footbridge that spanned the stream. A ghostly figure in a blue jacket was pushing a wheelbarrow into the mist on the other side.

It looked like the weather would dictate the course of the day, and maybe that was a good thing—he wanted to pick up the conversation where they'd left off yesterday. Oddly for Dan, who always felt the need to be doing something, he felt no pressure to rush into the day. He could go searching for Joe soon enough, but first, no point leaving the other croissant to grow cold.

Back in his room, Dan flicked through several messages that Kimberly had sent the night before. He typed a brief reply, apologizing for the lack of communication. He was aware of the uncertainty in the back of his mind and wondered what more he could tell her. His wife was giving him space to seek answers, but would she like what he found? What would happen if he moved forward and she stayed behind? Was their relationship strong enough to cope?

Before hitting *send* he added—*Joe seems like a good guy. Helping me to ask some better questions. Feels like God is in this. Love you.*

Dragging his attention back to the present, Dan showered, pulled on yesterday's clothes, and went to find his boots and jacket. He was relieved to discover that his things had dried out from the previous day's escapades, so he wrapped up against the cold and ventured out in search of his host.

Outside was still and gray, with a chill, damp mist hanging over everything. From the forest came a few solemn chatterings and chirps of birds, and the muffled background roaring of the stream. Dan turned to the right and headed for the little footbridge he'd seen from the window.

The bridge turned out to be not much more than thick wooden planks placed over what appeared to be rusty, old railroad tracks, with a moss-covered wooden handrail on one side. It spanned a rock-filled, angrily foaming stream edged with small trees, that had cut its way down from the heights above. Some of the larger boulders were the size of a small car, Dan mused.

On the other side, a rough track meandered up a grassy bank and disappeared into the darkness of the forest. Dan followed, looking around for any sign of Joe, but he hadn't gone far when the track split in two, bringing him to a halt. The trees rose up around him, tall pines next to slender birch trees bearing their new leaves of spring. The air was rich with the smell of new growth and decay.

Just then Dan heard the clunking noise once more, and Joe emerged from the mist on the lower track, wheelbarrow loaded with logs.

"Two roads diverge in a wood," shouted Joe cheerfully, the words of Robert Frost's famous poem quickly soaking into the surrounding trees. "And I..?"

"I was about to get lost, apparently," Dan finished with his own rendition.

"Well, don't make a habit of it. How you doing this fine day?" Joe inquired as he stopped next to Dan.

"Good. Thanks for breakfast. I feel ready for anything."

"Alright. So you can help me get the wagon going. Probably should do that this morning, then we can go down to the town." Joe's friendly eyes sparkled beneath his baseball cap.

"Of course. Anything I can do to help."

Joe pushed off with the wheelbarrow, concentrating on navigating the bumpy track. "Just remember, you're a guest. This place is your home for a few days, make the most of it."

Dan followed along behind. "That *Robert Frost* poem, I

thought about that a lot last year. It's all about making a decision and not looking back, I think."

"Could be," Joe agreed. *"The road not taken.* Because when you're on a journey, there's no point wondering what might have been. So many people are stuck in the past, it's not a good place to remain."

Joe crossed the rickety footbridge like someone who pushed heavy loads over roaring streams every day, and headed for the side of the house. "I'll just dump these logs."

Dan waited, hands in pockets, as Joe emptied the wheelbarrow onto a pile of fresh logs. He felt his phone buzz and pulled it out to find that Kimberly had finally replied to his earlier message.

I trust you. And trying to trust God.

He read it several times, then put his phone back in his pocket.

"Mist seems to be lifting a little, I'll show you the meadow," Joe shouted, waving Dan over. They began to walk along to the rear of the house.

"We've been here for about 5 years, I told you that, right?" Joe began as if he was telling a favorite story. "The first few weeks we just kind of sat here wondering what the heck we had jumped into."

Dan was happy to listen to the story. He'd always admired people who took big steps outside their comfort zone in search of their dreams, even if, he had to admit, there was also a hint of jealousy.

"We came here to get away and find some space to think. It ended up becoming our home. But we were still finding our way, I was still struggling with my faith, and there weren't any clear answers. It was really like God was only going to show us the very next step and that was all."

"One day at a time," Dan remarked, immediately wishing he'd found another phrase.

Joe gave him a quick glance. "It's cliché, but yeah. We had to fumble our way forward."

"That's why you look at it as a journey," Dan stated as he walked alongside.

"I guess so," Joe said. "I had to put myself in a place where I was content to learn, little by little, all over again. And to be honest, I couldn't think of a better place than this."

They now stood in the wet grass of the meadow, looking back at the house.

"It's wonderful. My kind of refuge." Dan said.

"Yeah, if you're looking for an idyllic get-away in the mountains, this is it. We try to make it a place of grace and peace, somewhere no one's going to place any expectations on you."

"So do you get many visitors?" Dan asked, curious to learn more about Joe's home.

"We get all kinds of people from all over," Joe said with a measure of excitement. "Not big numbers, but what we've found is that we attract people who are looking for something more than just a vacation in the mountains. There's a real desire to find a spiritual connection, you know what I mean? I'm biased, but I think there's no better place than a peaceful valley in the Pyrenees."

Dan was thoughtful for a moment. "I guess that's kind of what I'm looking for in a way, some kind of food for my soul."

"Well, we've got a whole lot of that, enough to feed an army," Joe reassured his guest. He raised his eyes to the heights and said, "You know, if God is anywhere, then he's in the process."

Dan was also looking up, watching the swirling mist hugging the ridge on the opposite side of the valley as the mountainside gradually became visible. For a few moments they both stood in silence, then Dan voiced his thoughts. "I feel like I've been walking through rain for a long time."

"Yep, I know what that feels like."

"But yesterday, well, that was the first time in a long while that I felt I was getting a little sunshine. A bit of clarity."

"Well, maybe you can get some more while you're here. Lots of people do, including myself."

Dan felt reassured by Joe's kind words. He continued to stand there in the meadow, taking in the beauty of the surroundings. The house seemed like a natural part of the landscape, nestling solidly among tall trees. Even in the dull light of a misty day, everything was green and verdant.

"It reminds me of a little farmhouse in Wales where we used to spend our summers. In fact, this whole area is very similar. Only on a much grander scale." Dan explained.

"Good memories come from the truest place inside us," Joe reflected. "Well, home is where the heart is, and it sounds like yours is here right now."

The two began walking back towards the house, heading for the rear gate. Joe explained that he would get the other car from the garage. "Where we keep all the fun stuff," he said. "Kayaks, mountain bikes, a quad-bike which is pretty cool. And my workshop up above. Man cave, really. I'll have to show you later."

Dan chuckled. "You need a man cave when you have all this on your doorstep?"

"You bet!" Joe exclaimed, opening the gate to let his guest through. "Anyways, I'll have to get the car keys. Wanna meet me down at the stream?"

"Okay, I'll try to not get lost in the fog."

As Joe disappeared into the house, Dan started towards the track that instantly began to slope down through the trees. Birds continued to sing in muted fashion as leaves dripped in the steadily clearing mist. Somehow there was a welcoming feel to the place, as if he'd wandered into an old childhood memory that still lingered on the edge of his subconscious.

The track ran straight for about fifty yards then turned sharply next to the large rock which he remembered seeing the day before. Rounding the bend he could see the ruined building, the shallow ford, and the SUV at the edge of the stream, white water foaming around the front wheels.

Joe had referred to it affectionately as a wagon, but on closer inspection, Dan could see that it was a somewhat dented Toyota that had seen better days. Yesterday, in the middle of a rainstorm, Dan hadn't paid much attention—he'd just been glad of a ride. Now he found himself wondering why Joe drove such an old wreck.

The sound of a car engine signaled Joe's arrival on the scene, and Dan turned to see a modern Volvo appear slowly around the bend.

"Had trouble finding the booster cables," Joe explained as he hopped out of the car, leaving the engine running. "If you can jump in here, bring her up close, and we can get that old thing going."

From inside the car, Dan watched Joe, now wearing high rubber boots, wade across the stream, almost slip over, pop the hood of the Toyota, and then wave him forward. As he edged the vehicle into the stream Dan couldn't help wondering about Joe. Here was a man who was clearly a million miles away from his life as a worship leader, and yet he seemed completely fulfilled and at ease in the new one he'd created. Before today, Dan would not have believed such a transformation was possible at that stage of life. It was certainly something he wouldn't forget in a hurry.

"Down on the left," Joe shouted above the noise of the stream, seeing Dan fumble around for the hood release. In no time Joe had connected the cables and poked his head in at the window. "Just keep the revs up and I'll give it a go."

Joe climbed into the Toyota, waved an arm in an upward movement, and the peace of the forest was momentarily shattered with the revving of first one engine, then another much throatier one as the Toyota came to life.

As Dan reversed back up the track he could hear Joe gunning the engine. Clearly his host was taking no chances. The Toyota powered forward through the shallow water and then came to a stop on solid ground.

Joe jumped out, a grin on his face. "You know, when you're stuck it's best to admit you're stuck and get some help," he shouted, walking up to the Volvo.

"Okay, I admit it, I'm stuck!"

Joe smiled. "You're doing great. Back up to the old building and you can turn around there. I'll guide you. Then I need to get changed real quick, and we can head down to town so you can get your things."

"And *you* can get a new battery," Dan quipped.

"Oh yeah. Mustn't forget that!"

CHAPTER 9

"It's the challenges, the dark times, that cause us
to grow the most."

Joe was driving the Volvo down the single-lane road back towards the town. The car passed scattered woodland and dark forest as it followed the path of the stream. In a matter of minutes they had reached the lake and Dan indicated his car, parked up next to a couple of others.

"Maybe we can pick it up on the way back," Dan suggested.

Joe agreed. He glanced over at the younger man, who seemed intent on enjoying the scenery, then fixed his eyes back on the road. After a few moments he spoke. "It doesn't have to be a lonely journey. You know that, right? There are a lot of other pilgrims on the track."

Dan brought his attention back to the present. "Hmm. I have felt pretty alone at times, I admit. Maybe I'm just growing used to it."

Joe slowed down to allow a pair of mountain-bikers to pass safely. "Whatever you currently believe about God, I know he's got your back. And I'm not just saying that, I've seen it time and again over the years we've been here."

"I hope so."

"You kind of get a feel for who's really looking to move forward at a spiritual level."

"Well, I don't want to stay where I am," Dan assured his new friend.

"It's difficult. When you're going through a transition it's always painful, and oftentimes we simply long for the good old days, the routine, the comfort of fellowship. We were once a part of something that gave shape and structure to our lives, and now that we've stepped outside that box it feels kinda scary. We might even consider that it's not worth the risk, and try to go back."

"Only we know," Dan sighed, looking up at the high valley sides, "we can never go back. We've outgrown the framework. It can't hold us anymore."

"Unfortunately for us, or maybe *fortunately,* that's exactly right," Joe reflected. "We know we can't fit ourselves back inside the box that is church. It's unsettling and exciting all at the same time. The good news is that we don't have to go back—God is bigger than we've understood up to now, and personally speaking, I find that incredibly freeing."

Dan looked over at Joe navigating the winding road. "I suppose part of the problem is that I don't talk about where I'm at. I've been thinking about this. I've tried to keep it all to myself, pretend everything is okay, and just work it through. I didn't want to be the one who rocked the boat, and I didn't want to be someone who ended up causing others to doubt their faith or be led astray because of my stupid doubts."

Joe smiled, but Dan could sense a sadness in the American's kind words. "The truth is, Dan, we do need to talk about this stuff. We do need to let people know where we're at, what our struggles are, and how we're doing. And...let the dice fall where they may. And it's not stupid. Yes, there are some Christians, even some friends out there who are not going to be happy for us, who will, unfortunately, see us as the enemy of all things good. It's just the way things are. Kinda sad, really."

The car slowed again as they passed a cluster of old houses huddled around a crossroads, and soon Joe was steering into the first of a series of tight hairpin bends. The land dropped away below them as it joined with the wider valley, and a spectacular vista opened up, mountain upon mountain stretching away to the north and west under wide skies.

"Not a bad view," Joe commented.

"Not bad at all," Dan said slowly, faced with the immense scale of the scene.

The mountain road leveled out as it joined onto the main road heading towards the town. Joe waited for a few cars to pass, then accelerated away from the junction. After a moment, he asked, "You talk things over with your wife, Kim? Kimberly, right?"

"Kimberly, yeah, she's been a real rock. But we don't really talk things through much. She's there for me, I know that. And all the time I was back and forth going to see my mother, she never made me feel like I should be pulling myself together or anything like that. Although she never let me get away with moping around either."

"Good for her. Just a piece of advice. Remember she needs to know where you're at. You don't want to close the door, even accidentally. That wouldn't be wise."

Dan thought for a moment. Kimberly was understanding. She was kind. But whether she was on the same journey as Dan or not, he wasn't sure, and that bothered him more than he could say. "Things were difficult last year. I think I was really going through a bad time. I know we've been better."

"You had a lot going on, by all accounts. There's a very real grief for what we once held so dear. You might even have been grieving in advance for your mom."

"Yeah, I kind of understand the grieving. Everything built up all at once and I didn't feel able to connect with anyone at church in the way I needed to. There was kind of a growing separation."

"I understand, I really do. We no longer connect with others in the same way. But we have to be available. Keep the lines of communication open. Because you will come through this, you *are* coming through, and there will be a time when you meet someone who's in kind of the same place you were, and they will need to know that they aren't alone."

Joe's words made sense, and Dan was starting to appreciate why this man wrote the way he did. "So you felt that separation?"

"It was like a loss. I'd lost part of who I was. We'd been so involved with that church for a long time, and on the surface all was going well. But..." Joe paused to find the words. "You know, it's not that church has it all wrong. It's simply that I found myself at a spiritual crossroads. And I didn't know how to move forward, but I knew I couldn't remain where I was either. It was a painful time. A very confusing time."

A few short miles along the road and the town came into view. Dan saw the church tower first above the trees, then the tall, gray buildings clustered around the river. *Pont de la Cruz* was beginning to look familiar, he realized, as Joe turned off the road into the parking lot and stopped the car.

"I'll come over to Casa Anna with you, then I have to pick up some supplies. *And* the new car battery, of course. Mustn't forget that."

Minutes later Joe, in a mixture of English and Spanish, was explaining to Anna that Dan would be staying a few days up at his place, and she wasn't to worry. Anna was pleased to see Joe, she didn't seem in the least offended, and as Dan ran upstairs to collect his things he could hear them chatting away like old friends.

***

Dan dumped his suitcase in the back of the car and jumped in next to Joe.

"What are all the flags around town for?" he asked, noticing again the colorful bunting between the houses.

Joe looked up from his phone. "Ah, I think it's a local *fiesta* this coming weekend."

"*Fiesta?*"

"Yeah, like a holiday. Or I should say *Holy Day.* Celebrating a local saint, I think. The town gets together in the square, everyone shares paella and they drink a lot of beer. It's cool, we went along a couple of years ago. They still have the old traditions here, it's nice," Joe commented. "It's not too overrun with tourists, we're far enough away from the big national parks, so there's still a lot of Spanish life to be found."

"Sounds interesting. I keep thinking my mother would have enjoyed spending some time here, she loved discovering new places." Dan paused to look around. "A week isn't long enough to get to know a place."

"No. Or five years," laughed Joe. "We still feel like we're just getting to understand the Pyrenees people. Some of these little communities, like the place on the way up to the house, they have a little farm with dairy cows, a couple of B & B's, and that's about it."

Dark clouds were building up once more over the peaks to the north as Joe collected the new battery from the town's only mechanic. Within the time it took for a quick visit to the small grocery store, the rain had begun to fall again. Large drops spattered against the windshield as the two companions headed back to the house.

Joe leaned forward in his seat. "Well, we need the rain. That's what I always say, anyhow."

The gray weather seemed to match the feeling in Dan's soul just then. He wasn't sure why, but being in the town had triggered some memories. Maybe it was the fact that there were people a thousand miles away from home who were celebrating someone who'd been dead for hundreds of years when he was still trying to navigate his way through multiple layers of raw grief and loss.

His mind wandered back in time to the funeral, and just for an instant the empty feeling returned. He recalled standing in the entrance to the old church, looking at the various photographs of his mother through the years. It was a lovely collection with plenty of flowers everywhere, but for Dan it had completely failed to convey the love and energy of the life that was.

A beginning. An end. Some photographs in-between.

He shook his head, bringing himself back to the present.

"You know, I always hoped I would be one of those people who would be able to wake up to the reality of life without having to go through some major trauma. I guess it doesn't really work that way."

Joe glanced sideways. "You're thinking about your mother?"

"Yeah, I suppose I went through it with her as much as I could. She used to tell me it was like waking up to a nightmare every morning."

"She must have been a strong woman."

"I never thought of her that way before," Dan admitted.

"Maybe she wasn't before," Joe offered as he concentrated on the road. "She had to look death in the face and stand up to her enemy. That changes a person."

Dan watched as the town quickly receded and the road followed the river into lush, green meadows and scattered woodland. "I guess so much has happened... I'm not the same guy."

"No, you won't be," Joe sighed. "Death does something. Something profound. And if we let it, it teaches us. I think about what Jesus said, a seed planted in the ground has to die before something new is born."

"Death can bring life? I figure that's Jesus talking about himself. That's the usual take, anyway."

"Often means a whole lot more, in my experience."

"Right, we have this very black and white way of dealing with death. Death is bad. Life is good."

"Death and life are part of the natural cycle in nature," Joe reflected.

"Could it be that death actually makes life?"

"Well..."

"We wouldn't know what light is if we didn't have dark," Dan mused. "Makes me wonder if without that knowledge of our own mortality we would never really live."

"You're right, we learn from death. And not just physical death, of course," Joe said. "Usually any kind of ending affects us. Even the end of the day. A sunset. Coming to the end of a good book. But also dying to self. I feel like I have to do that sometimes when I put up a new article on my blog."

"Really?"

"Oh yeah."

"So death isn't such a bad thing," Dan suggested.

"It's terrible for those losing someone they love. We've both experienced that, and that hole they leave never goes away. But I think death is supposed to move us. Things naturally come to an end. We can grieve the passing. But get offended by it? No, we should allow it to teach us."

"I always kind of thought that the eternal part of us was offended by death."

"But the seed dies so the plant can grow," Joe suggested.

Dan nodded. Joe's down-to-earth observations were making sense once again. "So if we stop seeing death as evil or wrong, we can start to see it as a teacher."

"What else can it be?" Joe asked rhetorically. "We always tend to fall back on the old narrative that only good things can teach us good, only good things can shape our lives in good ways. That doesn't take into account the human spirit."

"Hmm. We don't have to be the victim anymore?"

"Exactly," said Joe. "We can learn the lessons and grow."

The car wound its way back up the valley, passing through the small hamlet Joe had mentioned earlier. At one of the houses they came to a sudden halt.

"Just give me a second," Joe said, and leaving the engine running he jumped out into the rain and knocked on a red wooden door.

Dan watched as Joe stepped quickly inside and returned almost immediately clutching a small package, which he handed to Dan. A warm, sweet aroma began to fill the car.

"Cake?" Dan asked. Joe nodded and they continued on their way.

Presently the older man continued where he'd left off. "If you look back over your life I'm sure you're able to see that you aren't simply a product of the good times. We don't re-evaluate when things are going well. Winning doesn't cause soul-searching. No, it's the challenges, the dark times, that cause us to grow the most."

The wiper-blades swished back and forth steadily as the car snaked up the valley, dark forest seeming to close in around them.

"God teaches us through adversity, then," said Dan, and even though the weather seemed increasingly foreboding, he began to wonder if there really was a better way of facing his inner troubles and finding some hope in the darkness.

Joe was quick to reassure him. "To be clear, I don't believe life should be a continual trial that makes us stronger. What would that say about God? We have to be careful what we end up thinking—sometimes life is just hard."

"Hmm. Okay, he wants us to grow through the hard times. And he's still there in the background," Dan said slowly, as if testing the way forward on uneven ground.

This time Joe took a moment to reply. "You probably do exactly the same for your children. You want them to face their challenges, you want to see them overcome, figure things out and come out the other side better than they went in. In fact," he glanced quickly over at Dan, "we go through it with them. We share the struggle together."

Dan could feel a lump rising in his throat. His voice sounded tight. "I've never..."

"It makes a huge difference to how we perceive God. You might say, I guess, that his love actually prevents him from intervening. As if..." Joe paused, choosing his words. "It's as if there are times when all God can do is walk behind you, and keep reminding you he's there."

"Wow." Once again Dan found himself suddenly looking at things from a different perspective, and it felt both freeing and at the same time more than a little scary. "Not the all-powerful

God we hear about in Sunday school, after all."

"Not when we want him to be, no. Not in that sense, anyhow. Takes some getting used to."

There was a comfortable silence as the two men became lost in their thoughts. Rain continued to fall, little rivulets ran across the road in places, but Dan could feel the weight of expectations falling from his shoulders. How God worked, how this life worked, how his future was unfolding. Suddenly it all began to look much bigger. And that was something to hold onto.

"I just realized something," Dan said, as they came in sight of the house.

"Yeah?"

"I forgot to pick up my car at the lake."

They both laughed.

CHAPTER 10

"It's pretty obvious that God doesn't show up like he used to."

"What do you do when you don't have visitors?" Dan asked as he hung his jacket in the cloakroom.

Joe shut the front door firmly against the rain and kicked off his boots. "Well, that is a good question. Writing, mainly," he explained, telling Dan how, as his readership had grown, the blog had become more and more central to his work. "I try to do some every day—work on articles and such. I still play a bit of guitar. And I've got my workshop. Keeps me busy. Come on through to the kitchen."

"I have to say," Dan said, still clutching the cake as he followed after Joe, "coming across your blog was...well, it was just at the right time. I didn't appreciate that there were other people out there grappling with the bigger questions, you know? Working out their faith beyond the normal scope of church."

Joe switched on the coffee machine and topped up the beans. "Yeah, there's all sorts of people, and I wouldn't compare myself with some—I've had it easy in many ways."

"You've had it easy?"

"The thing is, when you take a walk outside the walls, it's a pretty messy place."

"Outside of church life, you mean?"

Joe's voice now came to Dan from the depths of a tall cupboard. "Yeah, beyond the safe boundary lines that we've been so used to for so long. Church, faith, doctrines, traditions." Joe grabbed some plates and then set about slicing up the cake.

Dan pulled a stool over to the breakfast bar and sat down. "It does seem a bit of a minefield. You mentioned you get hate mail? That must be tough."

"Well, hate is a strong word." Joe paused to gaze out of the window. "I mean, there are a couple of people who regularly email me about their concerns for my faith, and, well, I figure I can let them be concerned. It's not very often someone will be confrontational or anything like that. Most people are just searching. Struggling with faith, the church, their identity. Coming up against that wall I mentioned. A lot of *ex-evangelicals.*"

"*Ex-evangelicals* is a thing?" Dan mused. "Not sure I'd want to label myself as anything just yet."

Joe looked across at Dan with understanding in his eyes. "No, I know what you mean. I hate labels, don't you? Lived under them for most of my life. But it's a pretty good description. Been through the evangelical system and crawled out the other side, and we're trying to get our lives back together, make sense of the world once more."

The warm kitchen filled with the enticing smell of coffee mixed with freshly baked sponge-cake, and within moments Joe had placed a mug in front of Dan. "This stuff is the best. Just don't tell Sandy I said that." He offered the plate to Dan, then leaned back against the countertop.

Dan helped himself, quickly agreeing with Joe's assessment. "So is that how you see yourself? Christian, but no longer evangelical?"

"Well, it depends who's asking," Joe said with a laugh.

Dan was curious. He was also, as he often did with people he met, trying to categorize Joe. He was having trouble with that.

Joe continued his explanation. "Could be I don't fit some of the parameters anymore, so maybe that makes me *ex-evangelical*, or *post-evangelical*. Maybe I'm neither. Maybe I'm both and more." He raised an eyebrow.

"Not fitting into anyone's box," Dan commented, smiling.

"Man, I hope not. I prefer to look at it in terms of *journey*." Joe paused to take a bite of cake. "You know, a pilgrim is more defined by where he finds himself than where he's been, or even where he's going. Because a pilgrim knows they're always moving forward."

"Hmm. I like that, but I feel as if I'm carrying so much weight. Like rocks in my backpack."

"The thing is, we can't simply lose our past." There was understanding in Joe's tone as he continued. "We can't change yesterday, it's always with us, hovering in the background. But we *can* learn to embrace the now and be open to discovering God in the wilderness."

"Hmm. *Discovering God in the Wilderness*," Dan said dramatically. "Is that your next book?"

Joe chuckled. "It might be my *first* book, when I get around to finishing it. Yeah, discovering God again, *if* you still want to believe, that is. And I mean that in all seriousness."

"Well, I can see how easy it is to stop believing altogether. I came pretty close," Dan confessed. "I'll look forward to reading it."

"Let's call it a work in progress," Joe declared as he finally sat down next to Dan, holding his mug in both hands. "You see, Dan, you're probably like a lot of people, and I'm not just talking about Christians. You're beginning to lose faith in an all-powerful God who doesn't ever seem to intervene. A God who ignores suffering but seethes with anger at the slightest misstep."

"Yeah, but I'm still there, holding on by my fingernails," Dan mused. "Just about."

"Right, but I'm sure you've wondered—*what exactly am I holding onto? And what would happen if I let go?*" Joe sipped coffee, giving Dan a moment to process. "Because in my experience the god we lose faith in is nothing more than a reworked version of

Zeus or Apollo. A thunder and lightning deity who's only a little nicer now because Jesus stepped in."

"Ouch!" Dan exclaimed with a smile. "If you put it that way...and I always thought science was the reason for people losing their faith."

"Well, I figure that you want to have your beliefs challenged or you wouldn't be here."

"Okay. So keep going," Dan urged. "I can take it. And if not, I know where the door is."

Joe held back a smile. "We all need to be challenged once in a while. Hey, I *still* find myself talking about God as this singular, masculine *person.* Just easier that way. But more and more these days I think of God in terms of *community.*"

Dan raised an eyebrow. "You mean the Trinity? I guess you could say that's community."

Joe nodded. "It's a start, at least. How we view God says so much about ourselves. So for me, one of the hardest things to admit was this huge discrepancy between the God we experience in our everyday lives, and the God of the Old Testament." Joe pushed his stool to one side so he could turn towards Dan, then he made a fist and held it up. "I wanted the God who shows up in *power.* You know what I mean?"

Dan nodded.

"But the reality, my experience"—Joe's fist relaxed into an open palm—"tells me that God has different ideas."

Dan's gaze fixed on Joe's hand for a moment. "Part of me wants to disagree. But I guess that's my experience too."

"Well, we read the Old Testament interactions between God and people, and it's very dynamic—God is clearly at work, directly involved. Look at Elijah and the priests of Baal. Or God making the sun stand still so that Joshua could win the battle."

"Right, Moses and the Red Sea, that kind of thing?"

"Exactly. But in the New Testament?"

Dan took a moment to reflect. "Yeah, things are different."

"Very different. Why doesn't God work that way any longer? John the Baptist is beheaded; a close friend of Jesus dies;

Jesus himself is betrayed, he's beaten, whipped and finally crucified. Then look at what happened to Paul—he gets attacked by angry townsfolk, shipwrecked, bitten by a snake. Where was God in all that?"

"Well," Dan said, searching for an explanation, "it's more behind-the-scenes stuff, I guess. But I see the problem—we want that strong, warrior God who fights on our side, but he doesn't even do that for our New Testament heroes." He was intrigued by this new insight and wondered why he'd never seen it before.

"And not only a God who fights for us, but we get to decide who the enemies are," Joe added.

"Oh, exactly! But if you listen to Jesus, God must actually love our enemies, right? He's the perfect Father, the Good Shepherd."

Joe agreed. "And I think that's a great picture of a loving God. He *is* at work in our lives, interacting and even intervening at times, but not as the mighty warrior, not with thunderbolts, not with an outright show of power. It's all very much the invisible guide. Behind the scenes, like you said. And all motivated by a love we can't comprehend."

Dan felt a faint twinge of sadness as he realized how long it had been since he'd expected God to show up. "I know there have been times when I just wanted God to come along and make everything better. But"—he paused, considering Joe's words—"for God to step in and suddenly put it all right..."

"It's hard. But a loving parent doesn't step in and fix everything for the child!" Joe exclaimed. "We know that. We want to, but we also want our kids to grow. It's a continual process of the parent letting go, little by little, allowing the child the space they need to develop."

"But if I have this expectation that God is going to intervene, that he's always going to answer my prayers, like with my mother..." Dan was thinking things through as he spoke.

"And he doesn't seem to show up?" Joe raised a questioning eyebrow. "Your prayers feel like they're landing on deaf ears, and you begin to wonder if he's even bothered in the slightest."

"Or there's something wrong with me. Either way, after a while you stop praying." Dan nodded his head slightly, staring at the coffee cup before him, then exhaled. "I know I did."

"And you let God go. No matter how many times you hear that you just have to have more faith, keep on pushing through, the real problem isn't going away. We've bought into the Old Testament thunder and lightning God, but the reality is very different. It's not God who's to blame, it's what we've been led to expect."

"More expectations?"

"Exactly. We only expect God to work a certain way. We expect miraculous interventions every time. It's very narrow-minded."

Dan found himself reflecting on recent events. "You know, the only way I could handle it with the cancer, when I was praying every single day and nothing seemed to be happening except she'd get worse..." He stared at the ceiling. Talking things over with Joe was getting easier, but he was still finding his way through. He gulped air and continued. "All I could do was think about the care she was getting, all the treatment, the truly amazing doctors and nurses. I struggled a lot with the whole unanswered prayer thing—was I doing it right, didn't I have enough faith, all that stuff..." His voice trailed off.

"Before we even get started, God is there on the scene," Joe said in a reassuring tone. "And if we can begin to open our eyes to God being at work *in the world*, and not confined to our church or religion, then we can see this divine power behind all the advancements in health-care and science that made it possible for your mom to get the best care."

Dan nodded. "I guess it's a matter of looking at the bigger picture."

"Well, this is how I figure it. Is God able to work in the world? Of course. Is there a divine goodness at work in everyone and everything? I think so. More importantly, is God for us or against us? And by *us,* I mean everyone, not just believers."

"Ah. Big question," Dan stated, once again focusing his attention on the coffee. He shot a glance at Joe. "I know what I *used* to think. That it depends who's side you're on."

"And now," Joe offered, "you're beginning to see things differently. I believe God is for us, and I believe God can equip humankind to grow, to discover, learn, come together. And yes, we are great at making a mess of things. But when you look at how far we've come in 2000 years, I see a momentum that shows me God is very much working for our common good."

Dan was running Joe's words through his mind. "Alright, I can see that, maybe. But trying to see an all-powerful God only working in very small ways, seems to go against how I understand it. Raises a lot of questions."

"I always think about how Jesus lived," Joe continued. "He chose *humanity* over *divinity,* if you want a biblical perspective. He got involved in the everyday things of life, and he did it out of a place of love. That has to tell us something."

"So," said Dan, choosing his words carefully, "God is choosing love over power, in a way."

"That is a cool way of saying it, I should write that down. Next article—*Love not Power,*" Joe laughed, then continued with his thoughts. "But that's exactly it. God loves us *so much* he wants us to have the only power worth having—love."

Dan smiled. "Hmm. Maybe *I* should write that down."

Joe shook his head in wonder. "See, that's the kind of God I can believe in. One who is working in our lives, sure, but not taking the direct approach of an all-powerful God. Instead, it's the kind and caring approach of loving parents, parents who want the very best for their child, all the time knowing that the child has to find her own way as she grows. And, in fact"—Joe's voice became more serious—"just as parents love their *grown child* who's doing his own thing now. Like my son in California," he added softly, with a faint smile.

Dan noticed the far-off look in Joe's eyes, as if for a moment he was seeing something other than the room they were in. "So God *does* intervene, but not in the way we'd like."

Joe focused back on Dan. "If we knew God would always

intervene we would live very different lives, wouldn't we? We'd probably be a lot less cautious, take a whole lot of stupid risks, probably be a lot more lazy. I mean, it would be chaotic, if you think about it."

Dan found himself smiling in agreement as he drank his coffee. "I see what you mean. And at the same time, I know I've had those serendipity moments when I felt God had to be working behind the scenes. I was certain he must have set something up, you know?"

"Right, and I think that happens a lot more than we see. But it's not God controlling us, or our circumstances. It's God making possibilities. Sometimes we are led, sometimes we are left to figure it out. That's how I like to see it."

"Love, not power," Dan said to himself. "I'll have to let that sink in a little."

CHAPTER 11

"Before is what brings us to where we are now."

Thaere was a natural pause as the two men focused on their coffee. Dan reached for another slice of cake, telling himself that it was the polite thing to do. Kimberly's advice about being kind to himself played in the back of his mind. He could always be more disciplined with himself when he got home.

Joe rubbed his beard, something that seemed to help him process things. "You know one of the saddest things I hear? People who've been Christians their whole lives, twenty, thirty, forty years, telling me they weren't sure if they loved God enough."

Dan wasn't surprised. He'd often wondered the very same thing.

"That's why I wrote that article about God putting conditions on his love," Joe explained. "It was back in the middle of the pandemic. There was all the chatter about Psalm 91, the plague, the pestilence and God saving and protecting his people."

"Yes, I remember."

"I wanted to help people understand that it's not about us measuring up to God's expectations. God is about *grace*. His love is not in any way dependent on ours."

Dan couldn't think of anything to add so he let Joe continue, sensing the significance of the direction the conversation was taking.

"I wanted to give people permission to get on with their lives instead of wondering all the time whether or not they are good enough, faithful enough, love God enough. I wanted to remind people that it's all about grace. He's done it all, and if you believe that you'll get on with living that out and carrying that grace with you wherever you go, whatever you do. Not because you must, but because you can."

The younger man was enjoying the experience of witnessing Joe expound on something that was clearly very close to his heart. But more than that, it was shining a light on some of Dan's deeper questions. "We know it's about grace, but we still act as if it's about works. It's almost like the idea of grace is, I don't know, offensive somehow."

"Exactly!" Joe said with energy, excited by Dan's response. "We don't get it. We don't understand that if we go to church or don't go to church, read our Bible every day or only once a year, evangelize our workmates or live as a hermit..."

"It doesn't matter?"

"It doesn't matter! It's all about a life full of grace. Anything else is simply us trying to attain some kind of religious prize."

"I wish you had started your blog 20 years ago," Dan said with feeling, glancing sideways at the older man.

Joe chuckled. "So do I, man, so do I. Yeah, there is a big wide world out there full of confused, hurting, faithful and fearful Christians still trying to please God so they will receive his favor. And it's people like me, I admit, who only added to all that confusion."

"You were doing what you thought was right at the time, I guess."

Joe nodded. "No, you're right. That was before, and *before* is what brings us to where we are *now*. Mustn't forget that."

"Journey?"

"Journey," Joe affirmed. "So now, now I wanna help folk understand that each and every one of us is living in a place of grace. And grace doesn't have limits. All of us are recipients of limitless grace from God. It's our choice what we do with it, too. That, I guess, is at the back of everything Sandy and I do now. All of it is our attempt at giving some of that grace away."

"Well, you can feel that the moment you walk through the door," Dan commented.

Joe's eyes crinkled as he looked off into the distance once more. "We've seen so many people wrestling with the consequences of living lives full of guilt, shame and duty. And when you look at just how far removed that is from the offer Jesus held out 2000 years ago—life in all its fullness..."

"Yeah, that's been my experience," Dan added. "A plate full of duty, covered in shame sauce, with a side salad of guilt for good measure."

"Oh man, there's a picture! But what is the point of grace if it confines us to lives controlled by guilt and shame?" Joe asked rhetorically. "For grace to truly be grace, it means no limits, no boundaries. I don't have to feel guilty about the life I live."

"That sounds like...real freedom?"

Joe turned to his companion. "Grace," he said, slapping a hand down on the countertop, "is an open door to possibility."

Both men sat in comfortable silence, neither feeling the need to add anything to the conversation at that moment.

"I feel like I could do with some possibilities right now," Dan sighed.

Joe decided more coffee was needed. He topped up Dan's mug. "Coming here really saved my life, if I'm honest. I mean, I was seeing everything I held dear slipping away. Sandy, well, she was right there by my side, but God seemed so indifferent. When we came here, something happened. Out on those long walks, looking down on the valleys and up to the peaks, everything was new.

"And I remember one day I was up on the ridge there, it was a beautifully clear day, I could see for miles, and out of the blue it was as if God asked me 'What kind of life do you want to create? Where would you like this journey to go? Because it's all good.' And in that moment I knew that I wanted to be here."

"Maybe I should ask myself that question," Dan wondered.

"Truth is, I've always been a goal-oriented kind of guy," Joe explained. "I had goals for my career, my personal life, my spiritual life. And sitting up there on a rock, none of that was important anymore. It was the now, today. And what I could do with it."

"I always thought goal-setting was over-rated," Dan joked.

Joe grinned. "Well, goals are pretty restrictive in some ways. Now I kind of have a preferred destination, and my focus is much more on the journey, the unfolding of the moment. Rather than holding on to a specific dream and being disappointed, either because I never get there or it doesn't satisfy my expectations, I try to live with expectancy. It kind of takes the limitations away."

"Expectancy?" Dan weighed the word in his mind. "Ah, right, it's much more open-ended."

"Exactly. Expectations usually only create limitations," Joe affirmed. Then, as if remembering something, he continued. "Hey, I haven't properly shown you the *Journey Room* yet, have I? Let's go."

Still holding his coffee cup, Joe led the way down the corridor to the very back of the house, the part, he'd explained yesterday, that was the original stone building.

Dan stepped into a large, comfortable room divided into distinct areas. Much of the wall space was filled with shelves stacked with all kinds of books on all kinds of creative pursuits. He saw books on travel, books on cooking, books on wildlife photography. A whole shelf was dedicated to painting and drawing, and he could see that pottery, music, science, nature and astronomy were also catered for.

Comfortable couches invited Dan to just sit and chill. Exploring further, he came across a large table for craft-work, easels and paints for the artists, as well as a floor mat for meditation. A Spanish guitar hung on the wall next to the glass doors that opened onto the patio.

"We don't have everything, but we try to encourage being

creative. Sandy and I both discovered over the years that unlocking creativity is a real key for the journey. It's healing, it's freeing. We all have that creative spark in us, put there by the Creator, and this is a place for exploring and experimenting without any judgment."

"It's...very cool. My wife would love all this." Dan found himself drawn to a couple of cameras sitting on a shelf. "I don't suppose I see myself as creative. I guess what I do means fixing problems, making sure everything ticks along in the background. No room for creativity. I'm not even creative when I cook."

"Maybe you're trying too hard," Joe suggested. "Thinking of creativity as *doing* something rather than *being*."

"Yeah," Dan was thoughtful. "I always used to love photography back in my teens. Kind of an expensive hobby back then."

"Well, it still is. But these are nice cameras," Joe picked up one with a long lens. "This has a 300mm zoom on it, great for wildlife. Try it. Take it with you when you go out walking."

Dan took the camera from Joe and held it in his hands. Memories of a young man with the world at his feet suddenly flashed through his mind. "Okay, I'll give it a go. How do you..?"

"Switch it on? I thought *you* were the tech guy. There," Joe pointed out the power button and gave Dan a quick overview of some of its features. "I always keep it on auto mode anyhow, you can't go wrong. If you want to shoot video you just press the red button."

"Nice."

Joe finished the last of his coffee. "Okay if I leave you to yourself for a while? Gotta catch up with a few things, make some calls, that kind of thing."

"No problem," said Dan, looking around the room. "I think I'll chill out in here for a while."

"Good idea," Joe agreed. "Help yourself to tea, coffee, sandwich, whatever you want. I'll come find you later."

Dan nodded. "Okay."

Joe made to leave, then stopped at the door and turned

back. "Take some time out. Ask yourself some questions. And Dan," he pointed a finger in the air as he looked over the top of his spectacles. "Remember to listen."

Dan found himself alone in the silence, still holding the camera. An oddly familiar feeling had greeted him since the moment he stepped into the room, and he could still sense it lingering in the background. It was as if another piece of a puzzle had just clicked into place.

Sinking into a chair, he sat for some time in the *Journey Room* doing nothing. Instead of rushing into something, as was his usual way, Dan wanted to take a moment to be present, to allow his mind to slow down.

This room, Dan decided, was a room of possibilities, and that in itself was unusual. It was, he thought, a little like life—you don't get to do everything, you need to decide.

Eventually, he decided to look through some books. His eyes were drawn to a large wooden bookshelf stacked with hardcover travel books bearing evocative titles such as *Mysteries of India, Pictorial Guide To The South Pacific*, and *Australia From The Air.* One title in particular caught his attention—*Forgotten Spain: A Photographic Journey.* He removed it from the shelf and, still standing, began to flick through the glossy pages.

Dan was quickly immersed in photos of the diverse and timeless land he found himself in. Pictures of ancient Roman amphitheaters, ruined Moorish castles on remote mountaintops, desert canyons, dramatic coastlines and lush vineyards basking in golden sunlight. Page after page revealed beautiful vistas, striking landscapes and colorful towns. He was mesmerized, intrigued, and captured by the images as they stirred something deep inside. He let it continue to stir, enjoying the experience of allowing his emotions a little free reign.

The last time he'd been in Spain was the family summer vacation. A typical package deal on the *Costa Del Sol* along the southern coastline. It had been a pleasant two weeks at an average hotel with a large swimming pool, right on a long stretch of beach. Plenty of sunshine, plenty of sangria, and way too hot for

Dan. Still, it had been an experience they all remembered very positively, even though they'd never been back since.

But this book that Dan held in his hands as he sat back on the couch, this was showing him a land far removed from the popular tourist destinations. He could suddenly see a different world, and it spoke to him at a deep level.

He leaned back and closed his eyes. His thoughts were immediately filled with images of him and Kimberly walking together down winding roads to unknown destinations. It was something they'd done a lot of in the first few years of their marriage. It was something that was now only a memory.

Dan felt a sudden need to respond to what he was seeing. He picked up his phone and began to type a message to Kimberly, then he stopped. Was he just assuming that he could get himself sorted and they'd live happily ever after, wandering hand-in-hand just as they did before?

On the other hand, thought Dan, wasn't this all about the journey? He wasn't the same man he was 20 years ago, and she wasn't the same woman. They had changed, their relationship had changed, and maybe it was time to stop taking it all for granted and start working to make some positive changes.

He paused again, then laid the phone beside him. How could he communicate all these thoughts and feelings in few text messages? Impossible. They were too important.

Some things would just have to wait.

CHAPTER 12

"We live as if the future has already been decided."

It was raining again, and the sound of thunder could be heard rumbling in the distance. Joe was on a long phone call in the study, so Dan had fixed himself a sandwich, filled the biggest mug he could find with tea, and returned to the comfort of the lounge. Now he sat near the fire and let his thoughts wander. The world seemed to stand still as he closed his eyes.

As the peacefulness wrapped around him like a blanket he was more and more aware of how tired he felt. He'd been tired for a long time, long enough to have gotten used to it, and he found himself wondering why that surprised him. Two years of trying so hard to be there for his mother. Two years of holding up a career, of trying to be a father who was present and a husband who cared. And then the rising fear that he was losing his faith, all the time trying hard to ignore the turmoil inside whenever he went along to church or mid-week meeting.

He suspected that at some stage he'd even been suffering from mild depression. Maybe he still was.

At least this afternoon the tiredness felt more healthy. Like the natural fatigue he might experience after a long walk, lots of fresh air, and not being quite as fit as he used to be.

He opened his eyes just as Joe put his head around the door.

"Hey, just going to prepare some food for later," Joe explained. "Shepherd's pie okay?"

Dan snapped back to the present as if coming out of a trance. "Oh, yeah. Sounds good. Not too many shepherds for me, though. Can I give you a hand?"

"You can relax! You're the guest, and guests get to chill out."

"Well, I think I'm about to fall asleep," Dan stretched and stood up. "I'll come through to the kitchen anyway, I could do with some more caffeine."

"Sure thing. You fix the coffee, I'll get the food going."

There was something about Sandy's Kitchen that Dan found so inviting. As he sat with his coffee, watching Joe lay out various vegetables on the countertop, he could feel a welcoming, calming energy about the place. It was as if the memories of a thousand wonderful conversations were still echoing off the walls, or had been absorbed into the fixtures and fittings.

Joe chopped onions like a pro, tossed them into a large skillet, and started finely dicing the carrots. Red and green peppers were soon added to a healthy-looking pile of brightly colored ingredients. He added the meat to the onions, let it brown, then began to stir in the vegetables.

The wonderful aroma drifted over to Dan.

"You like cooking, Joe? You look like you know what you're doing."

"Yes, I do. *Look* like I know what I'm doing. No, I enjoy it. But I never had time for it back home. Sandy did everything."

"I can imagine a lot of baking going on in this kitchen," Dan said.

"Oh yeah. She makes this apple pie," Joe said fondly. "You wouldn't believe." He scanned a long line of herbs and spices, selected a few, and began to liberally add them to the mix. "Now, I try to do my share. And I love the creativity, I love the way different flavors and textures come together to make something unique. There's something so satisfying about cooking, it's really lost on so many people that live fast and furious lives."

Dan smiled to himself. "You're right. We go through a lot of microwave lasagnas in our house. Then again, we have teenage boys."

"But it's such a wonderful process, you're missing out," Joe said enthusiastically. "And look at all the life here!"

Dan played along. He was intrigued by Joe's energy, but could only see a pile of potatoes and vegetable scraps.

"Ah, you don't see the life."

"Um..."

"Look at this potato. I could leave that a few weeks to sprout, cut it in half and plant it out there in my little vegetable garden, and in a few months I'd have more potatoes. Or these bell pepper seeds. Each one full of the stuff of rebirth. Every seed holds a blueprint for not just a new pepper plant, but the plants that will come from *that* pepper plant. And so on. I love it."

"I never really thought about it. I mean, seeds are seeds."

"Seeds are incredible. We know what they do, but we don't understand the how or the why," Joe said, reaching for a jar on a shelf. He opened it and shook some of the contents onto the chopping board.

"Mustard seeds?" Dan guessed, looking at the heap of little black balls.

"Incredible. A tiny, lifeless seed, packed with potential. Just waiting for the right circumstances to grow into something more."

Joe returned to chopping the potatoes as the rich sauce bubbled away.

"Faith like a mustard seed." Dan was holding a few of the little black seeds in the palm of his hand. "I used to believe that a little faith would carry me through."

"Faith." Joe paused with the knife in his hand. "It's a pretty strange thing. Misunderstood."

"I think I understand it less now than ever."

"But faith is potential. Faith creates possibilities. And, if you believe what Jesus said, then you don't need a whole lot of it to create some big possibilities."

Dan was quiet for a moment. He found himself hoping that

Joe was not going to tell him something he already knew. "Okay, I kind of see that. So all those times I feel like there is no way forward, no way out of this situation..."

"It's not about trying harder. It's about allowing the little faith we do have to help us to see beyond."

"But doesn't it depend on what you have faith in? Faith in God, faith in people, faith in yourself?"

"You might say Jesus wants us to understand the potential of faith. Seeds are incredible, but only if they die. But what's more incredible is what's locked inside you and me. That is truly awesome. And if we die to our fabricated, false self we walk around with all day long, and learn to unlock that faith in what God has put inside us, and let it grow..."

The chopping continued as Joe's words dissipate into the air. Dan waited expectantly.

Joe laid the knife aside and gazed through the window. His next words were spoken with conviction. "Each one of us has the seeds of greatness inside, but most of the time we live as if the future has already been decided."

Dan raised his eyebrows. "Well, that's deep. But I can't force myself to have faith."

"No, it has a lot to do with trust. It's taking that first step, trusting that God will meet you there. It's not easy, though, when your foundations have been shaken."

"I think my trust took a real beating when I had to watch my mother go through it all."

"And that doesn't just get better overnight," said Joe, and Dan could see the kindness in his eyes once more. "The last thing you need right now is someone telling you that you don't have enough faith because you don't trust God or your spiritual leaders."

Joe left the potatoes to boil and sat on a stool at the breakfast bar. Dan had stepped up to the open patio doors and stood looking over the back yard. Sunlight was coming through the clouds and highlighting the pink roses against the dark stone wall.

"You're talking about moving forward from here," Dan pondered. "Something needs to change, I need to change, to take a new path with my life. But I don't really trust God with my life anymore."

"I can only tell you my experience. But the reality of the situation is this—there are no guarantees. God doesn't guarantee an easy life, or success, or promise to fix everything. But he does promise to be there, and that was something I could hold onto."

"Part of the journey."

"Yeah, he's there on the journey with us. And we can only stay where we are or walk with him into the unknown. No promises. But a whole lot of potential."

"So it's learning to trust God, not trust the outcome."

"Yeah, that's a good way of looking at it, because we always have this hope that once we arrive at our dream job or a certain amount of money, all our problems will disappear. Or with your mother, you were looking for a certain outcome that didn't happen."

"That is very, very true," Dan admitted, looking back at Joe. "I thought things would work out differently. I hoped."

Joe nodded in understanding. "So instead, how about seeing it as God inviting us to work things out as we go. Maybe even God does that too, in a sense. And that's a true pilgrimage. Still moving forward even when we know we may never have all the answers, and may never see all the outcomes we want to see in this life."

Dan let the thoughts run through his head as he realized the wisdom of Joe's words. He had lived with certain expectations for a long time. Maybe his whole life. Expectations about his career, his marriage, his faith. But things were so very different from his expectations.

"Our expectations do kind of put limits on things, don't they?" Dan mused. "Is that just kind of a mixed-up faith?"

Joe said nothing, allowing Dan the space he needed to process his thoughts.

Eventually, Dan broke the silence. His voice was far off. "I have so much to be grateful for, but things aren't quite how I expected them to be."

"If we live life from a place of expectations, we are never going to be truly happy."

"Because we limit ourselves? Limit God even?"

"We either continue to try to make our life fit into our narrow, results-oriented path, or we're disappointed when we arrive because it's not what we imagined it would be," Joe explained. "Same with having expectations of how God works."

Dan was looking through the open door, but his eyes were examining his heart. "I have to start asking questions of myself, I think."

"We all do. Where we find ourselves now doesn't really have much to do with chance. It has a lot to do with how we've chosen to fit ourselves into a box of our own making."

Dan chewed his lip as he continued to look inwards. "So what do we do? To break out of that?"

"Change one thing. *One* thing. Change how you see yourself, your self-worth or your expectations, and your future will unfold in a completely different way. Like discovering a new road just around the corner."

***

Joe hadn't had his usual writing time that morning; he'd wanted to get out for some quiet time before the day ran away with him. Gathering logs in the forest at daybreak, he decided, can be an almost meditative, ethereal experience, and it had given him a chance to prepare himself.

Having Dan around was a good thing. Joe had sensed a connection right from the beginning, and there was no doubt in his mind that his visitor was supposed to be here. But however he viewed it there was no question that Joe would be giving of himself, and he didn't want to do that halfheartedly.

Dan, as much as anyone else, needed him to be fully engaged.

Now, standing in his study, with the smell of baking pie coming through from the kitchen, he was thankful for how it had turned out. A busy day, yes. An unusual day, certainly. But a good one, nonetheless.

The conversations with Dan had surprised him. They were covering a lot of ground, fast. He reflected on the fact that Sandy wasn't here. How her presence would have completely changed the dynamic, slowed the pace and created more room for the *important things,* like family, kids and such.

He smiled. That was why they made such a good team—she balanced him out. Dan would just have to come back another time for the relationship counseling.

Still, he couldn't help but wonder at the timing. God's timing.

All so very perfect. This was the kind of divine interaction he wanted to believe in, but when it actually happened he still had trouble accepting it for the gift it was.

No problem. He was on a journey.

He took his place at the desk, opened a new document on the laptop, then flicked through the voice app on his phone. He'd recorded a few thoughts and ideas throughout the day that had seemed good at the time. Thoughts that could, maybe, turn into something more.

Or not. He'd just have to see. That was the fun of it.

He hit *play* and began to type.

What are you hearing? Because God is at work. There is an underlying call of your heart, there are signs, indicators, and if you learn to tune in you'll discover a whole new way of approaching something, even the everyday, normal things.

You're thinking there has to be a way forward, and it doesn't mean something scary like quitting your job or moving to another town, it's more likely that there is already something going on, some connection you feel to something or someone, some hints as to what the next step involves.

God wants to help you trust your intuition. You must have felt that when you came here. You trusted, you made a leap, and you're here. That's not normal. We're so often convinced that we have to leave things in God's hands. That we don't have anything to offer.

But we do.

So when something unusual happens, out of the blue, we need to take note. It is easy to overlook little things that we put down to coincidence, but a conversation here, an idea there, a chance meeting or a sentence from a book that you can't get out of your head. All these are indicators of something coming together, but it's up to us what we do with it.

Think about this in terms of prayer. We've been taught that God answers prayer, and answers to prayer should mean something pretty clear. A healing, an intervention, a change of direction. Our prayers, we understand, cause an effect.

But what if God is more about possibility? What if prayer is more about how we can respond to a situation, and that as we pray we learn to have an expectancy that we're involved in the outcome?

That would mean we can't fire off a prayer and forget. We have to remain involved, watch for the connections, and use our intelligence and initiative to bring about a shift, a resolution, a result.

The bleeping of the timer in the kitchen interrupted Joe's work. He stopped and sat back, carefully re-reading the words on the page, testing each sentence.

Prayer.

He would be the first to admit that his understanding of prayer was a work in progress. He didn't see it the same way, that much was certain, but then he wasn't the same guy either.

And, of course, God was not the same.

He stopped himself. Had God changed? His *perception* of God had changed, yes, and recent years had shown him, to his great relief, that there was so much more to be discovered. And honestly, what could he expect from the divine Creator of everything?

He shook his head. "You've got a long way to go, Mitch. Still a long way. Keep remembering that."

The bleeps from the kitchen continued to assault his ears. "Alright!" Rubbing his hands together, he decided to leave the writing as it was. More work to be done, he concluded. A lot more.

But now, time to eat.

He suddenly realized that he was looking forward to sitting down with Dan for some good food, a glass of wine and relaxed conversation.

Maybe he was making a new friend.

Stranger things had happened.

***

"I did some listening earlier," Dan said, watching Joe removed the perfectly baked shepherd's pie from the oven.

"Good! Just give me a second and you can tell me about it."

As Joe prepared the table for dinner, Dan thought over the experience of that afternoon. Something had happened, but if he was honest, he wasn't completely sure what.

"I think I was reminded of some things. You know, stuff that used to be important to me. Like seeing a bit more of the world."

Joe, stopping to fill the water jug, simply nodded.

"I found a book about Spain. It was challenging, in an odd way. The only other time I've been to Spain was the typical package holiday in a beach hotel. But that book, it was exploring forgotten parts of Spain, off the typical tourist routes."

"Spain is a big country. Haven't seen enough of it myself."

"I live in a little English town," Dan explained, continuing to work out what he was feeling. "It's got a bit of history, nice countryside. When the sun shines you wouldn't want to be anywhere else. But, I don't know…"

"There's so much to discover in this world?"

"Exactly."

"Being content with what we have is a good thing. Until it becomes a barrier."

"That's it. I always wanted to experience new places. But somewhere along the way..." Dan stopped. He knew why he'd laid those dreams aside—there were always more important things to do.

"You're a bit of an adventurer at heart, Dan. I think you wouldn't have come here otherwise. That says something to me. It's one of those fundamental truths about you that you dare not ignore."

"I can't remember the last time I wanted to go exploring."

"Well," Joe said, finally taking his place at the table, "tomorrow should be a good day to get out there. Something to look forward to."

"Yes," Dan agreed. "Something to look forward to would be good."

Just then, Dan's attention was drawn to a buzz from his phone lying on the table.

"Go ahead," Joe said. "Might be important. In fact," he added with a whisper, "if it's your wife, it's important."

"I'll just check." Dan reached over to opened the message as Joe went in search of wine.

Hey, just chatting with Debs and Reg about you. How's your day been?

How had his day been? Full, he thought. Full and unusual. And...

Good. Covered a lot of ground with Joe. Talked about faith. How God's grace has to be unconditional. That kind of thing.

And you're being kind to yourself? How's the weather?

Weather is awful but the house is lovely. You OK? The boys?

We all had dinner with Debbie and Reg. The boys have gone back now so we are having some grown-up time.

Good. You like being a grown-up sometimes.

Only sometimes.

Dan smiled. He knew how much Kimberly had wrestled with seeing her little babies develop into young men. They were both taller than their mother now, officially making her the shortest person in the house. Dan suspected he'd be in second place before the year was out.

When I get back it would be good to talk about some of this stuff.

Talking is good.

Dan smiled at her reply. She'd let him get away with *not* talking about this stuff for too long.

Joe has been helping me look at my expectations, how I expect my faith to work, how I expect God to do things. He talks about a more Jesus-centered approach.

Sounds interesting.

Dan thought about his next line carefully. He wanted to trust the instinct that told him his wife was willing to listen.

I don't want to carry on the same way, not for my faith, not for us.

Kimberly took her time replying. He could imagine her having a three-way conversation with their neighbors.

Neither do I. I hope you find some answers. I hope there are answers.

Dan paused. Answers seemed to still be a long way off. He looked up as Joe placed a glass of wine on the table and said a quick thank-you.

More questions than answers, I'm afraid.

Reg says to enjoy yourself.

I'll try, but Joe is really putting me through it. Non-stop torture.

There was another pause. He could almost sense Kimberly's restrained smile at the other end.

You haven't sent me any photos yet.

I'll send some tomorrow xx.

***

Before heading to bed that evening, Dan decided to take a walk outside. He pulled on his boots, zipped up his fleece jacket, headed out the back door and stepped into the gray expanse of the meadow.

Away from the house, with only a single, solitary light shining outside the kitchen, his eyes gradually adjusted to the darkness. It was an inky blackness he had rarely experienced in his lifetime.

The night sky was nothing short of breathtaking. Thousands of shining dots, each one a different brightness, all clamoring for his attention. The cloudy streak of the milky way arched over his head. He had never seen anything so wonderful, and it seemed so close he could reach out and touch it.

When I consider your heavens, the work of your fingers, the moon and the stars which you have set in place...

The familiar words of the Psalmist came to him from a place deep inside. It sounded like an invitation. Dan couldn't take his eyes off the immense show above him. After a few minutes, almost holding his breath, he lay down on the damp grass with his hands behind his head and simply let it all wash over him.

Here I am, looking into the vastness of the Universe as I hurtle through space at thousands of miles per hour.

He recalled his childhood fascination with astronomy. Names came to mind —Betelgeuse, Cassiopeia, Andromeda galaxy. He began to wonder how it had all become so ordinary.

How can billions of light-years, filled with billions of galaxies each with billions of stars, become just a nice evening sky?

Gradually he found himself reflecting on the day, at the unfolding conversation and the thoughts that had come out of it. He and Joe had covered so much today, it was impossible to remember everything. He decided that he simply needed to trust God in it and hold onto the things that seemed most important at the time.

Grace, Dan thought. *That keeps coming up. A complete grace, that doesn't depend on us. Not one bit. Everything is a gift.*

Why was it, he wondered, that the concept of grace had always been put across as an exchange. And yet Jesus had spent three years going around forgiving complete strangers their sins, wanting nothing in return.

Would God really be any different?

This conversation with Joe was revealing things that needed to be examined, exposing the shaky foundations more and more, and forcing him to look at his faith in a new way. And of course it raised more questions. Of course, the doubts weren't going to dissipate in an instant.

And he was beginning to feel okay with that.

It was some time before he realized that he was getting cold. At the same moment, he remembered what Joe had said about the wild boar roaming around at night. With that he stood up, looking around and feeling a little foolish.

The kitchen light was guiding him home, the mountainside was a deep black against the sparkling infinity of sky, and as he walked the short distance across the meadow back to the house, he said a quiet thank-you to the Creator.

Thursday

CHAPTER 13

"I just want to learn the lessons and move on."

D an awoke to a sense of anticipation in his spirit. The view from the window was promising—blue sky above the ridge-line and sunlight already painting the distant peaks with a red-gold tinge. The positive feeling stayed with him at breakfast, and after talking things over with his host he headed out the door, camera and snacks in his pack, clasping a well-used map Joe had given him.

Following the stony track that crossed the stream into the forest, he took the higher fork through the trees as Joe had instructed. Soon he was deep in sunlit woodlands filled with the happy sounds of birds enjoying the morning. Yellow butterflies flitted between purple orchids, and the undergrowth was full of pale blue flowers and moss-covered rocks. His boots beat out a steady pace on the soft dirt as the path meandered gradually higher, and it wasn't long before Dan had settled into a comfortable, almost soothing rhythm.

Emerging from the woodlands, the track soon met the empty road. Crossing over, Dan stepped onto another track, this one marked with a wooden sign indicating an official hiking route. It skirted a picturesque meadow that sloped down to where a small herd of brown cows grazed contentedly around an old building with a collapsed roof.

Something about the scene caught Dan's eye, and he

stopped. *Nice ruin,* he thought to himself, noticing how the early sunlight picked out every detail on the stone walls. After snapping a few photos with his phone he continued on his way, following the trail on a wide sweep around a dark, forested area, then climbing steadily upwards beside a glistening stream.

At one point the track crossed over to the far bank by way of large, flat boulders, and Dan took a moment to stop and dip a hand in the rushing water. The sensation of ice-cold snow-melt running between his fingers was exhilarating, almost mesmerizing. Just when it was beginning to get too cold, he plucked out a smooth, round stone that sparkled with traces of quartz, which he held tightly in his hand as he continued the climb.

Another wooden sign, this one faded and weathered, now presented him with two options, both of which meant nothing to him. A quick look at the map confirmed that turning to the right would take him up to the head of the valley. Joe, he recalled, had suggested he take the left fork. He smiled to himself at the thought of the choices before him—*it's impossible to go both ways, Dan; you have to choose one or the other.*

He decided to stick with Joe's recommendation which, from the number of boot-prints in the mud, seemed, at least today, to be the road *more* traveled by.

The trail took a straight line westward, rising gently, and presently he found himself coming out of the trees onto a grassy slope dotted with large boulders and edged with a riot of pink rhododendron. This higher vantage point presented a wide panorama of the valley, with the little ruined building in the meadow now dwarfed by the surrounding landscape. He stopped once more to grab some memories with his phone, feeling a sense of disappointment that Kimberly wasn't there to share the moment.

But I'm here, and I need this. And Kimberly knows that.

Dan was suddenly aware that he was standing still, staring down at the ruin. It seemed to fill his vision. How old was that place, he wondered. *Was it once someone's home, long abandoned to the elements? What stories did it have to tell?*

"Is it even possible to have a *nice ruin?*" he said to himself, shaking his head.

After the gentle rise, the track now forced him higher up the valley side. It became gradually steeper and more rocky, snaking back and forth among scattered pine trees and boulders until his ears caught the unmistakable sound of rushing water.

On the other side of a small stand of trees, he found a level shelf of rock offering a view of a series of waterfalls cascading down the steep mountainside. The sight and sound of the water foaming and plunging from high above, down to a deep pool far below, was inspiring, even if it were on a small scale.

Leaning on a solid wooden rail, Dan took a moment to catch his breath and take in his surroundings. Azure blue sky flecked with white clouds above the dark rock wall that stretched above him. Looking south, above the opposite ridge, green slopes rose gracefully up to bare rock summits, fading into haze in either direction. His ears were filled with the background roar of the falls; his lungs were filled with the cool mountain air.

He breathed deeply, held it for a few seconds, and exhaled.

This is beautiful. Dramatic, peaceful, exhilarating. Everything I need right now. If only life were so simple.

Below him, the valley continued to rise to the east, and he could see a cluster of large stone buildings among the trees and meadows that could be a farm. Dark pines hugged the rocky slope, reaching heavenward, and further below, nestling in the green meadow, he could still make out the ruin. The cows, it seemed, had wandered off to find fresh grass.

He stared at it as he munched on a chocolate bar. The old building appeared to be stubbornly fixed in place. It wasn't going anywhere, and it seemed to play on his mind. Once there was life, now only ruins. Desolation. Was that the reality of *his life,* he wondered?

Clearly, he was not where he wanted to be. Clearly, things could not stay the same—it wasn't doing *him* any good, it wasn't doing his marriage or family life any good. If he stayed on this road he'd be forever wondering what could have been, and he knew he didn't want to live a life of *maybe, someday.*

If I could just learn the lessons and move on. I want to understand. I want someone to show me the way.

He exhaled with a deep sigh and closed his eyes.

I want someone to tell me what to believe.

Dan caught himself. He'd been through this before, many times. Following someone else's lead had always been easier, more comfortable. He would be happier with Joe giving him some answers. Any answers. But what he needed, he knew deep down, was to figure out his own way.

The journey, as Joe referred to it, was starting to make sense.

He removed his hat, ran his fingers through his hair, and smiled wryly to himself. *It doesn't matter how far I go from home, or how high I climb, I'm still taking all my doubts and pain and frustration with me.*

His thoughts returned to breakfast-time that morning. Joe had once again left him a note on the table in the lounge—*breakfast is in the kitchen.* Walking back through the hallway he'd seen Joe at his desk, tapping away on the laptop. Not wanting to disturb his work, Dan had quietly walked past but Joe had noticed anyway and called out a greeting.

"Pancakes and tea in the kitchen, I'll come through in a minute." Joe had added, not taking his eyes from the screen.

Dan had made himself comfortable at one of the patio tables outside, worked his way through a couple of pancakes, and spent some time skimming through the list of walks he'd put together the week before. *I need to get out somewhere. Time for some wilderness.*

Joe had finally appeared through the kitchen door. *"Feels like summer is making its presence felt in the Pyrenees. Got your tea?"*

"Yep," Dan had replied, lifting his mug for Joe to see. *"Can't live without it."*

Joe had seemed tired. He'd taken a seat opposite Dan and was unusually quiet. Finally, he asked Dan if he was planning on going walking. *"You should make the most of it this morning, it's going to cloud over this afternoon."*

"Yeah, I should do a bit of exploring, that was always part of the plan. And this conversation, of course."

"And I'll be here when you get back. I can tell you how to find a great trail up the valley, goes up past some waterfalls then doubles back along the ridge. Incredible views. Very peaceful."

"Sounds perfect. And you'll know where to find me if I get lost."

Before he left, Joe had set him a task. *"I want you to think about something when you're out. I want you to think of three things. Three things that you love to do. That are important to you."*

Almost two hours had passed since he'd set off from the house. Looking down on the valley from his vantage point at the falls, Dan pondered Joe's suggestion. *Three things that are important to me. Three things I love to do.*

The sun was high now, and Dan was suddenly aware of how much warmer it was. He stripped off his fleece jacket and began to stuff it in the pack. It was then that he remembered the camera. He took it out of its case and tried a few shots, zooming in on the meadow with its now-familiar ruin. Then Dan flicked through the images on the small display, nodded to himself and turned back to the trail.

The path continued to take him higher up the steep valley side, and at times Dan would stop and take a photo, all the while feeling more confident with the equipment. Finally, with a bit of careful scrambling, he found himself at the top of the ridge —a long line of exposed rock that stretched westward. Here he stopped again to drink some water and experiment a little more with the camera.

His vantage point gave him an almost uninterrupted view of the valley. The pine clad slopes below, steaming in the warm sun; the small lake of shimmering silver set in green velvet; snow-capped peaks reaching up to the north, fading to gray as they marched towards the west. An eagle soared effortlessly on a thermal not far above his head. Dan felt like he was absorbing pure exhilaration, and he wasn't in the least distracted by his mediocre photographs.

The path now became less distinct as it passed over barren rock and wound between young pines, but it continued to lead him along the ridge-line that stretched generally westward along the edge of the valley. At one point he noticed Joe's place far below, with the little stream cutting down between the meadow and the forest, fed by a ribbon of a cascade, pure white against the dark rock-face directly opposite where he stood.

As the ridge began to fade into forest once more and the path took on a distinct downward attitude, he stopped again. Scrambling up onto a high, flat boulder where he could still see above the trees, Dan made himself comfortable, pulled an apple out of his pack, and let the presence of the mountains wash over him in a reassuring flow of strength and endurance.

Maybe I'm overthinking things. Wouldn't be the first time. I love this—trekking in wild places, exploring, camera in hand. The adventure of it all. It's been far too long.

Over two years ago. That was the last time he'd been out walking in mountains, Dan realized. A summer vacation among the lochs and highlands of Scotland's west coast. Apart from the brief, awkward visit with Kimberly's parents, it had been a memorable time together as a family.

A time before everything started to unravel.

He found himself wondering if those simple, *together times* were gone. If it would even be possible to get the boys to come along on an adventure now that they were older. He realized how he missed them.

Okay, so I love spending time with my family. That's another one on the list. And maybe we can talk about another trip when I get back home. Not camping this time, though. No way.

As Dan sat lost in thought, another eagle came into view, appearing to float on the air with wings outstretched, wheeling in wide circles above the trees. Dan sat still, transfixed by the beauty of the moment. The sense of timeless freedom was almost palpable, and he felt something like jealousy for the sheer enjoyment the large bird of prey seemed to take from simply being in its element.

Who told the eagle she was meant to soar?

The question came like a whisper on the breeze, floating down from the heights above. Holding the half-eaten apple between his teeth, he reached for the camera, aimed and hit the video record button. For a few brief seconds, he framed the majestic bird in the display and carefully panned the camera to track its flight. Then, as if aware of his presence, the eagle suddenly pulled her wings closer to her body and became a swift arrow that sped away out of view.

Dan held the camera in his hand. It almost seemed to be asking him a question. *Why aren't you doing what you love to do?*

The trail back down the mountain hugged the side of the valley and meandered through the dark forest. At times the sunlight would shine through but Dan hardly noticed. He'd become lost in his thoughts again, but this time things felt lighter. He wasn't dwelling on the past, he wasn't even thinking about his current situation. He found himself wondering about possibilities.

Good possibilities.

Joe had talked about dismantling and rebuilding. Digging up old, shaky foundations and reconstructing with the little pieces of gold that could be found in the rubble. Dan liked that analogy—it was at least a little comforting to think that his life was not a complete mistake, that there were some good elements to hold onto, and that it wasn't so much a matter of starting from scratch but of reforming things into a new, more flexible framework.

So had he found any gold so far? Dan wondered at all that had happened over the past couple of days.

Well, I was ready to throw out the Bible. Now I'm at least prepared to approach it with a more open mind and start reading it differently. That has to be worth something because I have found some good stuff in there over the years. Maybe I'm also beginning to see the difference between reading it for the insight it can give, as opposed to manipulating it, even weaponizing it, to give weight to an agenda. There seems to be a lot of that going on in the world.

And God. These conversations with Joe have been...enlightening. I like the way Joe has a much bigger view of God than I've had for a long time. That has to be a good thing.

Church. I'm still not sure about the whole church thing. I think I need to ask Joe what his take is, because in my mind church is a very enclosed, self-serving institution that is all about getting people in, getting people saved from God's wrath and judgment.

So the other thing is me. How do I see myself?

Dan let his thoughts wander as he navigated his way through the trees and shrubs. The track was winding back and forth now as it descended, skirting large boulders and patches of thick undergrowth. Birds sang in the branches of slender birch trees as squirrels jumped and skittered above him.

A long-forgotten memory seemed to appear from nowhere. A memory of a hot summer just before he was about to start college. A group of friends on a long hike in the rolling hills of southern England. *"And Dan? What about you? What do you want to do with your life?"*

"Me? Oh, I don't know. I just want to make the world a better place."

***

Joe's boots left deep prints in the soft ground as he stomped around on the shore of the lake, muttering to himself. Even though the sun was now high over the mountains, he felt like he was trying to crawl out from under a cloud.

He stooped to pick up a rock and sent it sailing through the air. It hit the water with a satisfying *plunk.*

Picking up another, this time he put some grunt into it. It sailed high and splashed down further out.

Plunk.

He tried again, and this time he found a suitable word to accompany the rock on its journey. *"Dammit!"*

Plunk. The surface of the lake was broken once more, sending ripples out across the water.

"I'm trying my *hardest*."

Plunk.

"I'm giving my *all*."

Plunk.

"Dammit."

Plunk

"This is not how it's supposed to be."

It wasn't the first time Joe had gone to find some space down at the lake for a serious talk with God. In the conversations he'd had over the years with various good people carrying burdens too heavy for them to bear, there often came a point when he had to get out and find a place to rant. One thing he was sure about—God didn't seem in the least bit phased.

This morning was a little different, though. The email he'd received from his old friend had brought it all back—the pain, the loss, the doubts about his work, along with a whole bunch of questions for tomorrow.

Steve had been blunt. He'd thanked Joe for the coffee-shop meeting, it had been good to catch up. But people were asking questions, and as the Pastor, he didn't want his congregation getting the wrong idea.

Joe had heard it all before. And maybe Steve had a point —hiding behind a laptop screen thousands of miles away, Joe didn't have to live with the consequences of his words. He wasn't accountable, and Steve loved accountability.

When it suited him.

There was no point pretending, though. Joe had known when he walked out the church door one last time that he was leaving a minefield ready to blow up at any minute, and good people were bound to get hurt. A senior leader of the church doesn't just change his mind about God without consequences— it seemed that the ripples of his leaving were still being felt even now.

No, he couldn't blame Steve that the bitterness remained, even if most of the hurts had healed with time.

He just wished things would have worked out differently.

Joe gritted his teeth. Who was he kidding, thinking he had something to say? What guarantees were there that Dan wouldn't be the next guy to implode, wrecking his life and those closest to him in the process?

He knew where this was leading. Somewhere much closer to home.

Stones all thrown, he sat down on his favorite rock and watched the lake become a mirror once more. Thoughts of his son flickered through his mind, and he let them come, knowing the healing was in there somewhere with all the regret, the sorrow and frustration. Anger still reared its head, of course—Grant must have known his choices were going to cause lasting pain. At least Joe was in a better place now.

He just didn't know how to tell his son that.

As the calmness returned to the surface he felt a sense of peace reflected in his spirit, moving him to reach out in prayer. He tried forming a prayer for Grant, but he stumbled. He'd keep on trying, though.

He prayed for his daughter. He prayed for Sandy.

Eventually his thoughts turned to Dan.

"God, I really feel for Dan. One more believer who can't believe it when the foundations start to crumble. Man, it's the same old story."

He stopped himself. The rant was over. He could go on and on but he knew, at this moment at least, that the problem was too big, too ingrained. The only thing he could do was to do the work God had put in front of him. And that, for now, was talking with Dan.

God did not need anyone to serve him. God did not need the corporate meetings and happy worship songs any more than he needed bulls sacrificed on the altar. God didn't need any of that. The church *did* need those things. It created a sense of community, a sense of belonging. A reason for being.

"I just want to be able to give Dan something to go forward with. I know he's not going to be able to deconstruct his life in a week, I know he's got a long way to go to arrive at a place where he's comfortable with himself and where he is on his own journey. But, well, I think you're in this. I feel it. So I'm just asking."

As Joe sat watching the swallows skim gracefully across the water he felt a growing reassurance that everything was okay. It wasn't his job to change the world, it wasn't up to him to dismantle old religious structures. It was up to him to listen, observe, and write and talk about what came up. He thought about Jesus's words—*For my yoke is easy, and my burden is light.*

Yes, when things became a burden it was time to lay them down.

Time passed, and presently Joe pulled his smartphone from a pocket and started an audio recording. He'd allowed himself some space, he'd gotten things off his chest, and now, trusting in the process, he let his thoughts coalesce into words.

It's the very process of asking questions that brings meaning to life. That's why it's so dangerous to think we have all the answers, or to exist inside a system that offers all the answers.

What happens is that we stop seeking.

We are taught that there is no higher wisdom than that which can be gained through the evangelical walk. This is as good as it gets. This is ultimate truth.

And so by investing heavily in the assurance of faith that promises life, we actually stop living.

We trade our passion for the seat of a cynical spectator, observing this universe, the trouble, the pain, the struggles, instead of heeding the invitation to get involved.

We have become mere consumers, almost entertained by the feeble efforts of mortals lost in their own sea of sin.

There is an invitation, all the time. God and the universe invite us to participate.

He stopped the recording.

The morning sun was beginning to create some real warmth now and Joe decided to walk back to the car. He figured he could get another hour of writing done before lunch, then maybe Dan could help him out with some odd jobs this afternoon.

Odd jobs, Joe reflected, always seemed to create space for thoughts to flow.

CHAPTER 14

"What does it mean to love your neighbor, practically speaking?"

"**Y**ou don't go to church anymore then, Joe? Don't you miss it?" Dan inquired, his voice raised over the background roar of the stream. He carefully balanced a pine log on top of a solid, old stump and stood back.

"I miss the fellowship, sure," Joe said as he checked the blade of his axe. "And yeah, I miss that sense of being a part of something. I think church fills that sense of purpose in our lives. But you don't need to go to church to find fellowship. I mean, you're here, right?"

"Yes, I suppose so." Dan agreed, hoping Joe would expand on his views.

"Well, to be a little controversial, how can you go to something that's inside you?" Joe asked pointedly.

The question seemed more of a challenge, hanging in the space between them.

"Ah, right. I still see church as meeting together." Dan was thinking back over recent months as if trying to find a clue that would explain the loss he was feeling. "I suppose I miss the community, being around like-minded people, sharing a common goal. I mean, there's a whole lot I don't miss, but there are some things..."

Joe looked at Dan from behind dark sunglasses. "Sometimes we just want to belong. There's nothing wrong with that, but our concepts of church need to be dismantled and examined very carefully."

Dan watched Joe swing the axe in a well-practiced action that split the log cleanly in two with a satisfying *crack*.

"How do you mean?"

"Well," Joe said, stepping back, "call it a work in progress. And I mean that with all honesty—I'm still trying to work this stuff out myself."

"It's a difficult subject."

"Sure is. And I was angry for a long time. Maybe I still am. Angry at how this thing called church could mess people up so much. I experienced it, and I've seen it in so many others."

"You mean the duty and the rules? The pressure to conform," Dan suggested.

"That and more. See, I used to be able to give you the biblical basis for what we call church. And, if you want it, I can give you a number of reasons why that thinking is flawed."

"Okay, that sounds pretty balanced," Dan said.

Joe paused to roll up his shirt-sleeves. "We know that the church is not the building, right? So we naturally assume that the church is the people, which is a step in the right direction, but that's still not close to understanding the original meaning of the word *ecclesia.*"

"*Ecclesia* is a congregation, I thought."

"Well, yeah. But doing what? Worshiping God?"

Dan shrugged. "Um. *Not* worshiping God?"

Joe chuckled. "In the Roman world, an *ecclesia* was much more like a political body than a religious one. Think of a town council, something like that. And it's so important to understand that because then you can begin to see what Jesus did in a whole different light."

Another log split in two as the air was filled with a dull crack from Joe's axe.

"Right," Dan said. "I think you'll have to...enlighten me."

"Don't worry, these are big questions we have to wrestle with," Joe assured him.

"I've got nothing better to do," Dan assured him.

"Okay." Joe paused. "So you know that Jesus lived in a time and a place where society was both a political and a religious system all mixed together. The nation was run by its beliefs. The religion was so ingrained into how they lived, their culture, that the two were inseparable."

"So their political laws were also cultural and religious laws," Dan reflected back, intent on understanding.

"Yeah, essentially. And you have to remember," Joe continued as he waited for Dan, "what the Bible reveals about a culture that had built a political and religious system on top of these ancient teachings."

"Lots of rules and laws, you mean?"

"Exactly. That's what made Jesus so angry at times—he saw the injustice, the power-hungry leaders manipulating the laws that everyone was supposed to follow to the letter, while at the same time considering themselves above it all."

Dan watched another log crack under Joe's axe and then quickly prepared another, all the time listening intently.

"Jesus stood for change. Change to the system. He was, if you read between the lines, actually quite a subversive kind of guy. He took aim at the leaders of society, the ones who should know better; the ones who manipulated the system to their own advantage and got rich in the process. He called them out as the ones who were really falling short of the mark."

Crack.

"He wasn't crucified for judging and condemning the people he met in the street. Not the tax collectors and prostitutes, not even the Roman oppressors. No, it was the religious leaders, the ones with the real power of life and death in their hands, that he saved his criticism for. He called them whitewashed tombs—they look nice on the outside, but they are full of death on the inside."

Crack.

Joe sat down on a log, removed his cap and wiped his brow with a gloved hand. He looked across at Dan.

"If you read the New Testament in context, you'll find it very political in the truest sense of the word. In terms of today's politics, it's pretty radical stuff. Justice for the oppressed; feeding the hungry; healing for the sick; release for the captives. The sermon on the mount is all about a re-balancing—blessed are the meek, the persecuted, the poor in spirit. Not the powerful, not the rich, not the pastors and preachers—they already have their rewards. It's the ordinary people trying hard to make a life that Jesus was concerned for."

"Hmm. So you might say..." Dan was processing information fast. "Or are you saying, that Jesus was more about changing the political structures than the religious ones? That sounds really out there."

"Well, I'd say it's a lot harder to separate the two than you'd think. It's actually the politics that affect people's lives where it matters, isn't it? Politics is how we shape society, and how we shape society shapes how we live."

"That makes sense."

"What does it mean to love your neighbor, practically speaking? Or love your enemy? What does it mean to give your extra cloak to someone who doesn't have one? Those aren't religious actions, they are *political*."

Dan threw a few split logs onto the pile to clear some space. There was already a huge stack of firewood next to the house, and he found himself wondering just how cold it could get in the winter. "So, I think I see where you're going. How we relate to others comes out of how we relate to God, but there's nothing exactly spiritual about it?"

"When you think about what we read in the gospels, like the rich young ruler. *How do I inherit eternal life?* Well, you're wealthy, go give your money to the poor. That's taking a step beyond simply observing religious laws, and moving into practical acts of kindness because you can. Because it's needed. Because it's the right thing to do."

Another log split in two. Joe paused to let Dan set up the next one, then he continued. "Ask yourself, why was Rome bothered about a religious zealot in Israel? It wasn't. But people who started proclaiming a different political system? Who offered an alternative to the *Roman* Son of God? Now that's an entirely different situation. That kind of stuff is what's going to get you persecuted and thrown to the lions."

Joe had probably spent many hours thinking over and writing about such things, but to Dan this was completely new. In his mind's eye, he had a sudden picture of squads of Roman soldiers rounding up Christian believers. People who weren't simply devoted to following a heavenly Jesus, but activists intent on bringing in a new world order.

He was still trying to take all that on board when Joe continued with his discourse. "So we have this political tension building up. The Empire has a new enemy, an enemy within its walls. And then something happens, something that changes the course of history, and it's genius when you think about it."

Joe had Dan's full attention. He realized he was holding a log in his hands, waiting.

"Christianity," Joe said dramatically, "became the *state religion*."

Dan nodded slowly, letting the implications sink in. "Right."

"Think about it. There was no way Rome was going to share political dominion with any religion. The empire recognized the influence it had, the power it could wield. So the lines were drawn, religion was nicely separated from politics, and the whole movement became"—the next log cracked down the middle—"sterilized."

Dan looked at the split logs fallen to the ground. He found himself wondering if Joe's words could be true. Had the church been split up, segmented off?

"In my humble opinion," Joe concluded, easing the axe out of the stump.

"That's pretty damning," Dan said. "Actually, that's...I'm not sure what you'd call it. *Earth-shattering* comes to mind."

"Well, you have to admit, most of our concepts of church, our rule-book, all goes back to that period of time, three or four hundred years after Christ. It was a hugely influential time. And the models established then remain pretty much the same today. Go along to any evangelical church and you'll see the same pattern—one leader, an educated, upstanding pillar of the community who is a shining example of righteousness. And he's there every Sunday morning standing up and preaching to a crowd of ordinary folk. Reminding them to watch their ways, to be right with God so that they will be found acceptable when he returns."

"Well, you've just described my church at least," Dan agreed. "And it's always a man, isn't it? Well, 99 percent of the time it seems."

"Male-dominated, like politics, oddly enough. And the focus is always on how to remove yourself *from* the world. How to move *towards* heaven. You never hear anything about getting involved in the politics of the world, in how we shape our societies—that would be wrong. We should set our hearts on heavenly matters."

Dan chewed on his lip. Joe seemed intent on turning his little world completely upside down. Or maybe it was right side up. "You aren't going to get many logs chopped at this rate," he pointed out.

Joe laughed. "Unfortunately, I could go on about this stuff all day. I think it's a fundamental building block that's missing from church life—a desire to be instruments of change in the world. *This* world, right now. See, we're taught to have nothing to do with the world. God is going to make a new one someday soon. He'll wipe away all that injustice and sickness, and we'll reign with him."

"So why get involved in trying to bring about political change?" Dan mused.

"It's not on the agenda."

"So if, let's say, God is more concerned with how we look

after the world and everything in it, including each other…"

"That should completely change how we work out our faith."

Dan nodded slowly. "Justice, equality, rights…"

"We'd be more concerned about the poor and the marginalized, about kids growing up in refugee camps, about our governments subsidizing oil companies, about the ingrained systems that favor the rich and sideline the poor…"

"Okay, so when the Bible talks about the body of Christ as the church…" Dan was trying to make sense of this revelation.

"I like to think of it as a movement."

"A *movement?*"

"A movement that's making a real difference in our societies, for the good of society. It's not just about how we relate to God, but how we relate to each other and the world we live in. How we live our day-to-day lives."

Dan was silent as he looked up above the tops of the trees into the cloudy sky. An eagle soared high, circling as it traveled down the valley.

"So if we're not making a real, tangible difference in our societies, then we're missing the point? I've never heard that before."

"It's big stuff. But it's nothing new. Moses leading the Israelites out of Egypt, that was about establishing a new religion, sure. But more importantly, it was about establishing a fair, just society. Free from oppression, free from the grip of empire. At least, that was the idea."

"The physical *and* the spiritual…"

Joe smiled. "It shouldn't surprise us. If we choose to look, we can find God already working in the world, in politics, in business, in medicine, in science. Just because we see God at work in our church doesn't mean we have some exclusive access to him. I think that's why I've come to the conclusion that *the Church*, whatever it is, is not limited by our religious interpretations. It's much wider, and not confined in any way to a label or an institution."

Dan set another log up ready for chopping, but Joe remained where he was. "Your turn," he said, offering Dan the axe.

"I'm not sure," Dan laughed. "But hey, I'll give it a go."

"Just let the axe do the work. Keep your eyes on the log. Sharp side down."

CHAPTER 15

"It's not about conformity, it's about diversity."

Thursday night was pizza night, according to Joe, and Dan wasn't about to argue. But since there was no delivery service at that altitude, he'd watched with interest as his host skillfully prepared a selection of delicious toppings and piled them on top of two pizza bases extracted from the depths of a large freezer. Now the two men sat outside the kitchen door enjoying the cool evening air, resting from their day's labor and waiting for the oven to do its work.

The conversation had ebbed and flowed throughout the afternoon, but now Dan was hoping to steer it back to what he considered to be the key question of the day. Joe had certainly given him a lot to think about, but any kind of answers still remained elusive—if not church, then what?

The older man was happy to talk about his own experiences, and Dan listened with interest to the story of a group of young friends starting a new church in California. Everyone had given their all, Joe explained with a faint smile in his eyes. With his friend Steven as pastor and Joe himself as the worship leader, they had committed themselves to the vision and seen the church grow beyond anything they thought possible.

"It was a dream come true, doing the stuff I loved, but

well...not all dreams have a happy ending. Eventually I had to get out. I had to walk away."

Dan rested a mug of tea on his knee as he listened. He was beginning to catch a glimpse of the commitment, the long days, the sacrifices Joe had made over the years. All for it to end in tears.

"I can't imagine...must have been devastating."

"But would I change anything? Well, maybe some things, sure. But it's the road that brought me to where I am now. No point being bitter about it."

Dan didn't quite share Joe's positive attitude. "You don't see it as a waste?"

"Here's something a good friend once told me—with God, nothing is wasted." Joe fixed his gaze on Dan. "Not one thing."

Nothing is wasted? Was that just wishful thinking? But if it were true...

"But what we call *church*," Dan tried pressing Joe. "It's basically lost its way over the centuries. It's not what it should be?"

"Well, it's never good to over-simplify things, and the danger is that we completely reject church and anything that remotely looks like one. But..." Joe paused for a moment as he weighed up his words. "Yeah, essentially I'd say it's nothing more than a religious, self-serving institution."

Dan held back a smile.

"Okay, I'm being unfair." Joe held up a hand in submission. "We can't generalize this stuff. Did I grow spiritually in those years? Of course. Could we have done things differently? Of course."

"Hmm. But *how*, that's my question. How do you do church differently?"

"Yep. We have to ask," Joe agreed. "I know of church organizations that work with orphans, with HIV patients. The people the world has forgotten about. When I see that kind of stuff happening, when there's no agenda behind it, when it's a grace thing, that's when I think we see a truer form of church."

An old memory flickered in Dan's mind. He could see his

wife standing up at a leadership meeting and enthusiastically suggesting the church start a soup kitchen for the homeless. It must have been four or five years ago, and nothing had ever come of it. He looked across at Joe. "Earlier, you seemed to be painting a picture of something much bigger."

Joe nodded. "I can only speak from where I'm at on my journey, but what I'm learning takes me outside the four walls of church. In fact, it asks new questions of how we can work out our faith within the broader context of the world we find ourselves in."

"But first off, you had to let go of the old, right?" Dan prompted. "You had to realize that whatever church was supposed to be, this wasn't it. I think that's where I'm at, but I don't see where it's heading."

"I have to be honest with you, Dan," Joe said slowly. "You know, we can all have different ideas about God. We can all have our different doctrines, different takes on how we interpret the Bible and how we work it out in our lives." He paused, looking upwards, then glanced at Dan. "Church is a whole different ball game."

Dan could feel Joe wrestling with his thoughts and remained silent.

"See, you could keep going along on a Sunday, joining in, singing the songs, pretending all is fine. But you've probably already checked out in here." Joe tapped a thumb on his chest.

That simple statement seemed to strike a chord with Dan. He nodded, letting Joe continue.

"So if you decide to walk away, you're turning your back on family. That's how they'll see it, anyway. You're leaving the tribe, the club, and that's offensive."

"And backsliding, I suppose. Turning away from God."

"That's how it's perceived. And that makes you worse than an unbeliever." Joe closed his eyes for a moment. "And if that isn't enough, you don't know for sure you're ever going to find what you seek. Church was my life, and walking away was like stepping into the unknown. Traumatic stuff."

Dan felt something resonating inside his soul. He was starting to understand where all the uncertainty and doubts were coming from. "So what was your experience?" he asked.

"Well, first off, I didn't go searching for a church replacement, and I think that was important for me. I had to discover that I could have a re-energized relationship with God without feeling the need for corporate worship and Sunday sermons."

"Makes a lot of sense. And goes completely against everything I've been taught."

Smiling, Joe opened a can of low-alcohol beer. "But there is a beyond."

"I hope so."

"Eventually, I began to meet people who seemed to have a deeper understanding of this *body of believers*. People who put *community* at the center of people, instead of the other way around. The community serves the person, the individual."

Dan interrupted. "Ah, I thought that's what church was supposed to do. We all become members of one body."

Joe nodded. "Yeah, one body, many parts. We've heard it all before. But it's not about conformity, it's about diversity. And honoring that diversity. The many parts are all individuals, all unique, all valued."

"So a community...you're not talking about an organization. Or a fellowship, even."

"No, I guess not." Joe tilted his head as he looked inwards. "I'm not even sure there's a label for it. If anything, it's holding space for people to grow. It doesn't exist to build itself up, it's there to enable and equip the individual. And as the individual grows, their part of the world around them is transformed."

Dan considered this. He'd read those New Testament verses numerous times, and what Joe was saying wasn't anything amazingly new. It was, he realized, simply reading the same words without church glasses on. He found himself wondering how it could be read any other way.

"So you could say that a church is only a church if it's bringing real change into the world," Dan suggested.

"Actually, Dan, I think we need to go a step further. Get our thinking beyond ideas of what church was supposed to be, or should be, even."

"So...what *is* beyond church?"

Joe took a deep breath as he considered Dan's question. "Jesus talked about the yeast in the dough, the salt of the earth. It's *kingdom* stuff, right?"

"Okay."

"But God's kind of kingdom is all inside out," Joe explained. "It has nothing to do with *domination.*"

"Ah, right. It's invisible. The yeast, I mean."

"And it doesn't dominate the dough, does it? It doesn't turn the dough into more yeast. Think about that next time you hear someone talk about Christianity influencing politics, or education, or the arts."

"Hmm. So it's not just about spiritual change."

"Maybe the spiritual stuff is secondary. Or maybe it's *all* spiritual. The whole thing," Joe said with feeling, opening his arms wide as if to embrace everything.

"Hmm. Is that what *you* think?"

"I think we love to classify things we don't understand. But our faith has to have real-world consequences, right?"

"I guess so," Dan pondered. "Like how we care for one another, look after the planet..."

"How we care. Period."

"Good point."

"See, I'm not completely against church as we know it. It *can* transform lives, to a point. It goes some way to filling a need, especially for those new to faith."

Dan found himself reluctantly agreeing to Joe's assessment. "What you're talking about, though, seems very...practical. Pure, maybe?"

"I think there's a waking up. Slow, but it's happening. When you strip away all the trimmings, the show, the traditions, what you find at the core is simplicity."

Dan nodded. He suddenly realized just how much he

wanted that to be true.

"This stuff doesn't need to be complicated," Joe continued. "It doesn't need rules. There's no spiritual ladder to climb. It doesn't need a physical place to get together or even have a name. It's all very organic, and anyone can play a part."

"I like the sound of that," Dan said, feeling an odd sense of relief rising in his soul.

Joe got up to check on the pizzas while Dan gathered his thoughts once more. He could hear the sound of metal baking trays emanating from the kitchen as Joe busied himself. There was something familiar and comforting about simply being around Joe, and even if he still had a thousand questions, at least he now had a new friend to share the burden with.

Returning with the hot trays, Joe proudly announced that the food was ready. The sight and smell of the richly-laden pizzas instantly changed the focus to more immediate matters, and soon the two men were eating and chatting like old buddies.

Joe looked up from his plate. "How did you get on with the camera today? Any good photos?"

Dan had downloaded everything onto a laptop in the *Journey Room* earlier and was a little disappointed with the results. He explained to Joe how he'd enjoyed the experience, even if he was a little out of practice. "A couple worth keeping, maybe. I'm not sure I'll be rushing to buy a camera when I get home," he laughed.

"Although," Joe said with a shrug, "it may be good to be open to possibility."

Dan was thoughtful for a moment. "Yeah. I have to get home first."

"It's going to take time," Joe said, sensing Dan's hesitancy. "No question that you have hills to climb. You need to appreciate that it's not all going to drop into place all at once. Be kind to yourself."

"That's what my wife told me."

"Well, that's good. I think you can trust her judgment, from what you've told me."

"Actually," Dan smiled as he spoke. "She messaged me earlier. She's been reading one of your articles. About Jesus being more human than we think."

"Oh yeah?" Joe chuckled. "You read that one?"

"No, I don't think so."

"That came out of something a friend said to me a couple months back. That Christians are so afraid, ashamed almost, of their humanity. It made me realize how much we have to change our perception of Jesus."

"Go on," Dan urged.

Joe concentrated on his beer for a moment, then put a question to Dan. "What did Jesus model? Did he model God or did he model humanity?"

The question made Dan pause. He thought he should know the answer, but he could see the implications either way.

"Put it another way," Joe suggested. "How human was Jesus?"

Dan squinted at Joe, trying to work out where this was leading. "On a scale of one to ten?"

Joe grinned as he reached for another slice of pizza. "If he were here now, if he'd spent the day with us, and he was sitting here in jeans and a sweater, chilling out? I don't think we'd experience God in human form, do you?"

"Ah. He's not walking through walls or anything like that."

"The word became flesh…" Joe's quote from the gospel of John trailed away as he took a bite of pizza.

Dan could feel more questions queuing up. "It's interesting because we tend to look at Jesus as not completely human. Holy, worthy, perfect…"

"But the man who wept at the news of his friend dying? Who got angry in the temple courts and overturned the tables…"

"Hmm." Dan could see the images in his mind. "Makes you wonder."

"We need to remember that Jesus laid aside his divinity and *chose* to be human. It really changes things, because then you find a man in all his wonderful, complex and imperfect humanity, able to fully connect with God and do what he did from a place of great love and selflessness."

"Which kind of makes Jesus more like us, in a way."

"Or...*exactly* like us? We're all made in the image of God, aren't we? And if God has poured out his Spirit on all flesh, as we read in Acts..."

Dan narrowed his eyes. "I can feel a revelation coming on here."

"Oh yeah!" Joe laughed, enjoying the fact that Dan was engaging with his little sermon. "But think about it, it's so easy to develop this mixed-up idea that being human is no better than being a worm. We grow to hate our humanity and long for spiritual freedom. That's a dangerous separation. Did Jesus see us that way?"

"Uh, no, I guess not."

"He *became* human, that has to tell us something."

"That he thought we were worth the effort?" Dan suggested, then stopped, seeing Joe's raised eyebrow. "Actually, that sounds..."

"Oh, I can hear my wife now—'*Don't be so hard on the kids, Joe. Remember, they are worth the effort.*'"

Dan couldn't help smiling at Joe's effort to mimic his wife, and he found himself hoping that Sandy didn't actually sound like that. "Oh dear, the things we say."

"The things we *believe*. God thinks I'm *worth the effort*? Is that what it comes down to?"

"But...we've all sinned," Dan commented. "I've been reminded of that a few times."

"Fallen short, missed the mark, yes. But perfectly human and perfectly god-like are two very different things. God doesn't ask us to be his kind of perfect."

Dan munched on a slice of pizza as he let Joe's words sort themselves out in his mind. He found himself reflecting on the picture he'd always had of lowly humans in their journey towards a Holy God. "Okay, so what would Jesus say, if he were here right now?"

"Well, you know, I don't come up with this stuff all on my own, and I don't expect everyone to buy it either. This is my personal journey. It's how I approach my walk with God."

Dan nodded. "So…"

"I think if Jesus were here now, listening to our back-and-forth conversation on how to sort everything out, I think his suggestion would be so simple."

"Like..?"

"Just be the best human you can be," Joe replied. "Something like that."

***

That evening Dan watched the sun go down in a wonderful display of pink and orange. Joe was right—when you could see it, the view from the apartment window was amazing, and just then it felt like a wonderful gift at the end of a very full day.

So much to think about, so many more questions looking for answers. But for now, he simply wanted to put a few thoughts down on paper. He picked up his notebook, sat on the edge of the bed and wrote a single line:

Who told the eagle she was meant to soar?

There is nothing, Dan thought, like witnessing something being in its element. Remembering how effortlessly the eagle soared across the ridge that morning, he felt once more that pure freedom. That bird knew what she was. Knew what she was meant to do. Knew from the deepest place inside that she was an eagle who was made to soar across mountains and valleys. If only life were that simple for him. To know what he was made for, and to pursue it with all he had.

A blip from his phone shifted his attention. It must be Kimberly getting back to him.

Sorry. Cooking. Love the photos. Especially the ruin in the val-

ley. Glad you had a good hike.

Dan smiled. As he typed his reply, he realized how much he wished Kimberly could be part of these conversations.

It's been a good day. Talked over with Joe about church, trying to make sense of how I feel about it.

Kimberly didn't respond immediately, but soon enough her words popped up. *I wish church were different, but it is what it is.*

Dan pursed his lips. He wanted to tell her everything, but he still had so much to work through.

Joe talks about a more Jesus-centered approach. We should be more focused on making a real difference in the world, rather than trying to get everyone off the world.

There was another pause before Kimberly replied.

I wish.

Dan decided not to pursue things. The conversation moved on to what the boys were up to, and then Kimberly gave him a quick summary of a difficult phone call she'd had with her mother. It was more of the same strained relationship, and he could feel her frustrations coming through. She had probably cried about it and just wanted to get the last of it out of her system.

Finally they said their good-nights. He laid the phone on the bed beside his notebook and moved over to the open window to look out at the night.

Bright stars had begun to shine between scattered cloud. Dan sighed. However much he might want things to change overnight, he knew that there were so many uncertainties still ahead. In a few days he'd be back home, back in normal life, and having to make this all work.

And he very much wanted Kimberly alongside him.

You can trust her judgment, Joe had said earlier.

It seemed like a good time to pray. He knew that's what he would have done, just a couple of short years ago. He'd been comfortable with prayer. He'd known the language, the right way to do it.

Now he didn't even know how to start. He wondered if he

was simply clinging onto a rope that was no-longer tied to any-thing, but just as he was about to let go he remembered what Joe had said about rebuilding with the good stuff. Surely prayer was one of those good things, and if there wasn't a right way any-more then that meant the pressure was off.

His prayer was simply a reaching out. It was really nothing more than a seemingly one-sided conversation between Dan and a single, bright star up in the void.

Soon he began to pour out his heart, and with it came more questions. He poured out his regrets. His longings and dreams. He told the star about his confusion over his mother's suffering, his concerns about his marriage, all the hidden doubts that had bubbled away for so long. He touched on the past, he touched on the future, he touched on the journey he found himself on.

Dan wasn't sure quite how long he sat there, but presently he was aware of the tears running down his cheek. He let them fall. Tears of sorrow, tears of thankfulness, tears of freedom all mingled together.

He breathed in sharply, suddenly aware that it had grown colder.

A wry smile touched his lips. In his mind's eye, he could imagine Pastor Alan patting him on the back and asking, *"So, Daniel, how's your walk with Jesus this week?"*

At last, he reached for his notebook and wrote one more line—*I want to be more human.*

Friday

CHAPTER 16

"The answers are subject to change without notice."

"Oh yeah! It sure feels good to be out," exclaimed Joe. "Haven't been on a good hike since the fall."

It was another fine morning. Streaks of white cloud drifted lazily in a sea of blue, the air was filled with birdsong, and the sun was already warming up as Joe and Dan crossed the back meadow heading for the trees.

"You must know these mountains pretty well now," Dan remarked. "I guess there are trails everywhere."

"There are, but finding them is the problem," Joe explained that in the first year of his new life in Spain he'd struck up a friendship with a retired Spaniard who lived back down the valley. Together he and Manel had explored many tracks and trails over the mountains, having long, meandering discussions in a colourful mix of English and Spanish. "Got lost a couple of times, too. I blame him, to be honest. More of a fisherman than a hiker."

Dan smiled at Joe's account of his adventures. "Sounds like fun times."

"Precious," Joe remarked. He was scanning the escarpment above them, squinting into the sunlight. "This one is a bit of a scramble, but it's worth it. We're going up to that ridge. See where those eagles are soaring?"

Shading his eyes, Dan looked up to see a pair of large birds effortlessly riding the thermals. He felt an excitement, a thrill stirring inside as if he'd just been handed an invitation to participate in some grand adventure. Adjusting his rucksack, he set his feet to the trail, a new eagerness in his step.

Leaving the springy grass of the meadow, the explorers soon found themselves on a stony track cutting its way through mixed woodland, with leaves of every shade of green adorning the trees. The path led them into darker pine trees, climbing gradually at first, then snaking between dense undergrowth and outcrops of rock the higher they went. Now and then Dan would catch glimpses of the looming rock-face still high above, rising sheer in places.

"We're actually going to get up there?" Dan asked.

Joe was quick to reassure him. "Don't worry, there *is* a way. There is always a way."

Dan's companion was right. After another sharp turn, the trees thinned to small scrub oaks and scattered clumps of wildflowers, and the track kept on a shallow climb almost right against the rock wall until a gully opened up.

Here a small stream cascaded down from high above, and Joe led the way, keeping to the side of the gully still in shade. He deftly picked his way between rocks and over uneven, broken stones and scree so easily that Dan wondered at his skills. At times the spray from a small waterfall would drift across them. It became more and more of a scramble, and Dan was glad that he wasn't carrying a heavy pack. Even in the shadow of the cliff, he was beginning to feel quite warm.

After navigating a difficult crevice over slippery rocks, Dan stopped and shouted up to Joe. "I just want to take 5, Joe, if that's okay."

The older man looked back and down at Dan just below him. "No problem. I could use a break too."

Dan scrambled up to the ledge where Joe was already sitting, sipping water from a bottle. "I'm not as young as I think I am," laughed Dan, catching his breath. He found a suitable rock to sit on and reached for his water bottle.

"I know what you mean. Not far to the top now, another 10 minutes should do it," Joe said, raising his voice over the background rush of the falling water.

Dan found himself gazing back down the gully, over the tops of the pine trees, to the narrow view of the valley stretching below. "You know, I realized something this morning. I used to believe God was completely in control of my life, which is kind of a strange concept when you think about it."

"And now?"

"Well, now I see it a little differently," Dan said.

"In a good way, though."

"Yeah," Dan confirmed. "But for a long time there's been this background worry, a fear almost, that it's all down to me to keep on making the right decisions."

"Well, you can see the shift, that's good," offered Joe. "Something's happening."

Dan didn't reply immediately. He looked back down at the valley, wondering what it could all mean. "But then it's become all about having the right answers. Like I've become obsessed with knowing. I have to figure it all out before I can make the right decision."

"This is why we have to appreciate that God is in the process," Joe reminded him.

Dan turned to his friend. "I'm learning."

"Takes some getting used to," Joe said.

"But it's good. It begins to feel more open. Like everything is much bigger and grander, and the God behind it all loves the process too."

Joe nodded in agreement. "It's a whole different philosophy on life. See, when you've spent years working towards that truth, to reach the top of the mountain, and when you get there all you find is a note saying *the answers you seek are not here...*"

Dan couldn't help chuckling. "Devastating! So...God doesn't have all the answers? Or are we asking the wrong questions again?"

"I'm suggesting that the answers are subject to change without notice," Joe said dramatically, pointing his water bottle at Dan. "It's how the universe works."

"Well, that's comforting to know."

Joe smiled at Dan's sense of humor. "No, seriously. Einstein once famously said that God doesn't throw dice. He believed the universe could be completely understood, nothing was down to chance, it could all be measured, you could do the math."

"Right. I hate math, to be honest," Dan said, looking up to see Joe holding his bottle high above his head so that the water sparkled in a ray of sunlight.

"It's really all about possibility, you know that? Patterns and probability," Joe explained. "Light hits the water, but is it a wave or a particle? Can it be both? What we think of as certain, when you look closely enough, turns out it's not so predictable."

"Hmm. That's quantum theory, right? And I thought you were going to turn water into wine."

Joe smiled and took a sip. "No, it's still water," he said. "But this is what Einstein couldn't get his head around. A universe that works on high probability, rather than certainty? Patterns and chance rather than exact outcomes? How crazy is that?"

"Hmm. So chance has a say in how the universe is run, essentially?"

"A big say, it seems. And I know we don't see the whole picture. I guess God sees patterns where we only see random mutations, but it does make you think—we can't know everything because uncertainty is built into the very fabric of creation."

Dan nodded, thinking of the implications. "So in fact, my quest for answers is only ever going to raise more questions. Kimberly's going to be so happy."

"What a wonderful paradox we are," Joe said kindly as he looked at Dan. "The important thing is that we never stop asking."

"Well, that's it!" Dan exclaimed cheerfully as he stood up. "I'm done for. I think I'll just have to pretend I got myself sorted out and make it up as I go."

"Hey, we aren't done yet. Come on, let's get up to the top of this ridge. The view is fantastic."

Joe took up the lead again and before long the pair scrambled onto a patch of level ground covered with verdant green grass and dotted with fir trees. It seemed similar to the ridge on the other side of the valley where Dan had spotted the eagle, except from here the view northward to the highest peaks was almost uninterrupted.

Dan stood in awe at the immense vista before him. Below them the valley stretched out, bathed in sunlight with shadows of clouds. Above and beyond the far ridge mountains rose over mountains, stretching away to the west as far as he could see. The air was so clear that it seemed he might reach out and grab a handful of snow from a summit.

"Now, if I was a good guide I'd be able to tell you the names of some of these mountains," Joe said quietly, careful not to disrupt the sense of peace and tranquility. "Always takes my breath away, this panorama."

"I should get a few photos." Dan pulled out the camera and was presently clicking away at the scenery.

Joe pointed out a few of the peaks he was familiar with, enjoying watching his companion forget his troubles as the questions drifted away on the breeze and Dan was able to simply find meaning in the moment.

"It's stunning. When I'm faced with something like this,"—Dan waved an arm in a wide arc—"I don't need answers. I just want to be."

Joe smiled. "I know what you mean. Gives us a little perspective."

"I kind of like this idea that God is more into patterns than precise outcomes," Dan said, sounding almost excited. "Somehow that makes more sense. Sounds more like a God of diversity and wonder."

Joe drew Dan's attention to the dark rock-face directly across the valley. "Look at that crag with the fir trees. See how the sunlight is hitting it? How rough and uneven it all is, nothing precise about it. Like God just made it up as he went along."

Crouching on one knee, Dan zoomed in on the mountainside as Joe continued. "And I know it's millions of years old, but that just makes it all the more wonderful, especially when you consider that it's changing slowly all the time. And we get to see it fully at this moment. That's pretty awesome."

"Awesome," Dan repeated, standing and pulling the camera strap over his shoulder. "We think we'll be happier, having the answers. But the questions are too big. I mean, can we honestly begin to fathom the immensity of a God who's behind *everything?*"

"Well, we live in an age of answers. Everyone has answers. The church has answers. Science has answers. And every other person on *YouTube,* apparently," Joe commented, then motioned to Dan to follow.

Joe now found an indistinct route taking them upwards over the shoulder of the mountain. The scattering of trees at the ridge gave way to an open grassy slope dotted with boulders, topped by a long, rugged escarpment stretching away behind them to the east. Dan followed close behind, stopping at intervals as the view continued to open up all around him.

Joe seemed to be in his element just then. Out on a high mountain, enjoying the views, taking the opportunity to talk about what he was so passionate about. But it wasn't a one-sided conversation. Dan was beginning to realize that with Joe at least, there were no stupid questions, and no subject was taboo.

They chatted about church life, about friends and family, about some of the self-help books Dan had read when he was searching for answers. That led Joe to riff on about gurus who feed on people's insatiable appetite for anything that might promise a better life.

"Money, health, sex, it's all sold the same way. The author makes sure you know exactly what you lack. You are in need. You don't have the answers or you would have figured it out by now. Only they hold the keys to make it all better. And they paint a picture of this wonderful life you can have, hold it out to you, give you just enough of a taster to get you wanting more, and then..."

"Buy my *masterclass?*"

"Exactly. But it's like a disease. And the way a lot of evangelical churches go about selling God, it's no different. That's why we always remind visitors that it's not about answers. We don't want to be gurus."

"Yeah, I have to admit I've been pretty disappointed this week."

Joe looked back at Dan with a smile. "You know, we can laugh about it, but it's always tempting to give answers when you know it's going to help them get on with their lives. And a lot of people are content with that. *Just tell me what to believe and I'll be okay.*"

"I found myself thinking that," Dan admitted. "I've been told what to believe for most of my life, I'll just find another version of faith and stick with that."

"But that guru model, that's used by just about every church. You have someone up front with the answers, and everyone else is a disciple. And no matter what Christianity teaches, the leader's job is not to empower people, it's to keep them coming back for more. It has to be that way for the system to work. Get them in and keep them in. Now, a real leader would take a completely different approach."

"How do you mean? Like empowering the follower to grow up?"

"Yeah, exactly." Joe stopped and turned to face Dan. "The true master is the one who wants to make themselves redundant. They aim to empower and equip, raise up the student so they can stand on their own two feet and not need the guru any longer. Can you imagine how that would work in a church setting?"

"Well...no, I guess that wouldn't work too well," Dan agreed. "*Bums on seats, fill the chairs, standing room only!* That's what our pastor is all about."

"There you have it," Joe confirmed, turning back to the trail.

"We have to grow in our spiritual journey or we are simply *consumer Christians.*"

The stony track was leveling out as it skirted a small, boulder-strewn plateau marking the end of the escarpment. Soon the landscape to the south opened up as they found themselves crossing the shoulder of the mountainside. Another green valley lay at their feet, thick with forest that gradually gave way to lower, less rugged mountains.

"Yet another amazing view," Joe offered with a hint of pride. "Good place to stop for five minutes. Then we'll start heading down towards the lake."

They sat on the soft grass, leaning against a large rock and enjoying the surroundings. Dan searched around in his rucksack, pulling out a variety of snacks.

"Coffee?" Joe held out a tin mug to Dan, which he gratefully accepted. They sat in friendly silence, watching the sun-dappled landscape, listening to the wind in their ears and the call of eagles high above.

"Let me know when you're ready to head home." Joe reached over to pour more coffee from a flask.

Dan took a sip from his mug, leaned back and looked up at the sky. "I have good coffee, an amazing view, great conversation, and I don't know when I'll come this way again. I need a few more minutes."

Joe nodded his understanding. "I used to have a special place back home, somewhere I'd take off to when I needed to get some real answers from God. It's a lake with some trails through the forest. Plenty of places to just sit and pray. So I'd take a coolbox with me, some food and drink, but I'd fast through the day until evening. Then, as the sun was going down I'd have something to eat and drive home, feeling very spiritual. Like I'd done something to get closer to God."

Dan looked over at Joe, who was staring off into the distance. "Did it work?"

"It was a good exercise, I'm sure. I always felt better for it, even if I didn't get a revelation. But there was one time, I remember it was a beautiful day, like today. There was no one around, I think it was mid-week when everyone was working. But I suddenly had a realization. I was so busy trying to get a breakthrough, trying to get some answers, that I wasn't really there. I wasn't being present. I was trying to impress God somehow with my humility, trying to show him how spiritually mature and devoted I was."

"What did you do?"

Joe turned to look at Dan. "I walked back to the car, grabbed my cool-box, sat down by the lake and enjoyed the day. I drank my coffee, I ate a candy bar, I watched the ripples on the lake and the birds on the picnic benches, the wind blowing the trees. I just opened my eyes to the precious gifts all around me."

"Sounds good."

"But what amazed me is that I suddenly appreciated this wonderful, physical world all around me that I could see and touch and taste and hear and smell. It was like a light came on —God is very much into the physical. Jesus was a physical being. He cared about our physical well-being. And of course, he made a very physical, incredibly beautiful world that we can experience in a very real way."

Dan glanced at his friend. "So all this effort trying to become *more spiritual*..."

"Sounds good, but I think we're missing the whole point," Joe suggested. "Look at all this. None of it needed to exist. But it does. That should speak for itself. That day by the lake, I had never felt so connected with God, so close to the divine, or so much a part of the world around me. It was a very complete experience."

Dan nodded. "I like that. God shows up when you stop trying to impress him."

Joe chuckled. He was putting things back in his pack but didn't seem in any rush to leave. "You know, we need those times of solitude," he reflected. "Moments to just be. But I used to think it was about drawing closer to God as I *removed* myself from the world."

"That's the way I've always understood it."

"If I have to work at getting closer to God then it wouldn't all be about grace, would it?"

"No, I guess not," Dan agreed. "Just more work."

"We need those times to get closer to *ourselves,*" Joe added. "Our truest self. That's what I believe. And through that, we begin to see the reality—that God is right there beside us."

Dan stood up first. He took one last look at the wide panorama, from the highest snow-capped peaks to the north around to the lower, more gentle mountains and green valleys to the south. He breathed deeply, as if he could in some way soak this snapshot of time into his very being. Then he turned to Joe.

"I've doubted God. For *so* long."

"And that's okay."

"I think I'm ready to head home."

"Then let's go."

CHAPTER 17

*"All we know is where we came from, and where
we are right now"*

With Joe leading once more, the two men began a snaking descent of the grass-covered alpine slope on the south side of the mountain. Dan noticed for the first time the patches of little blue flowers contrasting with the gray stone, all of them begging to have their picture taken. He found himself wondering what the flora would be like in the summer and decided he'd ask Joe later.

"Thinking back to that day at the lake, it reminds me," said Joe, interrupting his chain of thought, "how I had to find a completely different model for my faith. I'd lost that certainty, that assurance. All I knew deep down was that if God was truly in this then he would be there, guiding me through."

"You didn't ever feel like you were backsliding?" Dan asked, bringing up one of the questions that had been lurking in the background.

"Did I feel like I was backsliding?" Joe mused. "That's probably what everyone else thought. No, I knew I was in uncharted territory, that I was having to leave something behind. But no, it's not backsliding, it's *climbing*. Climbing out of a pit. And it was hard work at times, learning to lay down the load."

"A load we're not supposed to carry, I'm thinking."

"Right. And I figured, God doesn't demand that I do all this by myself. There are no demands. I could have stayed, serving the institution or trying to change it, and God would have met me there like he always had."

"Journey again?"

"There is so much about journey in the Bible," Joe continued. "Think of Abraham, Isaac, Jacob. Even David. Spiritual journeys linked to a very physical journey. Their faith had nothing to do with going to church on Sundays. They didn't carry Bibles around in their pocket. They fumbled their way forward and lived it out."

Dan thought about that as he picked his way down an awkward drop between the rocks. "They spent a lot of time out there in the wilderness..."

"A *lot* can happen in the wilderness," Joe said. "I know from experience."

"When it's just you and God?" Dan suggested.

"Exactly. Think about it. It was only after Moses led the people out of Egypt that they started to make a physical place for God's presence. And even that was a movable tent. It was really just a focal point."

"Hmm. You think..," Dan asked, testing his idea, "the more physical the presence, like the tabernacle, the temple, the church, the less it becomes a spiritual journey and more about the institution?"

"Well, if you can step into a church and be handed a faith, where's the journey in that? I think about where I was. I knew everything. I knew the theology, I knew the verses, I knew how God worked, how to worship, all that stuff."

"So this physical representation of something spiritual starts to get in the way, and it hinders the journey instead of encouraging it."

"When you think about it, Jesus was the ultimate physical representation of God. He showed us what it meant to be fully human and fully empowered by God. And we built a religion around that. I have this picture in my head of this big old bus lumbering along, people jumping on, people jumping off, people asleep on the back seat. And you suddenly realize it would be faster and more enjoyable to find your own way."

"So when you read the Old Testament now..." Dan paused. "*Do* you read the Old Testament?"

"I do, but when I read about these journeys, Abraham, Isaac, I remind myself that they were finding their way all the time. They had no organized religion, they didn't read their scriptures every day, they had no laws other than the ones that were written in here,"—he tapped a finger on his chest—"They had the Spirit of God guiding them, and they had stories. And they knew, I think, that they were part of a story. A big, unfolding story."

"And I suppose you could say that story is still unfolding today."

"Right," Joe agreed. "In me and you, and everyone who ever lived or ever will live. We don't know everything, all we know is where we came from, and where we are right now. The future is waiting to be written. I think the church, well, all the main religions, have this beginning and end. If we know the ending and we can't wait to get there, what's the point of the story? Abraham didn't know where he was going or what the future held. But he was prepared to walk the path to find out."

"All sounds a bit messy," Dan commented.

"Man, I wish I'd figured this out a long time ago instead of trying to fit my life into someone else's story." Joe had stopped and was taking in the view.

"I think I kind of lost my place in the story," Dan said, stopping beside Joe.

They had reached the top of the ridge on the far side of the mountain, looking over the tree-tops. Dan could see a steep trail leading down over sharp rocks, hugging the bank of a small torrent.

"Not afraid of heights are you?" Joe wondered.

"Well," Dan said, not taking his eyes off the track. "Depends what side of the height I'm on, if I'm honest."

Joe laughed. "Right. I think we'll take the longer route, there's an easier way down towards the lake. That one's for goats only."

As they followed the track slowly downwards along the ridge, Joe seemed in a thoughtful mood, whistling a faint tune as he walked. After a while, he called back over his shoulder. "You said earlier about God being in charge. How do you feel about God's will for your life? Have you thought about it recently?"

"God's will." Dan considered the question. "I used to believe God had a plan."

"So, an individual, tailored plan for your life?"

Dan didn't reply immediately. He knew it had been a long time since he felt he was living anywhere near some kind of plan. But he knew Joe enough now to trust that there would be some value in the questions. "I suppose so. And I used to be so scared that I would miss it. Then I moved onto being scared I wouldn't be able to handle it. Like God would ask me to be a missionary in China or something."

Joe laughed. "Yeah, it's a tough one. *'I know the plans I have for you. Plans to give you a hope and a future'*. It all sounds great, and it's something to hold onto at times. For myself, I've swung different ways over the years. I was eager to work out God's will for my life, but once I'd settled into a routine I stopped looking."

"So how do you approach it now? Is it so important anymore?"

Joe stepped over a small stream cutting through the track and turned to let Dan catch up. "I think the most important decision I came to in that regard was to stop being so damn fearful about it all. I know exactly what you mean when you say you worried about missing out. And then to worry that you wouldn't like it or didn't think you'd be up to the task. Worry, fear. And then to be bombarded all the time with the pressure to apply it to every area of your life. Am I inside God's will? Am I being disobedient if I listen to my heart? Constant second-guessing. It's a real mess."

Dan had stopped at the stream and was now kneeling as he

framed a shot in the viewfinder of the camera. "You asked me, yesterday, to think about what's important to me. It's all linked together, right?" He looked up at Joe briefly. "I mean, where do I get this love of photography, of nature? Of being out in a place like this?"

"Doesn't sound very spiritual, Dan. Are you sure there's not some deep desire inside you to take the Word to the lost?"

Dan was relieved to see the twinkle in the older man's eyes, and smiled. "You know, after being here this week, I could preach all day to the *saved,* I tell you that much."

"That," said Joe, turning back to the trail, "sounds like a *very* dangerous line of work."

Dan hopped across the stream and jogged a few paces to catch up. "I'll probably have changed my mind when I get back to England."

"Just remember, that's okay. God opens up doors, and it's completely up to you and me as to whether we walk through them or not. You can't make a wrong turn, because there is no wrong choice."

"*No wrong choice?*" echoed Dan, as if testing the concept in his mind. Taking that single statement to heart could have profound consequences on how he lived his life from today.

"Now sure, we can take that to the extreme," Joe added, quick to clarify what he meant. "Use it as an excuse for all kinds of foolish behavior, of course. The point is that we make our choices from a place of freedom, not fear."

"More possibilities?" Dan suggested.

"More possibilities than we could ever need in a lifetime," Joe said emphatically.

The two men continued to walk in amicable silence. As the track rounded the mountainside it began a steady descent over open ground dotted with flowers and small shrubs. Once again the lake became visible to the west, now much closer.

As they approached the forest once more, Joe stopped and silently drew Dan's attention to a tall, solitary pine. In the topmost branches sat a large bird, surveying the scene.

"Eagle, I think. Golden eagle, probably."

Dan had the camera to his eye in an instant, clicking away as he adjusted the zoom. "Wow. Beautiful."

As the two men watched, the eagle finally spread her wings and dropped from the tree, swooping down, then up and away towards the heights. Dan tried to follow it with the camera but in moments it was far away.

"Never stop looking for those possibilities!" Joe exclaimed, turning to Dan and waving a finger in the air. "Never stop!"

CHAPTER 18

*"I think we can trust that God's love is
unconditional."*

"You mentioned earlier about doubting God." Joe set a
tray down on the long wooden table then turned to
adjust the position of the parasol. After a morning
spent hiking he figured they both needed some cool drinks and a
bit of shade.

Dan reached for the jug and filled both their glasses as he
gathered his thoughts. "Well," he said finally. "I think back to
when I first wanted to seriously follow Jesus. He seemed to be
perfect, loving, kind, someone you'd want to spend time with, sit
down and have a cup of coffee with."

Joe sat down opposite and leaned back in the chair. "Right,"
was all he said, encouraging Dan to continue.

"But God, well, he's the one that keeps score, you know? I
mean, we say that God loves us unconditionally, but then we also
say that when God looks at us he doesn't see our sin, he sees the
Jesus in us. So it's not *us* that God loves, essentially, and that has
bothered me at times."

Joe simply nodded, so Dan leaned forward and continued.
"Alright, so here I am, as a father I love my children. No question.
I don't see them as something other than what they are. I see
them with all their faults and I still love them."

"Right," was all Joe said.

Dan held back a smile and took a breath. "Okay, like you said the other day, Christianity paints a very confusing picture of what God is like. I know I've made excuses for God, I've pretended to understand, I've tried to focus on Jesus rather than the Father, and I still have this messed-up idea about the nature of God. Is he good or is he nasty? You'd think it would be pretty simple."

Joe took his time answering. He suddenly realized how concerned he was for the younger man. How so much hung on what Dan chose to do, or not do after these days were over. He wondered if, in all their conversations over the past few days, he'd really given Dan some hope for the future, or simply added to the confusion. What, he wondered, would Jesus do? Finally he spoke. "It's just like The Prodigal Son."

Dan raised an eyebrow.

"The parable of the Prodigal Son," Joe explained, "is a story about the Father."

"Yes, I suppose so," Dan agreed. "I've sometimes heard it referred to as the Waiting Father."

"Right. But it's also about choices."

"I'm listening."

"So we have a loving father who would do anything for his two sons. Sons who are *both* unhappy, *both* ungrateful. At least the older one is obedient."

"And there's the younger, headstrong one who wants his inheritance," Dan added, hoping to speed things along a little.

"Yeah, he essentially says that he wishes his father were dead. But he's also saying *'I want to live my life my way. My choice.'* So he gets the money and takes off to a foreign land where he blows it all on wine and women."

"And it's probably a small fortune," Dan added. "Rich dad."

Joe smiled. "I think that's the idea Jesus was trying to put across. A young guy, only interested in pleasing himself, didn't care about his family, didn't think of the consequences. Just wanted to have a good time at his father's expense."

"But he has a change of heart."

"Right. So he's miles away from home, the money has all gone along with his friends, and he ends up with the worst job possible, feeding pigs. He's hungry, almost destitute, and all alone. It's the perfect picture of hell."

Dan was trying to recall the parable in his mind. Joe's words seemed to sum it up well. "Yeah, sounds like hell to me."

"A hell of his own making. Reaping the consequences of a selfish existence."

"But, as we all know, he repents and goes back home," Dan added, wondering if Joe really could pull something new out of this old parable. He certainly hoped so.

"We know the story, don't we?" Joe was gazing into the distance. "He has a change of heart. He realizes he can't go back to how things were. Impossible. He doesn't want to stay where he is, because that's hell. So he decides that he's better off working as a hired hand in his father's fields than feeding pigs. And," the older man brought his gaze back to Dan, "as we hear all the time, his father forgives him and restores everything to him."

"So it's a story about how God forgives when we choose to repent," Dan finished.

But Joe was just getting started. "Well," he said slowly, "I think it's so much more than that."

"Why am I not surprised?" Dan asked with a grin.

Joe chuckled. "Okay. I mean, if Jesus was trying to teach about the consequences of sin, it would have worked quite well, right? The son ends up in that situation because of his own choices. End of story. But no. He does repent, yes, but the fact is that the father had *already* forgiven him, maybe never even needed to forgive him, and was there waiting every day for his son to return."

Dan was thinking this new insight through. Maybe Joe *had* pulled a rabbit out of the hat after all. "Ah. The repentance part only really mattered to the son. Without that change of heart, he would never have returned home even if he *was* forgiven."

"Exactly. The relationship with his father wasn't nearly as

broken as he thought, he just didn't know it until he got back home. Sure, things would be different from then on, but this is essentially the story of a loving father who will do anything for their child, even if it means letting them go."

Dan leaned back and looked up, noticing for the first time the tiny white flowers among the purple and green leaves of the bougainvillea growing crazily over the archway.

"And there's no mediator. Ever wonder about that? The son doesn't send someone to negotiate his return. The father is simply over the moon at the opportunity to bring him back into the family home."

This was also news to Dan. "Ah, now *that* is interesting. There's no Jesus figure in the story. No one standing in the gap. Which is kind of odd since he was the one telling the parable."

"Exactly. It's a parable that doesn't fit your mainstream evangelical teaching at all. But then consider the other son. His reaction is just like ours would be. *'Dad, I knew you'd let him off, you're so soft on him. I'm the one working hard all day for you. I deserve that party, not him.'*"

"Yeah, I think I would feel the same way," Dan commented. "Doesn't seem fair."

"But here's something else—the father reminds the older son that he already has everything. From the very start, both sons had it all, they just didn't realize it."

"Ah. It was their perception of the father that got in the way."

"That's how I see it, anyways," Joe explained. "If God loves me in that way, that should change everything. Nothing to prove, no ladder to climb. It's not, like you said, that he sees the Jesus in me. God sees *me,* the everyday, regular me, and still loves me, no matter what choices I make. It doesn't get any better than that."

Dan topped up his glass. He watched the ice-cubes tumble into the water and bob around with the lemon slices. He was going to miss this place, he realized, and he was going to miss these conversations with Joe.

"So, just trying to get my head around that. Where does Jesus fit in?" Dan asked.

Joe nodded. "You're right, it's intriguing. I think there's no question that Jesus plays a part in the reconciliation. Whether he's the one to remind us that the relationship isn't as broken as we think, or he bridges the gap that *we've* created. Either way, I think we can trust that God's love is unconditional."

"I've never heard the Prodigal Son preached in that way. Makes me wonder what I've been missing."

"And if that's all it does, if it only gets us asking the deeper questions, then that's a good thing. It's so much more than repentance and forgiveness," Joe finished.

Dan glanced in Joe's direction and waited expectantly, hoping that Joe was going to continue. He could sense that there was more, but Joe seemed to be struggling to find the right words.

"Okay!" Joe laughed. "Since I now consider you a friend, I'm not gonna pull any punches, so listen good."

Dan smiled. "I'm all ears."

"You know, we have three ways we can go forward from today, and it has everything to do with what we believe." Joe tapped the table a few times as he considered his options, then picked up the knife he'd used to slice the lemons and placed it on the table. He took a spoon and set it at right-angles to the knife, forming an elongated 'T' shape, then pointed to the middle of the knife. "You're here," he said.

Dan leaned forward, elbows on the table, resting his chin on his hands. "Right, I'm at an intersection."

"Exactly. Like the Prodigal Son. Now, you can never go back to the way things were. That's the handle of the knife. You had a handle on your faith, you understood the rules, the boundary lines. It all made sense at one time, and you were doing okay with things. Life wasn't perfect but at least it was safe."

A long sigh emanated from Dan's mouth. "No. No, I understand I can't go back. I think I'm okay with that. Getting there, anyway."

Joe looked over the top of his sunglasses. "You could stay

where you are."

"Hmm. You mean, confused, afraid, doubting everything?"

"Yeah," Joe remarked. "Well, we know what that's like. I wouldn't recommend it."

Dan agreed. More of the same was not what he wanted at all.

"But that's good," Joe said, lifting a finger. "Knowing what you don't want, that's halfway to a solution."

"Alright," Dan said, squinting. "So what about the pointy end?"

"Ah. Well, the *pointy end* is one way forward, and it's what we've touched on this week. It's a walk into the unknown. Understanding that things have to change, that *we* have to change, that our *foundations* have to change. And trusting that whatever happens, God is right there, in the process."

The blade of the knife seemed to fill Dan's vision. Right then it seemed more like the tip of a compass, indicating the way. But it was a way he'd never traveled before. One with no guarantees. "Okay. And the spoon?"

"Oh yeah. The spoon. That way, there's no God, no purpose to any of this. No real journey other than what's taking place up here." Joe tapped his head.

Dan nodded again. "Yes, I thought it would be something like that."

Joe smiled but didn't say anything more.

"Choices. But no *right* choices." Dan leaned back and drank deeply from his glass. At that moment the ice-cold water was the most refreshing thing he'd ever tasted. He looked once more at the knife and the spoon. It was exactly the kind of quirky illustration he'd remember for a long, long time, and he could understand the temptation of choosing the spoon.

Forget everything. Start again.

It was a choice.

He took a deep breath and looked at Joe. "So, I'd better head off soon."

"Whenever you're ready."

"Ryan is arriving about 8."

After the week he'd had, Dan was in no rush to leave. He still wasn't sure how he felt about seeing his old friend, but at least he could look forward to a relaxed evening of good food and wine at the little Bistro Joe had recommended.

Dan now listened with interest as Joe explained how to get to what he described as one of the most picturesque valleys in the area. Half an hour's drive north from *Pont de la Cruz*, into the very heart of the mountains. To Dan it sounded like the perfect place for a walk and a talk with an old friend.

"You'd be very welcome, if you wanted to tag along," Dan said.

"Oh, nothing but work for me this weekend, I'm afraid," Joe explained, adding that he had a whole list of jobs to get done before Sandy came back. "Of course, you're both very welcome to stay here, but you guys probably want to do your own thing."

Dan nodded.

"Whatever you do," Joe continued, "see if Sunday afternoon you can both come here for some food."

"That would be great," Dan replied, grateful for the invitation to return so soon. "I'm sure Ryan would like to meet you and have a look at this place, I told him how amazing it is."

"And take the camera," Joe added. "I think you'll want to have it with you tomorrow."

Saturday

CHAPTER 19

"Christians don't get all the good ideas."

"**A**lright. Now, according to Joe," Dan explained, leaning on the steering wheel, "it's stunning to the left, dramatic to the right. Not sure what the difference is, to be honest. Said we'd be happy either way."

Ryan, who hadn't stopped reminiscing since breakfast, was looking up at steep-sided canyon walls that climbed up above clouds to snow-dusted heights. "Well, it's all pretty dramatic, if you ask me! Why don't we try stunning? We have to come back this way anyhow."

"Stunning it is, then" agreed Dan, steering the car down the left fork in the road. A narrow gorge quickly closed in on them as the road twisted along beside a sheer rock-face. At times the river could be seen below to the left, a foaming and raging torrent of aquamarine snow-melt hemmed in by huge boulders.

As Dan concentrated on navigating the road, which was becoming increasingly pot-holed and bumpy, he thought about his long friendship with the fair-haired man sitting next to him. He had always thought of Ryan as the older brother he'd never had. Best man at the wedding, Ryan was one of only a few people who could make him laugh, and in the short drive into the heart of the Pyrenees there had been plenty of happy banter and reminiscing.

Now his friend was straining forward to get a better view,

seemingly intent on distracting Dan from his task of driving safely. As the valley widened and the road leveled out, Ryan suddenly announced *"waterfall!"* A glimmering white ribbon had edged into view above the trees on the other side of the river. "That would make a good photo."

Dan slowed the car so he could take a look. "Nice! Definitely deserves a photo or two."

"You can pull over up ahead," Ryan said excitedly. "Let's take a look."

Driving a little further, Dan found a place to stop next to a couple of parked cars. Ryan was first out, passing under the trees growing on the riverbank, then picking his way carefully over rocks. With a few springing steps, he made it onto a large, sloping boulder edging the river and waited for his friend.

Dan followed at a slower pace, gripping Joe's camera firmly in one hand, and climbed up carefully next to Ryan. The roar of the water was almost deafening, swirling and foaming below their feet like a beautiful and deadly serpent snaking down the valley. On the far bank trees crowded together at the base of a steep, gray rock-face, glistening from the spray of the waterfall that leaped from a high crevice.

"How high do you think that is?" Dan asked, shielding his eyes from the sun and gazing up at the heights.

"Hard to say. Got to be a four, five-hundred feet drop. Stunning."

Dan smiled. "Stunning." He bent down on one knee, lifted the camera and started framing some shots.

"Nice camera," Ryan commented. "I've got one similar. Next model up, though."

"It's Joe's," Dan explained, not taking his eye away from the viewfinder. From experience he knew Ryan wasn't trying to be pretentious, that was just his way—Ryan liked expensive toys. It was also no surprise to Dan that his friend didn't have his camera with him—he'd probably not even thought about it. "I'm thinking I need to get one, though. It's all coming back to me. You remember going off places with our cameras? All those rolls of film we'd go through."

"Good times," Ryan reflected, pulling out his phone and aiming it at Dan. "Never went anywhere quite like this, though. Say *cheese*."

Dan was enjoying himself. He spent a few minutes on the rock, clicking away with the camera, then scrambled back down to find a better view of the waterfall. Ryan, on the other hand, was hopping around on boulders, intent on finding some treasure. When he reached Dan he held up a piece of driftwood and announced that he'd take it home.

"And I got you a nice pebble," Ryan declared, holding out his hand. "You used to collect them, I seem to remember. You can call this one Pobble."

Dan held the little rock up as if to inspect it closely, then with a faint smile, he put it in his jacket pocket.

Continuing their reflections on the good old days, the friends left the driftwood in the car and decided to follow the road on foot. Presently it crossed the river by way of an ancient stone bridge offering a wonderful view of the V-shaped valley. It was exhilarating—the river surging towards them through the forest, the mountains stretching up on either side, and snowy summits creating a majestic backdrop.

"I might not want to leave," said Ryan quietly as he took more photos.

Dan was surprised, and as they continued their walk he asked Ryan about life in France.

Ryan spent the next few minutes updating his friend. The consultancy business was paying the bills. He'd redecorated the house and changed his car. Things were quiet, but then it was rural France, Ryan explained. "Mum is well, but Dad is showing his age. He's 80 this year. Makes you think."

"Yes. Yes, it does," was all Dan said.

The mood became more somber for a while, and the only sound was their boots on the track against the background rush of water. Ryan was the first to speak. "Sorry I wasn't around when you were going through it with your mum."

Dan glanced at his friend, but he wasn't sure what to say.

"I liked her," Ryan added. "She was always so kind to me. And I was the naughty kid."

A faint smile passed over Dan's face. "Well, it's true what they say—you can choose your friends, but you can't choose your family. *Or* your neighbors."

Ryan snorted. "Very wise!"

"Yeah, it's good to have people around," Dan reflected, "but at the end of the day it's your road you have to travel."

"Well," said Ryan cheerfully, looking about him, "it's a pretty nice road at the moment."

He was right. The track continued to lead them beside the river, sometimes close by, other times higher up, with tall pines growing on the steep bank above the rapids. After the narrow gorge, the valley had quickly opened up, revealing a clearer view of the higher mountains that marked the frontier with France. Everywhere was, they agreed, stunning. Maybe even dramatic, too.

As they walked, the conversation naturally returned to days gone by. They chatted about old school friends, crazy old dreams, and childhood memories of Dan's mother. He appreciated the opportunity to talk with Ryan about her, and the more they talked the more the memories returned, releasing bittersweet feelings inside. Sensing the healing, he allowed a tear to run unchecked down his cheek.

"Oh, what a life!" Ryan exclaimed, "Seems like only yesterday we were building tree-houses in the woods, and now 50 is just around the corner."

"Well, you have a couple of years on me, remember," Dan was quick to point out. He missed these meandering discussions, as well as his friend's straightforward view of life—it was refreshing. "So are you going to stay in France? No desires to come back to sunny England?"

"I don't miss the UK, if that's what you mean. Maybe wasn't the most rational thing to do, but I just wanted to get away after I broke up with Rachel. So a little French village with my parents across the street. New start, you know. Seemed like a good idea."

Dan sighed. Ryan's seemingly reckless, almost clumsy decisions, seemed to have worked out for good, while *he* felt like he lived his life walking on egg-shells, trying hard not to upset anyone. The obvious, well-trodden road had always been Dan's choice.

"You're still the sensible one, though," Ryan remarked. "You're doing okay, aren't you?"

Dan looked across at Ryan, who was peering up at another high waterfall cutting its way down the forested slopes. "I wonder if I'm getting too old to keep on doing the sensible thing."

"What? Oh, has *Mister Sensible* stopped being sensible?"

"*Mister Sensible?*"

"Yeah, always doing the right thing. The sensible thing. But"—Ryan stopped to take a photo with his phone—"you might be right. I don't really do sensible. A few risks every once in a while, doesn't seem to have done me any harm."

Dan shook his head. Looking around, he tried to take in the grand scene that he found himself standing in. There was a sense of being on a stage, and the whole of creation was looking at him, waiting for him to deliver his lines. He looked back at Ryan. "I used to think I had it all together. Solid faith, solid church life, solid marriage. But when you're in that kind of situation, when nothing makes sense..." There was a pause as Dan gathered his thoughts. "You know, Ryan, it only takes you so far. All this stuff I'd built my life around for years. When it really mattered to me, it all began to crumble."

Ryan looked intently at his friend. "Don't tell me you've stopped believing? You know I depend on you for prayers when I need them, don't you?"

Dan smiled. Ryan was right. He would on occasion send a long email about his complicated, almost soap-opera life, and ask that Dan would put in a good word for him.

"No, it's not as simple as that. I think it's just that I'd grown so comfortable with my little version of truth. My little religion with all the answers. But then,"—Dan fixed his eyes on the track

—"the answers didn't fit the questions any longer."

"Maybe you're looking for the wrong answers?"

"Oh, not you too. I just wanted to go for a walk!"

Ryan laughed. "No, seriously. Being here today—mountains, streams, fresh air. For me, this is about as spiritual as I get, and I mean that. It's an experience that does something inside. There's no physical change, but there's certainly something going on in here." He put a hand to his chest.

"Yeah, being in the mountains certainly seems to ground you."

"Not just that. Inspiration. Energy. Look," Ryan said, drawing Dan's attention to a couple of climbers scaling a rock-face rising sheer above the forest. "People come here from all over for lots of different reasons. So is it that the mountains are inspiring, or is there a deeper connection? Something going on at a soul level?"

Dan looked up at the climbers, then further up at the mountainside basking in the sunshine.

"And I'd say God is pretty free with it all, don't you think? I mean, there's not many people who could spend time here and *not* be inspired in some way. You don't have to be religious to have a deep and meaningful experience, it's like we're all invited to the party."

Dan gave his friend a sideways look.

"What?" Ryan appeared offended. "I do think about these things, you know. Are we all spiritual to some degree or other? Is this whole thing a spiritual experience? Christians don't have exclusive access to God, do they?"

Dan almost couldn't believe what he was hearing. He'd had deep and meaningful discussions with Ryan on numerous occasions, but this seemed different somehow. He shook his head. "I know that's what I've always been taught. Well, more of an assumption, I suppose. But there is that line in the New Testament that says God made himself known through creation. Something to that effect, anyway."

"See, that makes sense to me. Much better than learning

some old rules."

"Except that it's normally used to accuse people of *not* believing the obvious fact that God exists."

"Now, doesn't that sound crazy to you?" Ryan laughed, spreading his arms wide.

Dan sighed, then he started to laugh too. "Yes, I suppose it does now!"

Ryan turned to face Dan, walking backwards as he spoke. "Okay, here's a question—is it only Christians who would be inspired by this scenery?"

"Well, no. I mean, you are, and you're a complete heathen."

"Exactly," Ryan agreed, raising a finger. "But let's take it further, my good friend. Is it only Christians who write moving poetry or inspirational books?"

"No, of course not."

"So, some of the most brilliant songwriters I can think of— John Lennon, for instance. Not a Christian."

"Not a Christian, no."

"So why aren't Christians the best songwriters in the world? The best artists, the best musicians? Because they should be if they have some kind of exclusive access."

Dan kept walking, but his mind was elsewhere for a moment. "Alright, I get what you're saying. I never thought about it that way. I suppose we're no better or worse than anyone else."

"Not too many writers like C. S. Lewis, are there? What I mean is, God is pretty free with the gifts, as far as I can see. Christians don't get all the good ideas."

"Ah. God outside the walls," Dan muttered to himself, then squinted at Ryan. "I think that's what Joe was talking about. Seeing God outside the walls of Church."

"So what's it all for, your faith?" Ryan challenged Dan. "Why church, if it doesn't make you any more clever, or creative, or inspired than the average Billy-Bob on the street?"

"I get you. Do you remember telling me, a long time ago, that you thought God was bigger than the Bible?"

"Did I?" Ryan had turned round to face the trail again,

walking beside Dan. "Sounds like something I might say after a couple of beers."

"I think it was just a throw-away comment, but it always stuck with me. At one level I agreed with you, but at another..." Dan hesitated, aware of how his beliefs were changing so rapidly. "I was always taught that the Bible contained everything we ever needed to know about God."

"Ah! But knowledge and feelings are two different things, aren't they? I feel something today that I can't put into words, and to be honest, I wouldn't want to even if I could."

Dan walked in silence. Feelings had certainly taken a back seat in his life for many years. Feelings were never to be trusted.

So if he was leaving all that behind, could he trust them now?

***

Kimberly kicked the front door closed with a high-booted foot and dumped the heavy bags of groceries in the hallway. She shook raindrops from her jacket as if to shake off her frustrations. The day was already beginning to weigh heavily on her.

A deep sigh seemed to emanate from her very soul as she leaned back against the door, closing her eyes momentarily as she silently prayed her one-worded, fall-back prayer that was all she could manage lately—*"God."*

On any normal Saturday morning, she would have enjoyed a couple of hours of peace and solitude down at the church office. Just herself and the computer as she worked steadily through the weekly administration. But today her little bubble had been burst by the unexpected appearance of the Pastor. Alan had stopped by to pick up some paperwork and briefly poked his head through the door to say hello. He'd seemed happy to see her, as always, and cheerfully remarked how he felt sure Dan was ready to come back. *"And we're all behind you both, you know that. Couldn't bear to see Dan falling away."*

With the sudden reminder that her man was still in Spain

and her carefree interlude was just an illusion, the weight of her troubles had returned and her shoulders had begun to sag.

On her way home, she'd found herself once again wondering how Dan was getting on. Whether the week had been worth it. Whether or not he'd found some answers. And what would happen when he got back.

There was so much she wanted to tell him.

For two years she'd watched helplessly as Dan had slowly but surely sunk into a mire of self-doubt and bewilderment. She had tried so very hard to be there for him through his mother's illness. She had watched, as Dan struggled to stop time and gradually come to terms with the fact that this battle was lost. She'd tried to remain faithful to their faith, tried to cover over the doubts, dismiss the questions, and carry on as usual.

She recalled the dark, cold weekends of winter when Dan would return home after the long drive and simply sit in his favorite armchair and stare into space. It would sometimes take him an hour to even say anything, and Kimberly could only be present, trying hard to maintain that sense of normality.

To her, it was all too plain that her husband's precious faith was hanging in the balance. She could see Dan's struggles, and it scared her. Their whole relationship had been built on the foundations of a shared faith, a shared commitment, and the timeless teachings of the church.

Now she didn't know what to do, she didn't even know how to pray anymore. And she didn't have anyone to talk to.

She stopped herself. No, that wasn't entirely true. She could talk to her neighbor. Debs was always so easy to be around, so undemanding, one of the few people Kimberly knew that accepted her for who she was. And right now, that was all she could be.

In an instant, her phone was in her hand and she was typing away. Debbie's quick response reassured her. *Yes I'm in! I'll put the kettle on.*

Kimberly said a quiet thank-you, put her phone away and looked up the stairs. "Tom? Are you in? I'm just popping over to see Debbie."

A voice came down from above. "Yeah, okay."

"Can you be a star and put the groceries away?"

A pause. "Yeah. No problem."

Minutes later she found herself holding a bone-china tea-cup carefully in both hands, letting the warmth soak into her cold fingers. She could feel herself begin to relax, her cares melting away as she sipped the hot liquid.

Debbie placed the tea-pot in the middle of the table and took a seat opposite Kimberly. "I hope Dan's got better weather," she said brightly. "I thought we'd put the winter behind us. All that rain, and so cold! I had to get Reg to put the heating on."

A faint smile touched Kimberly's eyes. At times she still couldn't tell whether or not her neighbor was being serious. She assured her that Dan would be having a great time. "Off walking in the mountains, I think he misses that."

Kimberly had never had a sister, and it was only in the last year that she'd begun to appreciate the chats with her older neighbor. For all her preoccupation with keeping a perfectly tidy house and having to look her best on every occasion, Debs continued to surprise Kimberly with her genuine concern and openness. And Kimberly didn't want to pretend anymore—she'd been doing that for far too long. "He's still struggling after the funeral," she added. "But there's more going on."

Debbie's kind but penetrating blue eyes looked at Kimberly over the top of her cup.

"It's not us," Kimberly assured her friend. "I don't think it's us. He's just unsure about church right now. I know Alan wants him to get back into it, but..."

"He's had so much to deal with," Debs finished the sentence for her.

Kimberly focused on her tea. "Yes. The thing is, Dan and I have always had church at the center of our lives. Everything we do revolves around our faith, and...I don't know. I can see him letting go. It worries me."

The older woman reached out a slender hand. "Oh, Kim.

You two are the only reason we go along, you know."

Kimberly smiled weakly. "We aren't supposed to have doubts. We're supposed to have all the answers, have our lives together. It's quite hard work, if I'm honest."

"Well, you don't have to pretend with us, my dear. Reg and I, we wouldn't have gotten through things without you and Dan. You were just the neighbors, but you were so kind, always so caring."

"I'm just glad we could help."

"Well, we needed it. You showed us what things *should* be like."

"Did we?" Kimberly was surprised.

"Of course."

"You're sweet," Kimberly said with a faint smile. "That's just who we are."

"And that's all any of us should ever be—ourselves! None of us are perfect. I'm sure there's not one single person at church who has complete faith all the time. That would be unnatural. Surely we're allowed to question things once in a while?"

Kimberly didn't answer. She'd been burying her doubts for a long, long time.

"What would that American say?" Debbie asked pointedly, eyebrow raised. "Joe Mitchel. What would he say? I've been reading his stuff, you know"

"What? You've read Joe's blog?"

Debbie shrugged innocently. "You sent me a link, remember."

"Did I? I've slept since then."

"*Questions are part of life. God is bigger than our doubts.* Or something. All that kind of thing."

"But I don't know who I am anymore," Kimberly said with exasperation in her voice. "I've had it with pretending everything is okay. I know what Dan's going through because I've been there. I've been there, and it's horrible."

Debbie placed her cup on the saucer, clasped her hands together and leaned forward. "Kim, do I look surprised?"

Kimberly looked up. All she could see in her friend's face was genuine concern.

"Tell me everything," Debs said as she topped up their tea-cups.

Kimberly blinked. She could feel the tears welling up.

"It was back when Dan's mother first got sick."

"Ah. Reg was in remission."

"Yes. She used to tell me everything was going to be okay, that God was going to heal her, that it was all in his plans for her. And you'd gone through it all with Reg's cancer..."

"And he was getting better, and she was getting worse," Debbie stated.

"It didn't make any sense to me."

"No, my dear." Debbie shook her head sadly. "It doesn't make any sense. But I'll always remember how you gave us hope, something to hold onto."

Kimberly simply nodded.

"I don't know if there's any plan in that," Debbie continued, "but Reg and I are better for it, that much I do know."

"I just can't see where it's all going."

Debbie seemed to be staring off into the distance. Her lips became a thin line. "None of us can. I can tell you from experience. I'm afraid that's the nature of life."

"I used to be so sure..."

"And *we* used to be so sure of *ourselves!*" Debbie exclaimed. "Thought we had our life in order. Now, well, there's always that little worry in the background. Will it come back? How long do we have? But we have to push through that, be thankful for what we've had, and what we have now."

Kimberly nodded. "*Every day is a gift.* That's what Reg told me once."

The smile returned to Debbie's eyes. "We never used to think that way. It was all about what we could achieve. How we could grow the business. How we could win. Now that *is* tiring."

"Sounds like we can all learn from each other."

"You know," Debbie said, a twinkle in her eye, "that's not a bad idea."

"What are you thinking?" Kimberly probed.

"I'm thinking that when Dan gets back, the four of us should get together for a good talk."

CHAPTER 20

"A shift in perspective can be life-changing."

"This looks cozy enough," Ryan declared as they approached the low, wooden buildings huddling bravely among trees at the foot of the mountain. A few hikers stood outside the little cafe in a group, chatting and laughing in the sunshine, and greeted the companions with friendly nods as they passed.

Inside they found a table by the window with a view of the valley. A fire was roaring in the large hearth, warming the whole room against the cold mountain air. A few people sat at another table, quietly talking over plates of food. To Dan it all seemed comfortably inviting and wholesome.

"Nice place," he said. "Wouldn't expect to find anywhere like this halfway up a Pyrenees valley."

"Yes, it does seem a bit remote." Ryan reached for the menu. "It's all a complex lure for unwary travelers. Might need to be on our guard against bandits."

Dan smirked. He looked over to the counter, noticing the trays of sandwiches and pastries. "I'll just have a coffee and a croissant," he said, unzipping his jacket.

Ryan looked at him, smiled mischievously, then focused his attention back on the menu. "Today's special. Grilled chicken breast, bacon, fried egg, cheese, tomato, lettuce, mayonnaise, all in a fresh baguette. With coffee or beer. That's what I'm having," he announced happily. "I'm on holiday."

"It's probably always today's special," Dan commented, sliding into his seat. "Okay. I'll have a coffee, and one of those."

Ryan ordered for both of them, appearing to be quite comfortable with a smattering of Spanish. They chatted until the drinks arrived, and Dan was pleased to see Ryan quickly relaxing, clearly enjoying his surroundings.

"When you coming back, then, Daniel?" Ryan inquired, reaching for his beer.

"Back here? I haven't left yet!"

"Yeah, but this is your kind of place, isn't it?"

Dan gazed through the wide window. He noticed the group of walkers setting off together, heading further up the valley. He wondered where he'd head off to if he had more time. "I think I'd like to come back at some point, maybe later in the year, even. I feel like there's still so much I don't understand."

"Hmm. So be honest, Daniel," Ryan said slowly, following Dan's gaze. "This Joe. Does he run some weird cult thing?"

Dan laughed. "No, I think Joe is...he's just someone who's further along the road than I am. But that doesn't begin to explain anything."

"Not a sort of guru type?" Ryan teased. "Christian guru, I can't think of anything worse."

"If I'm honest, there's a lot of things I've been struggling with—beliefs; the church. You know my faith has been such a big part of my life. If anything, maybe Joe just has a different perspective, a fresh take on an old story."

"And I thought you were going to have some big revelation about life and the universe, then you could tell me what it's really all about." Ryan sounded a little disappointed.

"It's complicated," Dan said, wondering as he said it if that were true. He still felt uncomfortable talking about spiritual matters with Ryan, knowing their history. "I think we all need to be challenged to see things a different way, from time to time. It doesn't sound all that amazing when I explain it."

"No, it doesn't. But I agree. A shift in perspective can be

life-changing. Sometimes that entails a physical change, such as when I went to France, or it can be an inner shift. Either way," Ryan reflected, "life never looks the same again."

"You're right. When I think about it, if I weren't searching, there wouldn't be anything revolutionary about the insights I've had this week. Maybe it's just that I'm ready for change."

"So?" Ryan was looking intently at Dan. "What's the problem?"

"Problem? What do you mean?"

"What I mean, my old friend, is this—why haven't you decided yet?"

Dan didn't know what to say. He could feel a faint swirling in his stomach—plain-talking Ryan was gently but firmly pushing him, and for a second it felt a little uncomfortable.

His friend leaned forward as he saw Dan's inward look. "Hey. It sounds like Joe's been giving you some good advice this week. I would even agree with some of the things you're telling me, for what it's worth."

Dan was surprised. "Okay, like what?"

"Well, God outside the box, for instance. God working in the world. Of course, God is bigger than your little closed-off view of him. Or her. Or whatever."

"That's obvious to you?"

Ryan shrugged. "And God being bigger than the Bible. Why shouldn't that be true? Especially since I said it."

"Hmm."

"To me, it's all bleedin' obvious. I think what's amazing, though, is that you're considering stepping outside your little ghetto. That's huge."

"Is that how you see it?" Dan asked. "Christianity is like a ghetto?"

"We all live in our own little ghettos, my friend. We all choose our version of reality, don't we? Our particular version of what we think the world is like, how it works—politics, money, relationships. We make our bubble, then we spend an awful lot of time finding evidence to back up our convictions, and only talking with people who agree with us. It's how the bubble stays floating. It's how we work."

"Now *you* sound like the guru."

Ryan grinned and shook his head. "No. This is personal development basics, mate. Our lives are constructed from opinions and experiences and things we've learned along the way. How much of it is truly us, we only discover *that* when we pull back the layers."

"Right." Dan nodded slowly. "Joe talks about deconstructing the foundations and finding the gold and silver."

"That's a good way of thinking about it. Who is the real Daniel Kendrick, when you lift off the veneer?"

Dan was silent, sitting back as the waitress arrived with their baguettes. Ryan rubbed his hands together excitedly, like a child who'd just received an unexpected gift.

"Ooh yes! *Bon appétit,* my friend!" Ryan lifted the foot-long sandwich from the plate and took an enormous bite. Dan, deciding that his mouth was not that big, opened his out and began cutting the meat into smaller chunks.

Ryan, even with his mouth full of chicken, still somehow managed to have room to get words out. "See, Daniel," he said. "I'm actually a bit excited for you, believe it or not. You're at this crossroads and you've been able to step back and take an objective look at the way forward. That's priceless, it really is."

Dan nodded. "Choices. Joe talked a bit about that."

"Look, how long have we known each other? Personally, I think you getting religion was good for you. It made you a better person, certainly opened up your world. You met Kimberly. All good stuff."

"But?" Dan pressed, sensing there was more.

Ryan finished his mouthful, wiped mayonnaise from his cheek and fixed his gaze on Dan. "It's coming to an end, Daniel. It's running out of energy."

"I feel like *I'm* the one who's run out of energy."

"Well, pretending is hard work."

There was a pause as Dan stared at the food on his plate.

"Look, you are moving beyond your boundaries, they can't hold you back any longer. There is more. *You* are more. So all this stuff Joe is saying, I say *yes.* Yes, and more."

As Dan munched on thick slices of grilled bacon he considered what his friend was saying. The whole situation seemed incredibly strange—sitting in a little Spanish cafe in the mountains, listening to Ryan agree with the spiritual insights of someone he'd never met, while at the same time offering his own down-to-earth assessment of Dan's life in very stark terms.

"I know you, Daniel. And I can't help thinking that you're more concerned with what people will think of you than whether or not it's the right thing to do, taking the unknown road."

Again, Dan wasn't sure what to say, so Ryan continued. "I think you're ready to decide if it's worth it or not."

With a heavy sigh, Dan looked intently over his coffee cup at his friend. "Maybe. But I can't help wondering what Kimberly's going to think if I start telling her I'm done with church and I'm rethinking my faith. Rethinking my *life,* in fact. I know she's generally pretty supportive, but it means things are going to change. Our relationship will change."

Ryan said nothing as he ate, only nodding in agreement.

"Joe was explaining to me a bit about choosing to go forward from here..."

"We have to choose every day."

"No, you're right. He was telling me about some of the problems he's had to face with his work. The reality of people making the wrong choices, I mean. Like not just walking away from faith but completely messing up their lives in the process and bringing others down with them because they feel angry or betrayed or manipulated."

"Well, I'm not too surprised. We hear about religious leaders taking advantage of people all the time. And I suppose spiritual abuse is a thing?"

"It certainly is. And with Joe, I think he's seen that from both sides. Maybe he played a part at some stage in his life—

there is so much manipulation going on in churches. But then, I've probably done the same thing with my kids now I think about it, telling them all kinds of stuff to get them in line. *Our sin hurts Jesus. What would Jesus do?* That kind of stuff. All very controlling."

"You were probably doing what you thought was best at the time."

"But isn't that how we all mess up?" Dan asked rhetorically. "A lot of the time we convince ourselves that we're doing it for the right reasons, but the ends don't justify the means."

"So Joe is still carrying around that guilt the same as the rest of us," Ryan suggested. "Are you afraid that's going to happen to you?"

"Maybe. But I guess the important thing for now is that I stop wandering around in no-man's-land like I've been doing for months."

"Only months?"

Dan shook his head. "You're right, now that you say it. I've always tried to please everyone, show that I'm part of the team, committed..."

"And now"—Ryan narrowed his eyes—"you have to start thinking in terms of self-preservation."

Self-preservation. The words echoed in Dan's ears.

"Huh. When you put it like that..." Dan paused, suddenly aware of the truth in Ryan's argument. "Self-preservation is right. And I just realized something."

"Do tell."

"I thought this was all about preserving my faith. And that's a big part of it, I've always believed there's more going on than what we see, that there's a reason to life..."

"But?"

"Suddenly it's about freedom and possibility that I find hard to grasp, and it all seems very self-centered, selfish even."

"Not to me."

"No, but when you've put church first for 20-something years, always there, always willing to serve, then you suddenly start re-evaluating what's important…"

"Ah."

"Crossroads, like you said," Dan concluded.

"So what is important to you? Or have you forgotten?"

"That's no joke. Joe asked me the other day to think of three things that were important to me."

"And?" Ryan raised an eyebrow.

"It wasn't so easy."

Ryan shook his head sympathetically. "We're in a constant battle. Wrestling with what we *want to do* with our lives, against this very powerful enemy which is *what we think we should do*, what others expect us to do. What we think is the normal, accepted path."

Dan sank his teeth into the baguette. He was beginning to understand how much of his life had revolved around what he thought he *should* be doing.

"When I moved to France," Ryan continued, "I stepped outside my box. I had nobody telling me what they thought I *should* be doing. I was a stranger in a foreign land and basically, nobody cared."

"And it worked out okay."

"Yeah. But I spent a lot of time wondering what I actually wanted to do. Asking myself what my future could look like without the constant need to live up to someone else's expectations. It's scary, to be honest."

Dan shook his head. "Possibilities are scary. I'm wondering what it all means."

"It's a big, wide world, my friend," Ryan stated wisely. "We love our boundary lines."

Dan turned his attention back to his plate once more as he let words and thoughts and feelings swirl around inside. Without knowing it, his friend had just confirmed what Dan had been suspecting for the last few days—that this was very much bigger than simply getting his faith sorted out, and that he was, without a doubt, only getting started on the journey.

"Anyway," Ryan continued, content to leave the deeper conversation for now and move on to other matters. "When are you guys coming to visit again? I miss our chats."

"Yeah. Kimberly would love it. Probably do us both some good."

"Well, it's been what, four years? I'm sure she's forgotten about that little incident with the brandy by now."

"Oh no, the dreaded French brandy." Dan pulled a face and reached for his coffee.

"She was not happy with me the next day," Ryan chuckled as he stared off into the past. "Never touched it since, anyway."

Dan looked across at his friend and smiled. He shook his head. He'd definitely forgotten about the brandy.

In fact, he had no memory of it at all.

Sunday

CHAPTER 21

"The questions you asked then are not the questions you're asking now."

Scattered clouds raced across a pale blue sky as Kimberly sat in the car, the words of the morning sermon still ringing in her ears.

Her hands were shaking slightly and she was almost surprised to find herself here. Having dropped Debbie and Reg outside their house she'd made a lame excuse about having to run an errand, messaged the boys to say she'd be a little late back from church, then turned the car around and headed out of town. It wasn't long before she was driving past green fields and scattered woodland in search of a place to stop and think.

She took a deep breath as she stared unseeingly at the English countryside around her, clenching her fists in a desperate effort to think clearly. What, she asked herself, was the problem?

What was the *real* problem?

On the surface, there was nothing wrong with the sermon. Alan had done what he did most Sundays—drawn on a few verses and built a compelling argument around them, and she would be the first to admit that Psalm 91 had been an important anchor for her at times. Over the years it had become a foundational piece of scripture, giving her hope that God *was* there, intervening, protecting, watching over her.

"God loves everyone," Pastor Alan had concluded. *"We know that, and we can take some comfort from that. He loves our lost neighbors. He loves our lost colleagues. He even loves the Muslim couple across the street. It's always been that way..."*

She couldn't disagree. She had even found herself hoping that Alan was going to bring some great revelation and insight that would have her neighbors begging for more.

It was a short-lived hope.

"But who is his special favor reserved for?" Alan had continued. *"Who gets the blessing, eh? That's what really counts in the end, right?"*

At a signal from Alan, the worship team had started playing background music as he continued to pace about on the platform. *"It's those who love God and do his will."* A long paused as he'd looked out at the congregation.

She remembered shooting a sideways glance at Debs, who was concentrating politely on Alan's performance.

"And it's easy to say we love God back. It's easy to pretend that God is the priority in our lives. But we would do well to stop and consider just how much of a priority God really is. Are we laying down our lives for him? Are we seeking his will? Are we committed to serving him through the church?"

The music was picking up volume and any minute now the worship leader would take them into the closing song.

"Remember, as you head back home this morning, it's those who love God and do his will. Those are the ones who are truly saved..."

Yes. A few years ago she would have taken that to heart. But somehow she didn't quite see it that way now. She saw the flaws in the argument, and more than that, she was genuinely concerned with the way Alan had manipulated it. What did that tell her neighbors about the nature of God?

That *He* wanted something in return?

A gust of wind buffeted the vehicle. Kimberly looked up at the clouds as she analyzed her thoughts. Did God want something in return? Was that her experience? Was that what she believed?

"No," she said finally, speaking quietly to herself. "God, I know you're not like that." Then, as if realizing that no one else was watching, she said it again, this time more fiercely. Tears were beginning to well up in her eyes as she felt a sudden release of emotion, and she quickly searched the glove box for a tissue.

As her resistance faded, and one by one the internal barriers came down, the tears seemed to bring with them a stream of memories. She looked back at the funeral, seeing Dan trying to read aloud the poem he'd written, choking on his words; then back to those days of hiding all her rising doubts and fears, which only seemed to widen the growing gap between herself and her husband; back to the day when Dan's mother first told them about the cancer. The day her world was shaken.

And finally, after what seemed like hours of looking back over the trials and traumas of the past few years, she saw a little girl, bursting with hopes and dreams, a girl who used to feel like she had strayed into a dark and forbidding forest only to stumble upon a magical, sunlit glade full of flowers and butterflies. That girl, who she truly was inside, searching for a life beyond the normal.

"What is going on?" she wondered out loud, suddenly aware of the pile of screwed-up tissues on the passenger seat. Leaning forward to look at herself in the rear-view mirror, she tried unsuccessfully to wipe mascara from her cheeks. A smile touched her eyes.

"No more," she said, feeling the tears start again. After a few more minutes she could see enough to reached for her phone and began flicking back through the week's messages from Dan.

There's an invitation to go deeper...

Joe talks about a more Jesus-centered approach...

God's grace has to be unconditional...

Going back further, she eventually found the one she was looking for—a link to an article written by Joe Mitchel that Dan had hoped she might be interested in. At the time she'd read it through with interest, but it was one more thing that she didn't want to think about. Now she opened the page and began to read. It was entitled *God Loves You, But Here's The Thing.*

If you've spent any time around Christians, you probably get the whole thing about God loving you. God loves you. It's so easy to say, and many of us take a great measure of personal reassurance from those three little words. Including me, I might add.

'God loves you, even when you mess up. These are hard times, but remember, God loves you. You've lost your job, sure...'

Except when times really are hard, like these crazy, world-shattering times that we find ourselves in right now. Then, it seems, God wants something in return before He steps in to rescue us.

At least, that's what you could easily end up believing if you read the Book of Psalms...

Kimberly quickly skimmed through the words, searching for what she remembered. Joe was digging into Psalm 91 in a way she'd never seen before, and she wanted to understand.

'Surely he will save you from the fowler's snare and from the deadly pestilence...'

She flicked the screen again. This was all familiar to her.

Unfortunately, if you want the benefits, there seems to be a proviso. We do, after all, live in a world of give and take...

Her head nodded slowly as she read. Joe was focusing on exactly the same verses that Alan had used that very morning. Only Joe's approach was different, daring to challenge the assumptions that her Pastor had used for his foundation.

'Because he loves me," says the LORD, "I will rescue him; I will protect him...'

The sad fact is that so many Christians will be quite happy to accept this at face value. "Well, of course you must love God in return," they will say. And anyway, isn't that what it's all about? Learning to love God makes you a better person.

It does.

But only when you truly know love in the first place.

And conditional love is not true love, is it?

As a father, I can't help but wonder why Father God is so often portrayed as the type of parent none of us would have wanted as a child.

That sentence made Kimberly pause once more. She leaned her head against the window and gazed up at the trees swaying in the wind. This, she thought, was what it all came down to—the conditions we place on God's love. Where was the grace in that?

I know my kids love me. They're all grown up now, but when they were younger I didn't ask them to prove it before I fed them and clothed them. I didn't measure their love or compare their levels of love between them so they could see who's winning. And yes, there were many times when I wondered if they deliberately did things to annoy me, but that never stopped me loving them.

To this day, I'd do anything for them.

Why would Father God be any different? In fact, why would our God treat us any differently than how Jesus treats us? Jesus, who taught us to love our enemies, not just with words but in deeds too?

Faced with conflicting views of God's nature that I find scattered among the pages of the Bible, I need to remember what James told us about the authority of scripture. It's useful. Useful, let's remember that. But helpful? Not those verses of Psalm 91. Not for me. Not today. And that's OK.

So can Psalm 91 speak into our current times? Yes, in a way. It encourages me that God is at work behind the scenes, as he's always been. And he wants us to get our hands dirty and get involved.

I look around at a world of people that desperately need unconditional love, a world that we've tried hard to remove ourselves from for way too long.

Time for the barriers to come down.

It's not about a chosen one here and a blessed one there.

Everyone matters to him.

As she finished reading, repeating the last line over and over again, a message popped up from Tom explaining that his brother was steadily eating through the contents of the fridge.

I'll be back in 20 minutes, she replied.

As Kimberly placed her phone on the passenger seat she

found herself thinking about their older son. Tom was a young man, starting to do his own thing, making his own choices, forming his own opinions. He was often out late with friends and having less and less to do with the other teens from church. Intelligent, good-looking, creative Tom who just a few short years ago used to curl up in bed and tell her everything about school and friends and feelings.

What could Tom do, she wondered, that would ever come in the way of her loving him.

Nothing, she concluded.

Nothing at all.

***

Dan couldn't think of anywhere he'd rather be on a cold Sunday afternoon than sitting in Sandy's kitchen drinking tea. The warmth and peace wrapped around him as he watched Joe set up his laptop on the table, all the while apologizing for his technical skills, or lack of them, when it came to conference calls.

Eventually, Joe managed to get things working. The call connected and Sandy appeared on the screen. Dan wasn't sure what he'd expected Joe's wife to look like, but his first impression was of an amazing smile, and dark, Spanish eyes that matched the color of her hair.

Introductions and weather reports out of the way, Sandy was keen to catch up on things. Dan shared a little of what he'd discovered in the past few days, even commenting on his walk with Ryan and the surprising confirmations that had come out of the brief time with his old friend.

"It's a shame he had to rush back so soon," Sandy said. "And I'm sorry I couldn't be there, sounds like I've missed out on some good conversation. I'm glad you had a productive week."

"Well, it's been challenging, certainly," Dan agreed. "I had no idea what to expect, to be honest. I just appreciate being able to dump everything on Joe and see what happened."

"He didn't really dump on me," Joe leaned closer to the laptop. "He's too polite. I had to kind of, you know, coax it out of him. He's too British."

"Ah, well, Joe, I'm sure you were gentle."

"It's been an amazing time," Dan said.

"So, what do you think, Dan?" she asked. "What does it mean for you, moving forward from today?"

Dan looked at the woman's kind face. She seemed, even across the wide space between them, to exude a sense of calm and acceptance. "Ah. Good question," he said. "I think one thing's for sure, I'm not about to rush into anything."

"No, you mustn't feel under any pressure. From us or anyone else," Sandy reassured him.

"Well, I've got a lot to unpack. Not just from this week, but all the stuff I've been carrying around for what feels like years."

"I think he's made a lot of progress in a very short time," Joe added, sounding pleased.

Dan nodded. "I can see God is in this, so that's a good thing. I'm a little clearer about this whole idea of the journey, and Joe has a great way of looking at things without making me feel like I have to buy into everything. I think it all feels so much more freeing."

"It doesn't make sense until you've been there," Sandy said in a reassuring tone, "but after our neat little view of God is shattered, our faith can really start to grow."

"That's what it feels like," Dan agreed. "A lot to take in, though."

"God in the wilderness," Joe reminded him.

Sandy nodded and continued as Dan sipped his tea. "Now, I want you to remember something. Two things. The first is that you don't keep anything back from your Kimberly, okay? God knows what he's doing. She's a part of your rebuilding process, you are a part of hers, you are partners on this journey."

"Okay."

"Now, it doesn't follow that she's going to completely agree with everything you say..."

A smile formed on Dan's face. "No, well, she never does

anyway."

"Good for her," Sandy teased. "What I mean is, just be prepared to have some long conversations to make progress. But there's healing to be found there, I'm confident of that."

Dan nodded his agreement. "Okay. So what's the other thing?"

The big smile returned again as Sandy laughed. "Oh good, you were paying attention. This is something Joe and I believe very strongly, but for years it was the exact opposite view. We used to believe that God had this one special plan for our lives, and we used to spend a lot of time and energy trying to determine his will for us. It all sounds wonderfully spiritual, but it's a scary way to live. There's a lot of good people out there so frightened that they can't hear God properly, they don't know his will for their lives, they're too afraid to do anything in case they get it wrong."

"Too true," Joe agreed. "We talked about this a little, right Dan?"

"Uh, was that something to do with particles?"

"Oh Joe! You and your quantum physics!" Sandy attempted to give Joe a hard stare, but the webcam wasn't conveying the emotion. Her voice softened as she directed it to Dan. "He's right about possibilities, Dan, but it's not the easiest thing to grasp. You just have to know that you can't make a mistake. There is no right way to go when you head back home. God is all about possibility, and he wants to give us the opportunities to grow into the best version of ourselves."

"Right," said Dan. "Sounds like something worth holding onto."

"I think so," Sandy agreed. "Now, there are better choices, and worse choices, and that's what being human is all about— we can never know where our choices lead. But don't be afraid to move forward in any direction that feels right to you. That's the best we can do. God will meet you, whichever direction you step in."

Dan looked sideways at Joe. "I did understand that a little

better than the particles thing, sorry."

"Oh well, I'll just have to work on my delivery."

"It's reassuring, though," Dan added, looking back at the screen, "to think of God as more of a companion on the journey than a divine GPS giving out garbled directions."

"Now there's a picture," laughed Sandy. "You know, I find it easier to think in terms of how Jesus would do things. He'd be right there with you. He might offer some guidance, he might tell you a strange story or two, he might laugh along with you when you get stuck in the mud, but he wouldn't be hitting you with a stick to keep you on the right road. Where would all the wonder and awe be if there was only one road to take?"

"Exactly. I'm pretty sure I said something like that," Joe stated.

Dan was enjoying watching the interaction between the older couple. Their differences seemed to complement each other perfectly, and he couldn't help but wonder how they'd managed to work things out when Joe started to rethink his faith. He put the question to Sandy, who raised her eyes heavenward and laughed.

"Oh my goodness!" she exclaimed. "Dan, the simple answer is that we're still working things out."

Joe nudged Dan with his elbow. "She's right. And I understand your concerns, all I can say is that it helps to remember that God is at work in your Kimberly just as much as he is in you. She may not have started to verbalize the questions yet, but that doesn't mean she isn't growing."

"We've talked with a fair few couples over the years, Dan," Sandy assured him, her eyes once again reflecting a deep kindness. "And one thing we see all the time is that if there is genuine commitment to each other then there is always shared growth. It might not always be at the same time, one of you is usually further forward on the journey than the other, but it's happening."

Dan bit his lip as he tried to absorb all that he could of their wise words.

"She will need reassuring, though, I think," Joe added. "She'll want to know that you are there for her, that you aren't checking out."

Sandy was quick to agree. "Right. It took me a while to understand what was happening with Joe. I used to pray that God would click his fingers and I'd have my old Joe back. I didn't want him to change. I even went to get some counseling."

"Really? Was it that bad?" Dan asked.

"Well, it's kinda funny now, but it wasn't back then. But this couple were old friends, they'd been working with pastors and leaders all over the States for 20 years or more and they'd seen it all. So they just asked me some questions. *Is Joe treating you differently? Is he pulling away from you? Is he open with you about what's going on?*"

"Basically, she thought I might be having an affair," Joe interjected with a smile.

"Oh, that's not true! Honey, be serious! No, the truth is, I had to admit, that Joe was being more open with me, more present than he had been for a long time. And our friends, well, they didn't really give me any answers. They just reassured me with some wise words. I remember so clearly, they said—'*Sandy, all of us are on a spiritual walk with God. If Joe were really falling away you'd be crying on the couch. You aren't and he's not. It's okay to be concerned, but more than anything Joe needs you by his side even if you don't understand what's going on.*'"

Joe continued from his perspective. "But it is strange. I was scared of facing such an uncertain future. I mean, what does an ex-worship leader do? As it turned out, Sandy was okay with that. She trusted God, and reminded me that we'd already done some crazy things together."

"It wasn't really so out of sorts to me," Sandy added. "Just the next stage of the adventure."

Dan found himself appreciating their honesty and openness more and more. "Doesn't sound so scary," he said.

"All you can do," Joe said, turning to Dan, "is make sure you're open with Kimberly. And your kids too. They all have to know that you're working things through, you're questioning things so that you can move forward. But you're still there for them. Show them you're still present."

Sandy agreed. "We do walk a fine line, though, Dan. I won't pretend it's easy. We just have to remember that God is more concerned about you now in this place on your journey than about whether you go to church or never set foot inside one again."

"Right," Joe affirmed, nodding.

"And," Sandy's eyes shifted to Joe, then back to Dan, "we are here for you. And Kimberly, and your boys too. I know you're a long way away but I want you to know you can reach out any time."

"In fact," Joe added, "we hope you'll all come visit. We'd love to meet the family."

Dan could feel the genuine invitation filling him with a sense of hope.

"But it's time to get rid of what you think you should be doing," Joe continued. "No more should. No more feeling guilty, okay? No more putting yourself down for feeling the way you do. And no more doing things out of a sense of duty. The way forward from today is an adventure that you can approach with an open heart and an open mind."

"Living life as an adventure does sound more appealing than what I've been going through." Dan's voice trailed off as he looked first at Sandy and then Joe. "This is an adventure right now."

"It sure is," Joe agreed. "At least, that's what we've found to be true."

"You know, Dan," Sandy said, her voice conveying a deep wisdom. "Someone once told me that one conversation can change your world. And it's almost as if those conversations are just waiting for you to join in. Our conversation, between Joe and me and God, has been going on for quite a few years now. And you've joined in for a time. But when you go back home, it doesn't have to stop."

"That's right," Joe added. "Sooner or later you'll find others who will join in. Kimberly hopefully, and God will guide others to you. Then you'll be having your own conversations, helping others change their world."

"And figuring out the way forward," said Dan.

"Exactly," Sandy said with a smile. "The answers are often in the conversation, as Joe always reminds me."

"Hey, I'm more convinced than ever," Joe insisted, holding up his hands.

"This is new ground for us too, Dan," Sandy continued. "We certainly don't pretend to have it all figured out. It's kinda like we had to reinvent our life from a pile of rubble, but in all that mess we found some silver and gold, just enough to start again."

"Well, you've built something pretty amazing here," Dan said.

Joe smiled. "We have a new fan."

"So you're heading back tomorrow, Dan?" Sandy asked.

"Yeah, I think I'm ready. Lots to think about. Lots to talk about when I get back."

"Just remember," Joe said. "You have to see it as a journey, and this journey has been going on your whole life. Once upon a time, you had a vague belief in a God up there. The questions you asked then are not the questions you're asking now."

"No, I see that," Dan agreed, looking from Joe to Sandy. "I've moved forward."

Sandy only nodded, allowing Joe to continue.

"Exactly. Would you have been interested in discovering faith outside the walls back then? Or even a few years ago?"

"No, I guess not."

"God has brought you to this place very gradually." Sandy's words were full of understanding.

"Who knows how this all fits together," Joe continued. "Maybe God simply opens the doors. Maybe plants the questions in our mind that can take us forward, should we dare to ask them. If we *want* to ask them."

"If we choose to follow the trail," Sandy added. "And you

have, Dan. It's taken a long time, it's been hard going, but you have ended up here."

"At a new beginning," Dan mused.

"It's a great place to start," Joe confirmed. "A great place to start."

CHAPTER 22

"Eventually, you will get through the rain."

"**C**locks," Dan said in surprise, looking around the dusty workshop.

"Clocks," Joe repeated, a look of pride on his face. "I meant to show you around before now."

Dan was taking in the workbenches, the various woodworking tools and machines, and a number of time-pieces in various stages of completion. "I would never have guessed."

"Something to do with my fascination with time, especially the time we find ourselves in. By which I mean, *this present moment.*"

"Ah, yes. So the clocks in the house, you made those?"

"Well, I really only make the face," Joe confessed, selecting one from a bench and handing it to Dan. "The mechanisms I import, of course. High-quality, silent. No ticking."

Dan held the smooth piece of wood in his hands. It was about the size of a dinner plate, an inch thick, with no particular shape to it. "Nice. I noticed that the clock in the lounge doesn't tick. My wife has this aversion to ticking watches. She can hear them a mile off."

"Yeah, and notice," said Joe, pointing to a finished clock hanging on the wall, "there's no second hand? And no numbers, ever."

Dan was intrigued by Joe's little side-business. "So what's it made out of, is it oak?"

"I mainly use olive. Easy to find here in Spain, and it looks amazing when it's all sanded down and varnished. Has this wonderful smell to it, too."

"Well, well. Making clocks," Dan mused. "Not something you've always done, then?"

"My dad taught me some carpentry. Takes me back to those golden days. And I wanted a hobby, something that didn't require a whole lot of thought, something that would give me time to think and pray and be. You'd be amazed at the ideas I have when I'm working away."

Dan placed the clock-face back on the bench, seeing the little particles of dust picked out by the sunshine, floating in the air. There was a sense of timelessness in the room, almost a detachment from the world that Dan found incredibly peaceful.

"You know," Joe continued as he absentmindedly moved some tools around, "it's a wonderful process, making these. I think God has taught me more sanding down a piece of wood than in a thousand sermons. See, I don't choose a perfect piece of wood to work with—I want one with some character, some grain, some unusual knots. Imperfections are better, it makes the finished product more interesting."

"Like this one," Dan said, stepping forward to take a closer look at another of the finished clocks hanging on the wall.

"That's a current favorite of mine. I don't know what it is about it, but I love how uneven it is. See, you can smooth things off a little here and there, no rough edges, but I want to make something unique."

"I've never seen anything like these, to be honest."

"And I'm just bringing out what's already there. I think that's a little like what God is doing in our lives. Sure, he has to knock off some rough edges. But he's not making us all the same, that's not what it's about. It's our uniqueness that adds something to the bigger picture."

Dan considered Joe's words of wisdom. "Hmm. Not just painting us with the same brush, so we all look the same. All that uniqueness covered over."

"Any time we're afraid of our uniqueness shining through, I think we need to look at where that fear originates from. It's usually a need to conform. To be part of the tribe, you know? So we aren't rejected. But those days are gone, Dan. God very much wants us to live lives that are laid bare for the world to see. All our pain and hurt and joy and sorrow, the passion *and* the dreams."

With his finger, Dan drew a line through a thin layer of sawdust on the workbench. "I've found a little fear creeping in again today. Like I don't know what I'm going back to, I still don't know where my life is going. I still don't know if Kimberly and I can make it work."

"No, we don't know. But what we can do is trust in the process. God might still be knocking off the rough edges on you. Or he might be sanding you down a little so the imperfections can show through better."

"I guess I just want some more certainty. More clarity." Dan looked up. "I want to be sure that God is actually doing something. That all the ups and the downs actually had some meaning in there. That when I look back it all makes sense."

"Yep," said Joe, and for a second the smile disappeared from his eyes, replaced with a deep understanding. "It gets easier. A little."

"It was helpful, though, hearing you and Sandy talk about things."

"The more I look back, the more I'm aware of the unfolding. I'm able to see God's hand in it, in all the pain and the sorrow and the tears, as well as the laughter and the fun times."

Dan nodded, saying nothing.

"We all want life to be easier, of course we do. But the truth is, and we know it when we look back, we are better for the struggles."

A thin smile formed on Dan's lips. "I know you're right, but..."

"Can you imagine a poem with no heartfelt anguish, or a

life story with no struggles and hurdles to overcome? What kind of book would that make?"

"Hmm. Yep."

"Don't we want to listen to music that stirs our soul? Violins that pluck at those heartstrings and resonate with our lives? It's then that we know we're human, in the best sense. This kind of stuff doesn't need to make sense. It just needs to be heard."

"Or seen. Like the knots in the wood."

"A perfectly running stream would make no noise. It's the rocks in the water that give it the music."

Dan looked over to his friend. "I think...I think you're trying to say that life is not going to be straightforward from here on in, and that's okay."

"Well, I'm trying the poetic approach," Joe admitted, smiling.

"You're a poet too?" Dan chuckled.

"At times."

"I used to write poems for Kimberly. I don't do that anymore." Dan moved to the window. The rays of the afternoon sun were filling the valley, highlighting the rocky ridge-line. He wished he could get up there with Joe's camera, one last time before he left. "I guess that's another thing I need to figure out."

"Your creative side?"

"Yes, I guess. It seems important, somehow."

Joe came and stood beside him, looking out at the valley. "God is a creative being. He takes great delight in bringing things forth. And I believe he takes great delight in watching us take hold of that creative spark in us."

"And you seem to give it a special place here."

"There's healing in creativity. Art, writing, music, you name it. I don't pretend to understand it, but maybe through the process of creating we draw closer to the Creator and closer to our truer self."

Dan nodded thoughtfully. "I'm just going to have to come back, I'm afraid."

"We're already looking forward to it."

"So," Dan turned around and surveyed the workshop. "Clean up?"

Joe reached under a workbench and pulled out a small vacuum cleaner. "Let's get to work."

The afternoon skies were clearing as the two friends finished their work and headed back to the house in search of refreshments. Descending the outside staircase, they crossed the graveled parking area in front of the garage, but Joe halted halfway. He looked in through the big open doors as Dan stopped beside him, following his gaze.

"I was just thinking," he said, turning to Dan. "Got time to take out the kayaks? The lake should be perfect now. It would be a good end to your week."

"Take some coffee with us?"

"All things are possible."

***

"This journey thing. It's a process. A continual, emerging process." Dan balanced the paddle on his knees and watched the water trickled off the blades, forming rings on the surface of the lake that rippled out like molten silver in the evening sunlight.

"It is," Joe affirmed. His kayak drifted along gently next to Dan's as they headed back towards the shore.

"Everything that's gone before has brought us to where we are, that much I understand. But we're continually needing to have faith for the next step." Dan was trying to put his thoughts into words, but he was in no rush to come to any conclusions. "We can't really see any further anyway, can we?"

"No one can. And there are no guarantees. See Dan, we all start in different places. We all take different routes, different paths. We,"—Joe motioned with the paddle in his hands—"we're walking together for a few days and that's great. And we need companions, we all do. But there are no guarantees this road is going to take you where you want to go."

"Okay."

"There's no guarantee about tomorrow. We only have today."

"Yeah, I think maybe I'm beginning to see that. It's so obvious on one level, but I don't think I've been living on that level."

Joe pulled his Kayak around to face Dan with a practiced backstroke. "Man, I wish we had more time. There *is* life on the other side, if you keep on walking through. There is an *invitation*. An invitation to discover a new way, a better way. And a whole new kind of inner freedom."

"If I keep on walking."

"You *can* come through, Dan. Eventually, you *will* get through the rain."

Dan looked ahead, seeing the tops of the mountains and the clouds reflected on the water. His thoughts immediately went back to Tuesday morning, when he'd first looked out across this very lake, not knowing what was ahead. The clouds of confusion and doubt seemed much more daunting then. Maybe it wasn't so scary after all. Maybe, like Joe was saying, there was a way.

Clearly something had changed in him over the past week. He wasn't the same man who'd got caught up in a rainstorm on the way to find some answers. Something had begun to shift inside, he could feel it. He just wasn't sure he could put his finger on exactly what. He only knew that it was time to move forward.

Maybe he should be listening to that invitation.

"You see, once you start taking hold of that journey," Joe continued enthusiastically, "once you own it, embrace it, then you're ready for the *next step.*"

"*Next step?*" Dan stared at Joe from behind his sunglasses. "You mean there's more?"

Joe grinned. "I sure hope so." He began to pull his paddle through the water, turning the kayak again.

"Wait! Hold on, it's not all about the *journey?*"

"It is," Joe confirmed. "But it's much more than simply understanding that we're on a journey. I think of it as expanding my world. Waking up. Me, I'm just getting started."

"Hmm. And here I am thinking you've arrived."

"No, I don't think so," Joe said, shaking his head. "I'm 57 years old. There's still so much I wanna do with my life, and now I'm learning to take hold of every day. Sure, I'm getting older, but at the same time I'm enjoying life more than ever."

"You know, you're right," Dan reflected. "Sometimes I think I'm past it in many ways, but I look at you and you're more alive than a lot of younger people I know."

"My philosophy is this—you can worry about the future, carry on worrying about your faith, about money and your marriage and your kids. Or you can choose to find some joy in the moment, because at the end of the day"—Joe dipped the tip of the blade into the lake and with a flick sent a spray of cold water in Dan's direction—"that's all we have!"

Dan smiled as he considered Joe's latest insight. "Find some joy?"

Joe had pushed off ahead a little, aiming for the stony beach close to where they'd parked the cars. "Yep. Joy."

With a few powerful strokes, Dan caught up with the leisurely progress of his companion. "Didn't I tell you that I'm a professional worrier?"

Joe gave him a sideways glance. "No, I think you told me you look after computer systems. Does that make you a professional worrier, then?"

"Of course! People pay me to worry all day about their stuff so they can sleep soundly at night."

"Well, at least they pay you, you could find some joy in that," Joe offered. "But seriously, don't you have a lot to be thankful for? If you can't find the joy right away, find something you can be grateful for and learn to see some joy in that."

"Like being here."

"Exactly. It's something you might need to practice."

The kayaks drifted effortlessly across the lake. Dan felt like he was in another world, a magical world of sunlight and water. Thoughts of his mother suddenly came from nowhere—her smile, her kind eyes. His defenses were down and he resisted the impulse to put them up again. Instead, he let the grip on his heart continue as he held his breath, hearing in his mind some of the last words she spoke to him—*Everything will be okay.*

He breathed out, the inner pain seeming to dissipate across the water. For a moment he felt disoriented, detached from reality. He shook himself, which only made matters worse. "Whoa!"

Joe saw the kayak wobble and called out. "Hey, you okay?"

Dan let out a nervous laugh. "I'm okay. I got it," he reassured his friend, steadying himself with the paddle.

"Ready to head back?"

"Yeah. I'm good. Just...thinking about my mother." Looking around at the impressive scenery, he felt his soul uplifted and filled with a timeless peace. "She would have loved it here."

Joe nodded. "It's okay to miss her. It's okay to have regrets. And it's gonna take however long it takes to find the healing."

Dan dipped the paddle in the water a few times but he wasn't in a rush to get anywhere. The shore drifted slowly nearer as they immersed themselves in their surroundings, their shared experiences steadily feeding their conversation. He could now see the bottom of the lake once again through the ripples pushed out from the kayaks.

"I've still got so many questions. Maybe more than before, actually. Questions about my questions."

"Welcome to the club!" Joe exclaimed. "Asking questions is part of life, why should it be any different with our faith?"

"Oh, I can think of a few," Dan ventured.

"Pretty much everyone who's come here over the years is asking hard questions, some have been through real trauma and pain, and they feel confused because it's like they think there's something wrong with them. They are almost embarrassed by their doubts."

"I can relate to that feeling," said Dan.

"You know what I realized when I first started asking questions? It unnerved people. It's not right to question a faith or a doctrine that holds all the answers. Questions expose our inner battles, our deepest thoughts, and people don't want to deal with all that raw stuff."

"Well, I certainly felt like it was wrong to question things. Like I was being disobedient or deliberately divisive, challenging the leadership. That kind of thing," Dan paused, thoughts running through his head as fast as lightning. "You know, now I come to think of it, I used to say *yes* a lot. I had questions but I didn't want to rock the boat, so I just found it easier to agree and push down the doubts. I didn't want the confrontation."

"No, it's uncomfortable," Joe agreed. "Like the sheep asking the shepherd if he knows what he's doing."

"Yeah," Dan laughed.

"Just be glad you aren't the shepherd."

"Ah, right. What happens when the shepherd starts asking questions?"

Joe adjusted his baseball cap as he gazed away into the west. "Man, that is it. The more you're invested in this thing, the harder the fall when it happens."

"When you're a professional believer?"

Joe shook his head. "Yeah. You know, it must have taken me a year to pick up my guitar again, after I left. I just didn't know what to do with this big part of my life."

"But you found a way."

"I'm a work in progress. But I sometimes wonder about my old Pastor friend, Steve. I know he's asked questions. I know he's had doubts. I think he's just so afraid of letting go. For him, it would be a long fall to who knows where."

Dan said nothing. He wondered at Joe's assessment of his friend, wondered what happened to Pastors who stepped beyond those comfortable walls. He could imagine what the church leadership back home would say if Alan showed signs of going off the rails—they'd probably give him some time off to get his act together.

So that he could carry on with the act.

The scrunch of pebbles underneath signaled the end of their little voyage. Stepping into the shallows, they pulled the kayaks up onto the cropped grass and sat down, facing west towards the evening sky, a sky scattered with clouds that seemed to be gathering together with them to watch the show.

"Not in a rush to leave, I hope? Looks like it's going to be an amazing sunset."

"No. But I do wonder," Dan confessed, not taking his eyes off the scene before him, "what does the future hold?"

"Now that's a great prayer."

Dan turned to Joe. "A *prayer?* That's not a prayer, it's a...."

"Sure it is."

"But it's a question," Dan insisted.

"Not a heartfelt cry? A searching?"

"Well..."

"Come on, we've got to push the boundaries. Break the mold."

"Hmm. You could be right," Dan agreed. "*What happens now?* Because I want to be open. Open to doing things differently. Doing *life* differently, in fact."

"Good," said Joe. "And to me, that kind of prayer is simply opening up the conversation. Embracing the future, not fearing it. Possibility, remember?"

"Well, it seems too easy."

"And it shouldn't be easy," Joe muttered under his breath.

Joe's realistic appraisal of the situation was enough to lift Dan out of any last shadows. He smiled and let it turn into a chuckle. "You're right. Thanks, Joe. Thanks for this week. It's not something I'm going to forget."

"Hey, it's been a pleasure. I hope you'll be able to look back and see this time as a milestone in your life."

"A milestone," Dan mused, testing the word in his mind. "Yes, I think so. That's a good way of looking at it."

"And you'll let me know how you're moving forward, right? We've all got a long way to go. We're fellow pilgrims finding our way, and just knowing someone else is walking beside you helps more than I can say."

"Well, since I now have more questions than when I arrived"—Dan joked, realizing the truth of his words even as he spoke them—"I guess I'll keep on walking!"

The two men watched the setting sun complete its performance, all the while reflecting back on the week's events like old friends. Then, both sensing a conclusion to their time together, they stood as one and set about loading the kayaks onto the trailer.

"I know some people in England," Joe stated, pulling tightly on a strap. "I'm gonna hook you guys up, I think you'll get on well."

"Fellow pilgrims? That would be good. Thanks."

Joe smiled. "Fellow pilgrims. They're on a similar journey. And we all need each other, right?"

Dan nodded thoughtfully, wondering briefly what that would mean. Leaving Joe to finish fastening the Kayaks in place, he returned to the shore to collect the paddles. There he paused, taking in the grand scenery. Around him the mountains stood firm in the gathering gloom, reflecting on the surface of the lake which was now being stirred by a gentle breeze coming up from the south. He took a moment to breathe it all in one last time.

As he reached for the paddles he stopped once again, crouching down to admire the stones and pebbles lining the shore. There was nothing special about the small, smooth stone he picked up. It was one ordinary pebble among many others. But another little reminder, he thought as he placed it in his pocket along with the others, of the ordinary in the wonderful.

On an impulse he pulled out his phone and snapped a couple of photos, trying to frame the lake between the stony shore in the foreground and the pink streaks of cloud above. He felt like he was trying to capture something that could not be expressed with words. It was something to do with connection. There was a new connection between himself and this place, and he could already feel the pull to return. He had forged a strong connection with Joe, and who knew what could come out of that. And beyond that, Joe was talking about more connections with others on the journey.

You're just getting started. A whisper on the wind, an echo of his heart, or something more, it didn't matter. He was listening.

Dan quickly flicked through the photos. They didn't do the scene justice but they were good enough. Choosing one, he attached it to a message, then typed out a brief thought to Kimberly—*I want to come back here with you. There's an invitation to go deeper, and I think I want to take notice.*

He hit send.

Monday

CHAPTER 23

What would things look like from now on?

Dan held the paper cup carefully as he slid the backpack from his shoulder and placed it on an empty chair. Before he sat down he looked around, taking in the sights and sounds of the bustling airport terminal—people of all shapes and sizes and colors, queuing at departure gates, eating breakfast in cafes, shopping for perfumes and wine, all to a gentle background hum of voices from every corner of the globe.

Making himself comfortable he made a conscious effort to relax, reflecting on his situation. Dan didn't particularly like crowds, but he began to wonder at the sense of connection he shared with the thousands of people who would pass through the airport that day. For some it would signify a beginning, for others an end. And for some, like himself, it would be both an end and a beginning. The end of an incredible week he would never forget, and the beginning...

The beginning of the rest of his life.

On an impulse he reached into his jacket pocket and pulled out three pebbles. He'd found them there when he was going through airport security and had almost thrown them in the trash can. Instead, in a moment of sentimentality, he'd tucked them away again and hoped they wouldn't be confiscated.

As he held the small, smooth stones in his hand, he found himself recalling what Ryan had said back at the river.

His friend's observations were correct—Dan would often collect interesting stones when he was out on a walk, and over the years many of them had ended up adorning the kitchen windowsill at his mother's house. She'd always seemed to treasure them.

When he and Kimberly had cleared out her house, he'd gathered all the stones together and dumped them in the fishpond. He hadn't known what else to do, but at the time it had felt like the end of an era, all the little mementos of past journeys sinking into the depths.

Now...now, as he rubbed the pebbles together, somehow they felt like a promise.

His reflections were interrupted by the low rumble of an aircraft taking to the skies, which drew his attention to the outside world. From his vantage point he watched in fascination as jets taxied to gates, ground crews busied themselves with luggage and refueling, and buses ferried passengers to and from the terminal. It all seemed to tick along, like clockwork. A well-oiled machine.

Would there ever again be that kind of order in his life? What would things look like from now on?

One thing he was sure about—he was ready to go home. Yes, he would miss the Pyrenees, but something told him that he'd come back, sometime, and he took some comfort from knowing that Joe and Sandy were only an email away.

The conversations with Joe had certainly opened his mind, no doubt about that. He'd been challenged beyond anything he'd imagined, and oddly, after spending the other day with Ryan, he was more certain than ever that God would continue to be there from day to day in unexpected ways.

It would be different from now on, of course, and it looked like he was going to have to figure a lot of things out as he went. Prayer, for instance. That was a big one. How to relate to a God who wants *you* to be part of the outcome, an integral piece of the solution.

That alone would change everything.

After the experiences of the last week he could sense a

growing awareness of God's involvement in his life. And even if God was not *intervening* the way he'd believed in the past, meeting people like Joe did not happen by accident. He felt sure he could still trust the Creator with the behind-the-scenes stuff and start to find some joy in the process.

The relationship had changed, certainly. Now it looked more like a partnership, a walking alongside.

On this wonderful, mysterious, incredible journey.

Questions remained. Joe had made it was pretty clear that there were always going to be questions. Dan could see that his life was now somewhere in between the questions and the answers, and that would probably mean learning to hold space for other people's questions, too.

No matter where those questions lead to. And that was okay.

But what he wasn't going to do anymore was try to please everyone. That was not going to be an option any longer. He would keep going forward from today, and people would just have to make of it what they would.

Yes, it might still be lonely. And painful at times. But Dan was beginning to appreciate why Joe did what he did with such conviction—faith was an active process. And keeping his faith alive meant stepping outside the safe walls, walking through the rain of doubt and confusion, and into the big, wide world.

Something that would have seemed completely insane just a short time ago.

He felt a hint of sorrow as he thought of Joe, sitting at his desk crafting articles that would at times rock the boat. As this wise and caring man helped others navigate their spiritual journeys, it was inevitable that he'd be misunderstood. Someone somewhere would use his words used against him to prove a point. But that wouldn't stop Joe, Dan was certain.

And clearly the boat needed rocking.

It struck Dan that Joe had become a catalyst in his life. Change had already started months, maybe years ago, but meeting Joe had accelerated that change at a rapid rate. And now that he had some clarity, now that he could see the possibilities, it would be his decision alone to follow through and take that next step.

He knew he had to keep moving forward.

His thoughts strayed to Kimberly and the boys. He wondered how different things would be when he got back, and what that would mean. Change, it seemed, was the only certainty—a necessary consequence of growing up.

As if reading his mind, a message appeared on his phone—Kimberly was checking up on him. Dan leaned forward, resting on his knees as he tapped out a response.

Waiting for the flight, got an hour.

Decided to come back, then?

Her question made him smile. He realized how much he missed her.

Well, you know, commitments. Got a wife waiting for me.

Right. I'll let her know.

For a brief moment, Dan glanced around him. Life was going on as normal, but the impulse to retreat from it was no longer there. At least, not like it used to be. He sighed, but it was a sigh of resolution, not resignation.

I thought maybe you'd help me figure some things out.

When did I stop doing that, might I ask?

Dan paused again. There was so much he wanted to say, and suddenly he very much wanted to hear Kimberly's voice.

Call me if you're free.

OK, 5 mins.

He waited, phone in hand, thinking about where to begin. A major shift had taken place inside, things had changed, but unpacking it all was going to take time. Dan knew that if he and Kimberly were going to move forward together and make things work, then they had to start having a deeper conversation.

The phone buzzed quietly and he swiped the screen.

"So," Kimberly said.

"So. Can I just say...I'm sorry. For not being there lately."

"Hmm. You can say it, of course. But there's no need to

apologize for what you're going through."

"It's just that I was wondering if you ever felt like I took you for granted, or took us for granted, you know. If maybe I haven't made you the priority in my life that I should have..." Dan was struggling to express what he was feeling, but he knew he had to try.

"Hey," Kimberly's voice was full of kindness and concern. "I really hope you didn't go all the way to Spain for marriage counseling."

"No. Of course not. It's just, I've been thinking a lot this week. I mean, over the past couple of years I've gone through a whole lot of changes and..."

"Dan!"

He knew when it was time to shut up and listen.

"Look, I'm not the same woman you married, am I? Think of all we've been through together. We've both changed."

"Yes, but I think I realized some things in my chats with Joe..."

"When I was on the prayer team I used to hear a lot of stuff, things you wouldn't believe. We're actually doing okay, you know. We're doing pretty well, in fact."

"But things could be better, right?"

There was a pause. "They always can, I suppose," Kimberly reflected. "But Dan, listen to me. Whatever it is you're working through, I want you to know, I like the changes I see in you."

"Really?"

"Yes! You're better for it."

Dan took a second or two to let her words sink in.

"You still there? I can hear the announcements in the background."

His gaze drifted to the outside world once more as another jet thundered along the runway. "Yes. Yes, I'm here."

"I want to be involved, okay? We're a team, aren't we?"

"Yes. And I don't want to keep anything from you anymore," Dan explained. "I want to be able to talk to you about what's going on inside."

There was a silence. Dan could almost hear Kimberly thinking about her next words.

She spoke slowly, feeling her way. "I think, if I'm really honest, I've kind of been where you are."

"Where? Barcelona airport?" he joked, trying to lighten the mood.

"I'm serious! All the doubts and questions, just the same as you."

"Ah." Things were suddenly starting to make a little more sense. "And you didn't know how to tell me."

"You had so much going on."

"And you didn't know what to do about it," Dan stated softly.

"No. I just hid it all away."

Dan took a deep breath. He closed his eyes. As he exhaled he felt the weight fall from his shoulders. "So from now on, we're going to work this out together?"

"Yes. I'd like that."

"So would I."

EPILOGUE

Step out into thin air, and find me there.

W*hy does the eagle build its nest so high?
The fledglings are hatched, they are fed and nur-
tured. Safe and secure, they have everything they need.
Why does the eagle build its nest so high? It's a long way down.
A long way to fall.*

No safety nets, no ropes. Nothing to hold them. Gravity will take over, and it's only their wings that will keep them up.

And that's where I find myself.

Out at the edge of the nest. I can feel the wind on my wings. Something is happening inside.

It's the call to fly.

You aren't made for the nest, I hear you say. You're made for the air.

But it's a long way to fall. How will I know?

You don't. You'll never know. Until you try. Step out. Step out into thin air, and find me there.

But I'm still so unsure.

You can soar, you really can. You're not supposed to fit in that nest. Look at your wings, you've outgrown your surroundings. It's only up in the air that you'll discover who you really are.

Soaring? I don't know how.

You've been learning. I've been teaching you. You've flapped those wings a few times now, stretched them a little. You've felt the power, felt the wind. My breath blows on them and something stirs inside.

You're right. I've felt something I can't explain. It feels like fear but...

That's me calling you to fly. But you have to step out into the air. Those wings I've given you can't wait to hold you, lift you, carry you far and wide.

But what if I fall?

What if you fly? Something tells you things will never be the same. It's scary I know, but you cannot remain. This is how it's supposed to be, soaring on the wind and relying on me.

I wasn't made for the nest? But I was so happy there.

No my child, you were made for the air.

Gravity takes over, a rushing wind, tumbling in confusion to meet my doom. But no, my wings know what to do, all that was needed was faith to step out.

Spreading out, catching the air, rising steadily, lifting me higher and higher. This is what it means to live by faith.

Constantly falling to earth but lifted up.

A little faith to live today.

Not tied to the ground but free to soar.

"I like it," Kimberly said, looking back over the last few lines. "It's positive. Encouraging."

"Well, it needs some work. It's just a way of me processing what's going on. Writing it out helps, apparently. Therapeutic."

Kimberly's eyes seemed to be looking into his very soul as she held the sheet of paper in her hand. "It's more than that, Dan. You've got something good here! You used to write stuff for me once, remember."

Dan nodded. "Hmm. It did feel good to get some ideas out, start to verbalize things."

She laid the print-out to one side and tapped it with a finger. "So keep at it."

"I think I will. It's actually based on a verse in the Old Testament. My attempt to take some of that ancient wisdom and make it my own, reshape it into my own words."

"Well, well," Kimberly mused. "Look at you, reading the Bible again."

He grinned. "Something Joe said about leaving the religion out of the wisdom. It can still teach us, we can still get inspiration from it."

"But in a different way, maybe? I should try that."

Dan glanced at the verses on the paper, then up at Kimberly. "I wish I'd understood sooner what you've been dealing with."

"Well, I could say the same thing. We haven't been very honest with each other, have we? You trying to protect me, me trying to shield you. All a big, confused mess."

"Right," Dan agreed. "But we're still together. And we'll work it out."

"But you're not going to boot me out of the nest, are you?" Kimberly challenged. "I like my nest, it's got tartan cushions and everything."

Dan chuckled. "I can imagine! But I don't think eagles actually do that. They just withhold food, chocolate, that kind of thing."

"Ooh. Don't mess with my chocolate!"

"Wouldn't think of it. Anyway, from what I gather, you've been flying longer than I have."

Kimberly looked heavenward. "Well, I wouldn't call it flying. More like free-fall."

"That makes two of us."

"More importantly, what are we going to do?" She reached out across the kitchen table and held Dan's hand firmly. "What are we going to do? We don't seem to have the answers."

"No." Dan was more serious for a moment. "No, we don't. But if there's anything I learned last week, it's that we kind of live in the space between the questions and the answers."

"Ah, that sounds very profound." Kimberly gave her husband an inquiring look. "Are those Joe's words?"

Dan couldn't help smiling. He shook his head. "No, I thought that up all by myself."

Kimberly nodded thoughtfully, then glanced quickly at the kitchen clock. "Well, back to reality for a minute, because I work for the church, and Alan wants you back. Remember?"

"You're right," Dan agreed, thankful that Kimberly could always think in practical steps. "We have to make some decisions. Not easy decisions, either."

"So we just figure things out as we go? We've done it before."

"If you're okay with not knowing."

"Hmm. Sounds fine to me," she reflected. "I could do with a bit more adventure."

"You mean that?"

"How long have we been married?"

"People change their mind about things."

Kimberly held his gaze. "You're my man," she said quietly. At that moment those words told Dan everything he needed to know.

A knock at the kitchen door interrupted their thoughts.

"Good evening, good neighbors," a woman's sing-song voice came through the opening door. "The wanderer has returned, we hear."

Dan looked up to see Debbie, with Reg close behind her carrying a covered plate with care. As they greeted each other he noticed that Kimberly didn't seem in the least surprised, and he found himself hoping the plate held one of Debbie's delicious creations.

"Well," Kimberly explained as she motioned their neighbors to the kitchen table, "I thought you'd want a chance to chill out and tell us about your week."

"Ah," said Dan. "I'm not much of a storyteller, you know that. But if that's a cake..."

"See what I mean, Kim. I told you he'd come back!" Debbie exclaimed with dramatic flourish, giving Dan a mischievous smile.

Kimberly gasped at her friend's little joke. "You said nothing of the sort!"

"I said nothing of the sort," Debbie confessed, a twinkle in her eye. "But I heard a thing or two, Dan. Kim told us you've been hanging out with an old guru in the mountains."

Dan held back a smile and looked at his wife. "Did she now?"

"And," Big Reg pulled up a chair and leaned forward, "we've been reading Joe's blog. Very interesting stuff, Dan. Very interesting."

Dan was lost for words. He looked from Reg to Debbie, then over to his wife, who was busy preparing snacks. He wondered if this might be an interrogation. An interrogation by friends.

"Which of you is the good cop?" he asked, eyes narrowed.

Kimberly placed slices of chocolate cake on the table alongside a bowl of carrot sticks, dips and a fresh pot of coffee. "Oh Dan, Reg is right. We've all been reading the blog, and Joe makes some really good arguments in his articles. I know you had some good talks with him."

"And we thought we'd like to be in on the conversation," Debbie added in a low voice, as if their little gathering was in some way clandestine.

"Well, what can I say?" Dan sat back, eyeing the cake. It looked like he was going to have to earn it. "I needed some advice, Joe invited me to stay for a few days. The truth is, he has a very different approach to faith. He used to be this full-on, Bible-bashing evangelical..."

"A bit like us, then?" Kimberly remarked.

"Yes, I suppose so. Not so different."

"And now?" Debbie asked.

"Now, well, now...I guess he would say he takes a more Jesus-centered approach to things. But he made Jesus sound much more human, somehow. I'm beginning to see how church-focused my faith has been, for such a long time."

"As if getting people into church is the point of it all," suggested Debbie, looking to the ceiling. "I bloody-well hope it isn't."

"Exactly!" said Dan, surprised at his neighbor's honesty. "This is more of a *faith outside the walls* kind of thing. Or maybe even a faith that breaks down those walls..."

"Since we built the walls in the first place," Debbie remarked.

"Right," Dan agreed. "I think it's about learning to see God at work everywhere, in everyone, regardless of who they are or what they believe. If we lose that church focus we can get out there and join in. If we want to. It's an open invitation."

Kimberly had sat down next to her husband. She sipped herbal tea as she looked across the table at her friends. "That sounds interesting, Dan."

Reg clasped his hands together. "Yeah, see Dan, we've been talking, the three of us." His deep voice resonated through the whole room. "You know, it's all very new to me. I'm still finding my way. And Debs, well, she's done religion before in the Catholic school..."

"And that was enough for me, if I'm honest," Debbie interjected.

"So anyway," Reg continued. "We thought that it doesn't make sense to go along to Alan's new group. Not when we could just come round here and talk among ourselves."

Dan found himself once again looking at each one in turn.

"Uh, hold on. You want me to lead a group?"

"No, Dan. More of an advisory role. Besides, Kimberly would be in charge." Reg sent an exaggerated wink in Kimberly's direction, who held back a smile.

Dan was about to reply when Debbie picked up the printout that Kimberly had left on the table.

"Oh, what's this? Poetry?" she asked.

"Just a bit of creative writing," Dan explained. "It's nothing, something to pass the time on the flight back."

"Shush! I'm reading."

Dan looked over at Reg.

"She's reading," the big man said with a shrug. He sipped his coffee. So did Dan. Kimberly munched on a carrot as they waited for Debbie to finish.

"This is good, Dan. Getting out of the nest. Trusting in your wings. Very insightful." Debbie slid the paper over to Reg, who glanced quickly over the words.

"Well, that's settled then," Reg announced. "You're the man, Dan."

Dan sucked his teeth. "I don't know. I mean, having another meeting, I'm not sure that's what it's about."

"But we have to start somewhere, right?" Reg stated.

"Makes perfect sense to me," Debbie added. "And there's more hands to give out sandwiches."

"Sandwiches?" Dan raised an eyebrow.

"For the homeless guys. It was their idea," Reg explained, nodding towards the two women.

Dan looked at Kimberly, who just smiled and said nothing.

"Ah. You actually want to *do* something."

"If we aren't making a difference, Dan..." Debbie said.

Glancing up, Dan caught sight of the sunset through the window. Clouds touched with pink in a pale blue sky. One single word kept resonating in his mind. *Invitation*, it said.

Invitation.

"Okay," he said finally. "I might have to agree with you."

Debbie clapped excitedly. "Ooh! Does that mean you won't be joining Alan's group?"

"I suppose it does."

"But what are you going to tell him?" Kimberly asked.

"What am *I* going to tell Alan? I thought *you* were the leader."

"Yes," she replied innocently. "But he asked you."

Dan looked at Reg and Debbie. "So you guys would rather not go along to the group?"

"We already have a group, Dan!" Debbie rolled her eyes. "And we like it here."

Kimberly smiled and leaned sideways. "So?"

"What?" Dan felt three pairs of eyes fix on him.

"Alan. He asked you, and he's waiting."

"Okay. Yes, I suppose I'll have to tell him something. I'll tell him..."

They waited for Dan to finish. Reg looked at Kimberly "I

hope Alan's not holding his breath."

Dan held up a hand. "The thing is, I really want to leave the door open. Joe isn't about telling people to stop going to church, he's more about getting a bigger perspective. So, just in case others in the church want to come through the door..."

"That's not going to be easy," said Kimberly. "He might get the wrong idea."

"Might? I think whatever I tell him he's going to get the wrong idea."

"And *I* have to work with him. For now, anyway," Kimberly reminded Dan.

"You could tell him you're taking flying lessons," Debbie suggested with a rye smile, picking up Dan's poem once more.

"Oh!" Kimberly exclaimed. "Oh, that's it. That's exactly it."

"We all are, I should think," Reg offered. *"Kimberly's Flying Club.* There you go. Everyone welcome. Bring your own parachute."

Dan sat back and smiled. He shook his head. *"Kimberly's Flying Club?* What have I gotten myself into now?"

His wife was fighting back giggles as she slid the plate of cake towards him. "I think it's all part of the journey, Dan. All part of the journey."

***

The northern Spanish town of Zaragoza basked in warm afternoon sunlight with not a single cloud in sight. The drive down had been a pleasant one, giving Joe plenty of space to reflect on the past week and the newly-formed friendship with Dan, as well as time to consider the weeks ahead. New visitors would soon start to arrive and new conversations would begin.

Joe felt energized as he considered how things had unfolded. He was still amazed at how much could change in a week. Only this morning he'd sat down at the computer and realized that he had new ideas for a whole series of blog posts. And maybe there was even a book in there. He'd have to find out.

After all, it was a journey.

Turning into a side road a couple of blocks away from the train station, he found a place to stop. Joe wasn't a big fan of the narrow, underground parking lots, and tried to avoid them whenever he could. Besides, this street had free parking every afternoon.

Leaving the car, Joe once again checked the time on his phone.

Train is due to arrive about 4, Sandy had said in her last message. No need to hurry.

As he approached the angular, concrete edifice that served as the modern bus and train hub, he looked with interest at the original station that still stood, intact, right next to the main building. He appreciated old architecture, and there was plenty of that in a city like Zaragoza, with its Gothic cathedrals, medieval castles and even more ancient ruins dating back to Roman times. Shame about the new stuff, he thought, as he walked up to the entrance and, seeing no benches, found a place in the shade to stand and wait.

A new message popped up on his phone—*Just coming into the station now.*

It was another five minutes or so before Sandy appeared through the sliding doors, pulling her bright yellow suitcase and waving energetically. She held back a smile as Joe approached.

Putting his phone away, Joe walked towards her, removing his baseball cap on the way—he never kissed Sandy with his hat on. Never.

"Hey Honey," she said, sounding relieved. She reached out to take Joe's hand and planted a quick kiss on his lips, then she looked him in the eyes.

"Good trip?" Joe asked.

"Yeah. Long day."

"You okay?" Joe could sense something in Sandy's demeanor, but he wasn't sure what it meant.

"I found someone on the plane."

"You *what?*" Joe smiled, but he squinted into her eyes.

Sandy turned to look back at the entrance. Joe followed her gaze. A tall young man in blue blazer and jeans was pushing an overnight case along, heading slowly in their direction.

Joe blinked, then opened his mouth as he realized who it was.

"Grant?"

"Hey Dad," the young man said. He stopped at a distance and tried a smile but it didn't quite reach his eyes.

Joe looked from his son to his wife. "You brought Grant back?" Then he looked back at his son.

"Grant?" Joe was having trouble finding words. He felt his throat tighten.

Sandy squeezed his hand. "He showed up at Mom's place last week. We've been talking."

Grant took a step forward. His mouth was a tight line. "Lorraine left me, Dad. Gone back to her folks in Seattle..." His words trailed off.

"Oh God," Joe said under his breath. He could feel his eyes beginning to smart. He found himself letting go of Sandy's hand and taking a few uncertain steps towards Grant, but Sandy was right by his side. She took his hand again and reached out her other hand to Grant. Both men stood facing each other.

"Dad, I'm sorry." Grant's eyes searched his father's face. "I'm sorry."

Joe closed his eyes. He took a deep breath and time seemed to slow down. Suddenly all the conversations with Dan over the past week seemed to run at lightning speed through his mind. He could recall every question, every thought, every feeling. His heart was beating wildly in his chest. He opened his eyes and couldn't stop the tears falling. As he reached out to put his arms around Grant all he could say was, "There's nothing to forgive. There's nothing to forgive."

As they walked back to the car, Sandy holding hands between the two men, Joe listened as his wife and son both chatted about the flight over, the last few days at her mother's house, and the plans they had made for the coming week. Joe found it hard to take in. He wasn't really listening, he was just glad to hear their voices over the steady rumble of the suitcase wheels and the noise of passing cars.

"Hey, Dad! I picked up a bottle of red wine at the Duty Free. It's a *Rio*-something."

"*Ree-oh-ha,*" said Joe, carefully pronouncing the name. "I didn't know you liked red wine."

"Well, you know, when in Rome..."

"It's *Rrree-oh-ha!*" Sandy announced, effortlessly trilling her R's. "It's the name of a small province. Not too far from here, in fact. Lot's of vineyards, quaint little towns..."

Joe glanced sideways at his wife, eyebrow raised. "Worth a visit, maybe? How about Saturday?"

"Now that would be cool," Grant said quickly.

"If you like picturesque landscapes and good wine, *Rioja* is the place," Sandy explained.

"How do you do that? Roll your R's like that?" Grant asked his mother. "I've never been able to."

Sandy shrugged. "Oh, I don't know. Just comes natural, I guess."

Joe laughed. "Natural? She couldn't do it when we moved over here. *Rioja.*" He tried but failed.

Sandy shook her head. "Come on, you boys! If you want to go there, the least you can do is learn to say it."

"*Rioja! Rioja!*" They all joined in as they walked along, laughing together and completely oblivious to the looks they were receiving from people passing by.

THE END

WHAT NEXT?

Writing this book has been an incredible experience for me, and I'm happy to say that I'm not the same person I was back in 2019 when I first began scribbling notes in a journal. Through the process I've been challenged and forced to look deeply into my own experiences, questions and beliefs.

There is no way I could include everything I wanted to in these pages, but I do believe it goes some way to fulfilling its primary purpose—to give myself and others permission to ask difficult questions about faith and religion, as well as encouraging those exploring spiritual paths outside the walls of traditional church.

Dan still has to work out his way forward, which is the same for each one of us. But if we decide to inhabit that space between the questions and the answers then I know we can begin to live out of a place of greater freedom and love.

Reflecting back on the twists and turns in my own spiritual journey, I'm keenly aware of how much help I've had along the way. Much of it is from people I've never met and aren't likely to, but their stories and timely wisdom have given me the courage and strength to keep on moving forward and keep seeking answers, even when it felt so lonely.

I'm so thankful for supportive friends and family who have been there to listen, give me space, and encourage me to continue writing. There are others, too many to mention, who've given of their time to read through my drafts, point out mistakes and make suggestions.

It turns out that I wasn't alone in my journey after all.

So then, what next? Well, the conversation doesn't have to

end here. I want to leave you with some resources—books, web-sites and groups that I and many others have found to be timely and helpful on the journey. You can find all these and more on my website.

I hope to see you there.

C. R. Pennell
Valencia, Spain.

nowlivingforward.com/rain

Printed in Great Britain
by Amazon

85005767R00141